MINIMUM MAINTENANCE

MINIMUM
MAINTENANCE
ROAD
TRAVEL AT YOUR OWN RISK

MINIMUM MAINTENANCE

Carolyn Colburn

Bonnie's Mews Publications
Duluth, Minnesota

Author's Note

"Minimum Maintenance" and "Drawing from Life" originally appeared in slightly different form in *Onion River Review* and *One Minute of Knowing*.

MINIMUM MAINTENANCE. Copyright © 2010 by Carolyn Colburn. All rights reserved. No part of this book may be used or reproduced in any manner whatsoever without written permission except in the case of brief quotations embodied in critical articles or reviews.

ISBN: 978-0-557-54669-5

For Tim

Acknowledgements

This work was supported by the Loft Literary Center, the McKnight Foundation, the Minnesota State Arts Board and the National Endowment for the Arts.

This activity is made possible by a grant provided by the Minnesota State Arts Board, through an appropriation by the Minnesota State Legislature. In addition, this activity is supported in part by a grant from the National Endowment for the Arts.

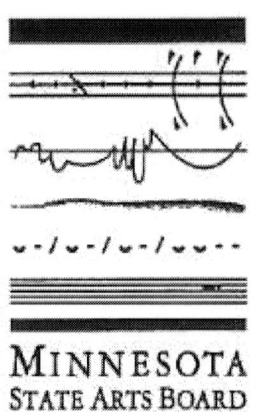

MINNESOTA STATE ARTS BOARD

NATIONAL ENDOWMENT FOR THE ARTS

Contents

1	Minimum Maintenance	1
2	The Last Poodle	19
3	Still Life	61
4	Here Comes the Sun	87
5	Drawing from Life	119
6	Homestudy	139
7	Xmas Story	177
8	Roadsong	201
	Epilogue	235

MINIMUM MAINTENANCE

"If you wish for something hard enough, you might lose your mind."

Twilight Zone notebook
(August 1984)

1

Minimum Maintenance

M a pierced my ears as a bribe. She used a pin and a potato. She said I could always grow the hole out, if I changed my mind. She didn't care if I smoked, I could always quit, or what color I dyed my hair, I could always dye it back. Only what I wanted more than anything was a tattoo.

"There's some things you can't change, Sugar," she said, "they're goddamn forever." She thought for a minute. "For instance, diamonds," she said.

"For instance, my name," I said.

It was funny about Ma. Sometimes she got mad for stuff like swearing or refusing to eat or refusing to eat anything that had a face. Then other times, she'd be like it didn't matter what I did.

Once I stayed downstairs at my friend Lucille's for two weeks, back at the old apartment. Ma'd locked me out, I can't remember why, I wanted her to sweat it. I'd watch her through Lucille's kitchen curtains, bringing out the garbage, getting in and out of the Olds, standing by the clothesline smoking. The smoke sat in the air above her head like I could read her thoughts. I couldn't decide, was she thinking about me? When I finally went home, she was like, What's new? We had popcorn for dinner, she let me drink two beers, we played Monopoly all

4   MINIMUM MAINTENANCE

night. The phone kept ringing, but she didn't answer. After awhile she unplugged it.

The night of the trouble, I was in my room in the old apartment, not exactly sleeping. I was worried I'd wet the bed. All of a sudden there's this explosion. I run into the living room looking for Ma. Jack's standing there with a gun. Around his feet are pieces of ceiling, above his head is a big black hole. Some other guy says, Come on man, get the fuck outta here. Jack just stares. The guy says, Come *on* man, and hightails it. Jack turns to follow, then he sees me. We look at each other, then he's gone, too. I thought he looked sad, but it was dark. Ma was in the hall closet, back behind the sheets.

It took us a whole day to move to the shelter, four loads in the Olds. My dad, before he went to Montana, left the car with Ma. This was awhile back. He said where he was going all he'd need was spurs and a prayer, besides, he didn't think the Olds would hold up. Long as I can remember, my dad was always coming and going. Only this time he stayed gone, this time he took the Greyhound.

The day he left, I still remember, he came by to clip my nails.

"I swear I could see 'em grow," he says, "if I watched careful enough." He picks two of my nails up off the linoleum, like tiny moons, puts them in his pocket. Then he smooths my ponytail.

"Just you remember, Sugarpop, don't let anyone, ever, fuck with this mane," he says, "it's all the luck in the world, this hair." Then he says, "My baby sister has her a mane like this. That'd be your auntie . . . " I was waiting for him to say more about this auntie, maybe snip off some ponytail, too, put that in his pocket, but he never did.

I tried to write to my dad. Ma had a new job and was worried about getting fat, so she spent her free time doing situps and deep knee bends. I'd sit at the kitchen table and write letters to General Delivery, Missoula, Montana. A couple of them came back, Return to Sender. A couple seemed to take, though he never answered. Once he called, but Ma answered. They started hollering and hung up. He didn't call back.

At the shelter Ma had to sneak to her job. All day she pretended to be looking through want ads, running her long Midnight Magenta nail along the columns for Waitress and Receptionist. She'd leave the ads laying around in strategic places, then shove her fishnet stockings and false eyelashes into her purse and say she was going to clean houses. The shelter ladies believed her.

Once Ma was sick, lying in bed all afternoon. She had me go pick up her pay.

"Now you just tell the ladies you're going to see a friend, Sugar," she said, and gave me a five and a little map drawn on a napkin. "Make sure you get cash!"

I took the 21A. I almost missed the place, "Girls Girls Girls" threw me off. Then I saw "Kum On Inn." So I did. The lady behind the bar gave me a coke, let me smoke. She said her name was Grace. She had long bangs, dyed black. They'd get stuck in her eyelashes and move up and down like a garage door when she blinked. She was wearing a silver tube top, there was a spider web stretched across her chest. She saw me staring.

"Yeah, hon," she says, "a tattoo is forever."

"Like a diamond," I say.

"Where'd you hear that bull, your old lady?" I nod. "Yeah, well, ain't none of these nudniks gonna give a girl no diamond, that's for sure." She lights a cigarette. "That one dude, with the scar and the old brown Plymouth ..."

"Jack?" I say, and Grace says,

"That's the one. But don't you worry none, I eighty-sixed that one a long time ago. Your old lady sure knows how to pick 'em."

She takes a long drag of her cigarette. The spider web expands.

"So where's the spider?" I ask, and Grace laughs. One of her teeth is gold.

"That's the gig, hon," she says. "Spider builds herself a web, goes into hiding, waits for something to come along. You don't see her, but she's there, you better believe it."

She leans closer across the bar. "D'ya know how the black widow gets her name?" I shake my head, take a long drag of my cigarette. "On account of she kills her mate," says Grace, "right after mating." I blink. Grace leans back.

"Well, not always," she says. "Just often enough to keep the boys nervous."

She laughs again, stubs out her cigarette, pours herself a shot. I exhale and look around the room. I'm practicing smoke rings.

"What's with the straw on the floor?" I ask.

Grace raises her bangs, studies me for a minute. "Absorbs the piss," she says.

A smoke ring sits in the air between us, growing wider. I'm watching a guy sweep up the straw with a wide broom.

"The piss?"

Grace says, "The guys who come here, they piss on the floor while the girls dance. Straw makes it easier to clean."

I'm listening to the broom. The smoke ring breaks up. After awhile Grace pats my head across the bartop and pours herself another shot.

The shelter kicked us out because Ma was dangerous, they said. Not her exactly, but Jack, who kept driving by late at night with his lights off. It was fall out. He'd park his car across the street for hours with the motor running, exhaust coming out the back like ghosts. When the cops showed up to ask Ma some questions about that night at the old apartment, the ladies heard the word "shotgun," that was that. Plus one of them had discovered Ma's stockings and eyelashes.

"We've got our other tenants to think about," they said.

I crossed my eyes at Terrell, one of the other tenants, he crossed his back. He had three earrings and a baby brother. Later in the hallway I said, "Who's gonna get you smokes now, huh?"

Next day me and Ma drove out to the country. Ma had directions on a piece of paper. I read them out loud as we went along. We drove all morning and all afternoon. Once I saw a deer, standing in a field. The moon came up before the sun went down. Ma kept looking back and forth between them.

She said, "Who's to say if it's day or night?"

I said, "Turn where the sign says 'Minimum Maintenance'."

◆ ◆ ◆

The first time I saw Elroy's, I named it the House of Cars.

Ma said Elroy was one of those people who, when they moved to a new place, didn't feel at home until they'd scattered a bunch of dead vehicles around. She told me she'd met Elroy at the Kum On Inn. She said he was a regular. He looked pretty regular to me, skinny, with those pointy-toed boots and sunglasses like mirrors.

Elroy never said much. Like that first day. There's me and Ma, in the middle of nowhere, driving up that long road to the House of Cars, and there's Elroy, standing on the porch like he'd been expecting us, though Ma said he wasn't, at least not right then. He walked down to meet us. Ma's nails and lips were Petal Pink, she'd done Miss Clairol before leaving the shelter. She was wearing sandals and talking a mile a minute. I stepped on her foot to shut her up.

Elroy pointed to the backseat of the Olds. "You want all that shit in the house?"

Ma said, "Oh no, that's for my hope chest, ha ha." Elroy followed her around to the trunk and helped with our suitcases.

"Your ma's a piece of work," Elroy said, while we watched her lock all four car doors, then double check. I guess Ma'd lived in the city too long. All she had to do was take a look around. There wasn't another house in sight.

Later, when I was wandering around counting dead vehicles, this tall skinny girl comes sputtering up on a Honda, which belonged to her cousin, she tells me right off, who got killed by a tractor.

I said, "Attack of the killer tractors."

She stared at me, her eyes were big and green. Then she turned her head and spit. The spit went about six feet. We became friends.

Junie lived down the road from the House of Cars. On the way I told her about Jack and the shelter, about Grace and the spider web and the gold tooth. I skipped the part about the straw. Junie told me she lived in a split level on forty acres with her dad and mom. When we got there nobody was home, she showed me around.

Junie's house was only half finished, so you never knew when you'd open a door and there'd be nothing there. Like in dreams, when there's a long hall and a long line of doors on either side, and you can choose any door, only you always choose the one with a tornado behind.

We ended up in the garage. I looked around, spotted the line of guns along the back wall.

"My dad's," said Junie. "Hey, you like guns? See that one?" She pointed to a long dark gun propped against the wall by the door. "That one'll tear a tree in half."

"Aren't you the lucky one," I said. "A dad who shoots trees."

Junie's cheeks turned color. "It's for the coyote," she said, "there's a coyote around. They're evil, everybody knows that."

Then she said, "I heard it once, real late, least I think it was him. Made my hair stand up. You keep an ear out, you might hear it, too."

I spotted the bench with all the tools.

"Hey, you want bangs?" I asked.

I used a pair of clippers. Before me and Ma left the shelter, I'd dyed my hair black, so I figured bangs would look good on me, too. My dad wouldn't mind, bangs weren't like real hair. I handed the clippers to Junie.

"You have a blonde stripe," she said, studying my part. "Like a skunk."

When we were finished we swept up our hair into a little pile and set it on fire. I lit a cigarette. Junie asked if she could have one. We blew the smoke toward the open garage door. This was November, you couldn't tell what was smoke and what was breath. From the garage we could see the back of Junie's house. In the middle of the second floor was a door leading nowhere. No porch, no stairs, nothing.

"You afraid you might sleepwalk out that door some night?" I asked, blowing a smoke ring.

Junie watched the smoke. "Nah, it's locked." She pointed to the ring. "Can you teach me that?"

"Shit," I said, blowing another one. "It's a secret. You'll have to trade, a secret for a secret."

She thought for a minute. "Elroy's crazy. His sister, too."

I rolled my eyes. "So's everybody. You'll have to do better."

She was quiet for awhile longer. Then she said, "I can give you a tattoo."

I lowered my cigarette, looked at her.

"It's true," she said, "with ink and a needle. It's no big deal, afterward you wear a Bandaid. My cousin did himself, before he died. I watched."

"Did himself?" I said.

"Gave himself a tattoo," said Junie. "A cross, on his arm.

10 MINIMUM MAINTENANCE

First he drank whiskey."

I wasn't sure which part of this information was the most interesting, so I said, "So what?"

Until Junie told me, I didn't even know Elroy had a sister.

I knew he had a wife—I'd seen a photo in his room—but I figured she was dead or living in California. In the photo Elroy was wearing a tuxedo and standing next to a bride. They were very far away, mostly it was a picture of space. I found it in a bottom desk drawer in his room, so I couldn't very well ask about it. But things seemed clear enough. I guess alot of stuff can already have happened when you got to be Elroy's age. Or Ma's age, for that matter, though Ma said a woman would rather be goddamn boiled alive than tell her age.

When he wasn't working on cars or selling parts from the cars to some guy, Elroy whittled. He had this little red pocket knife. He'd spend hours sitting on some rusty fender whittling away, little curls of wood piling up around his feet. He whittled cars and trucks, busses, tractors, trailers. As if he looked around his yard and got inspired. When they were finished, he stood them around inside the house. Everywhere you looked in that house, you saw some little vehicle parked, like it was about ready to take off somewhere.

And all those little cars and trucks had to be parked just so, because another thing about Elroy, he was neat. Inside the house, that is. He had these House Rules, he called them. You had to line up the magazines, just a little overlapping, on the coffee table. You had to fold the towels on the rack, leave only one square of toilet paper drooping. You had to wait until everyone was sitting at the table before you could lift your fork.

That's where we were, having dinner, when Bob walked in. I thought it was some guy coming about a part. But then the guy said something.

"I'm Bob," she said, "Elroy's sister. What's for dinner?"

Minimum Maintenance 11

She sat right down, didn't even bother to wash her hands, another rule. I glanced at Elroy only he wasn't saying much, just swallowed a mouthful of potato and popped open another beer. Before they sat down, he and Ma lined up two beers each beside their plates. Ma wouldn't have cared if I had one, but Elroy said, No fucking way. He'd already caught me smoking and gave me a snake bite until I dropped the pack, which he stomped into the dirt with his pointy boot.

Bob ran her hands through her hair—it stood up on her head like grass—and started eating. She ate faster than anyone I've ever seen. By the time she was done, me and Ma had forgotten our own food, we were watching her. She looked at Ma and winked, looked at me and belched, then started on seconds. Meanwhile Elroy finished his food and drank his beer. He pushed back his chair, picked up his plate, disappeared through the beads into the kitchen. The back door opened and closed and boots crunched across the driveway.

After awhile Bob sat back and unsnapped her jeans. She pulled a little pouch and some papers from her shirt pocket and rolled the most perfect joint, it could've won an award. She took a hit and passed the joint to Ma, who took a hit and passed it back. Bob had another hit. Then she raised her eyebrows like two crows, and held the joint toward me. I glanced at Ma, but she was already off.

We got pretty stoned. Next thing I knew I was eating another piece of pie, my third. Something was on the stereo, the Stones, I think. Ma and Bob were dancing. There they were, dancing and laughing and acting mental the way people that age can get. I finished my pie and went outside.

And this amazing thing: it was purple out. Everywhere I looked—dead cars, barn, long dirt driveway, woods across the road—like purple paint got poured on the world. I looked at my hands, they were purple. I touched my cheek, thought, This is how purple feels. I looked through the purple air back to the house, at the open window, yellow like a sun. Bob stood in the window laughing. Ma twirled in a circle behind her.

I was halfway down the driveway when I spotted Elroy, a purple shadow sitting on the hood of a dead bus. I made my way over to him through the clutter, my hightops bright as headlights. He was whittling.

"What if your fingers slip?" I said. "It's hard to see."

Elroy's knife moved. A little purple curl drifted to the ground. I sat on the bumper and watched the pile of curls grow. The sound of the knife was steady, like a cricket. Sometimes at night at the old apartment, when there was a break in traffic, I could hear the crickets from the pond in the park across the street. For a long time I thought it was the sound of electricity.

"It's purple out," I said. Elroy kept whittling.

I tried again. "Your sister sure likes to eat." Elroy shifted his boot.

I thought for a minute. "Black widows kill their mates, did you know?"

Then I said something which caught his attention. "Think the Olds'll hold up?"

Elroy's head turned. "Why, you goin' somewheres?"

"Well, no, it's just we're so far away from everything out here..."

"Like what?"

Elroy stopped whittling and stuck a Lucky in his mouth. He snapped a match with his fingernail. A little flame jumped up. He blew purple smoke in my direction. I couldn't tell if I was still stoned.

"Now I ask you again," says Elroy, "what is it you're so fuckin' far away from out here? Huh?"

I couldn't see his face too well, but I figured I knew the expression. I thought hard, wanting a cigarette in the worst way.

"Well, school, for one," I said. "I haven't been to school in awhile..."

Elroy snorted. "School? Now you're gonna tell me you miss school, you wanna go back to school?"

"No, but, it's a law..."

"Well, then, little lady, looks like that makes you a outlaw."

He flicked his cigarette far into the yard, where it glowed like a tiny planet in the purple dark. Then he jumped down from the hood of the bus, shook out his feet in his boots, started walking away.

"Wait a sec," I said. "You leaving me here?"

Elroy stopped walking. I said to his back,

"The coyote, I mean. What if the coyote comes sniffing around?"

Elroy turned and looked at me. I said,

"Junie's dad said..."

Elroy spit into the dirt beside his boot. "Guy's a fuckin' moron," he said. "Besides, wouldn't be no coyote around here. Be a wolf." I stood up.

"A wolf?" I said. "Shit! That IS evil!"

Elroy walked right back to me, leaned over, shook his finger in my face. The finger smelled like wood curls.

"There's evil in this world, little lady," he said, shaking that finger, "but it ain't no fuckin' wolf mindin' his own fuckin' business." He straightened up, spit into the dirt again.

"You'll fuckin' figure that out someday," he said over his shoulder as he walked away, "or you fuckin' won't."

I watched him fade into the dark in the direction of the house. The purple was gone.

The next day was Saturday. Ma and Bob were going into town for supplies, they called it. I hopped a ride and sat in the bed of Bob's truck and smoked and watched the dust billow while Bob tore up the empty roads like all hell was after her.

14 MINIMUM MAINTENANCE

After we'd been to Checks Cashed Here and Piggly Wiggly and Municipal Liquors, Bob slapped me on the back and Ma handed me a ten and told me to be at the Spur station in forty-five. Then they disappeared into the Lumberjack Lounge. I went into Ben Franklin and pocketed a bottle of India ink, a package of sewing needles and a box of Bandaids. At the counter I asked for change for a ten. At the Spur I used the outside cigarette machine and sat on a pile of tires to wait for Ma.

On the way back to Elroy's I asked to be dropped off at Junie's. Bob slowed the truck, I jumped down, ran across the lawn—there was no sidewalk—and rang the front bell. Junie's mom came to the door.

"Ju-nie!" she called over her shoulder. I could feel her staring at my hair. Junie appeared behind her at the top of the stairs.

When we were alone in her room, I gave Junie the plan.

"Tonight's the night," I said. "My wrist. A spider."

"What're you talking about?" said Junie.

"The tattoo. I got everything we need. Except whiskey, you got any whiskey?"

"Down in the kitchen, but ... we'll have to wait til they leave for the Legion."

I looked around Junie's pink room, at her pink walls and pink bed. "Who's in a hurry?" I said, and kicked off my shoes.

Halfway through the tattoo, Junie's pink phone rang.

"I gotta answer," she said, "it might be my mom."

I was sitting cross-legged on the pink rug, my hand above a white bowl. The water in the bowl was pink, from blood. I was dizzy, from whiskey. Junie kept saying, Don't worry, the bleeding will stop. I raised the bottle with my good hand, had another swallow. I hated the taste of whiskey.

Junie crouched down, handed me the phone. "It's your

mom," she whispered. She wrung the water from a washcloth and held it on my wrist. My arm felt hot, I bit my lip.

"Ma?" I said carefully.

"Sugar? You okay? Listen, never mind. There's been a change of plans. You gotta come home." She sounded far away.

"Wh-where?" I closed my eyes and saw pink swirls.

"Don't get smart with me," she snapped, her voice suddenly very near. "We're goddamn leaving. Tonight. I'm sending Elroy to pick you up, he'll be there in fifteen."

I hung up the phone and opened my eyes. There was Junie's hand on my wrist.

"How far'd you get?" I asked.

Junie peeled back the washcloth, we leaned forward. There on my wrist was a wobbly circle. It looked like it might be caught in my veins, like it might be trying to get away.

"What the fuck is that?" I blinked, trying to see.

"The body," said Junie, "of the spider." She sounded hurt. "I'm not done. I've got the legs left, then I'll fill it in."

"You don't get it," I said, "you're finished. We're finished. I gotta go." I focused my eyes on the circle, studied it for a minute. "Sort of looks like nothing."

Junie studied it. "Or, like a 'O,' maybe? The letter? It could stand for something."

We tried to think. "Old Crow? Oldsmobile?"

Junie told me it had to be done, just grit my teeth. Then she poured some of her mom's peroxide over my wrist. I screamed. She covered my wrist with the biggest Bandaid in the box.

"Just keep it clean," she said. "And take that off in a couple days. No big deal."

I stood up, one of my legs had gone to sleep. I sat on the edge of the bed, looked around for my sweatshirt. My leg felt electric, like any minute sparks might start jumping from my jeans. Just then lights flashed in the window, out on the

16   MINIMUM MAINTENANCE

driveway a horn honked.

"Junie!" I hollered, grabbing my sweatshirt, trying to stand. Junie stuck her head around the corner of the door.

"I've got it!" I said. " 'O' as in 'Outlaw'!"

Elroy was driving a car I'd never seen before. Long and wide, low to the ground, with silver fins. He narrowed his eyes at me, then looked back at the road. Cattails waved from the ditch, then disappeared. I was thinking about that wolf. Elroy cleared his throat.

"Some guy's hangin' around town, askin' after your ma. Name's Jack. It's got her shitless. I said no way nobody can come sneakin' around out here, ain't nowhere to fuckin' sneak. But that don't seem to matter, she's determined to get outta Dodge." I looked over at him.

"An expression," he said. "But never mind, all you need to know is, you're leavin'. The two of youse, with Roberta ..." he paused, " ... my sister ... tonight. She'll take the pickup. Not the Ford, the Chevy. Chevy's in good shape, worked on her myself."

None of this surprised me. What surprised me was Elroy saying so much all at one time.

"What about the Olds?" I asked, and yawned. The whiskey was making me sleepy.

Elroy looked sharp at me. Then he punched in the lighter, pulled a pack of Luckies from his jean jacket.

"That car wouldn't hold up," he said, "not where you're goin'. I bought it for parts, from your ma."

He shook out a cigarette, stuck it in his mouth, shook out another, held it toward me. I stared at it.

"Take the fuckin' thing," he said, so I did.

"Where they going?" I asked, trying not to cough. This was my first Lucky.

"Where *you* goin', you mean. Montana, or somewheres.

Though it sounds like more open space, to me. Could as well stay here."

My heart beat. "Montana?"

"That's the plan," said Elroy. "Roberta knows some broad has some land out there." Two trails of smoke curled from Elroy's nostrils. He said, "It's a big place, Montana."

He said, "Probably ride horses to school, out in Montana."

Then he steered the big car into the long driveway, just as I blew the most perfect smoke ring, it could've won an award.

◆ ◆ ◆

As it was, we didn't leave the House of Cars until the next morning. I slept like there was no tomorrow. When I finally staggered out of my room into the sunny hallway, there's Bob staggering out of Ma's room, with Ma right behind. The sun hurt my eyes. I blinked.

"Move your ass, girl, we're outta here," says Bob, I'm not sure to who. Ma headed for the bathroom. Nobody noticed the Bandaid.

We ate breakfast, loaded up the truck, and left. Elroy was nowhere to be seen. A couple miles down the road, Bob pulls over.

"Who's in a hurry?" she says, and rolls a joint.

"Oh, yeah," she says, "this is for you." She hands me a box of matches. "DIAMOND" it says, "STRIKE ANYWHERE."

I slide the box open. Instead of matches there's a tiny horse, carved out of wood, painted purple. I lift it out. "Diamond," I'm thinking, but I keep this to myself. After awhile I put Diamond back, and slide the box closed.

It took us two weeks to get to Montana, criss-crossing the countryside, while Ma ran her finger over the map. We kept to the gray roads, stayed away from the black or red ones. Ma's nails grew short. I wore long sleeves. After a few days, when no one was looking, I dropped the Bandaid out the side vent and stole a glance at my wrist. There was the 'O,' plain and blue, against my white skin. Junie was right, it was really no big deal. By the time we reached the Black Hills, I was healed.

2

The Last Poodle

M a told me hickeys were a sign somebody loved you. I studied her neck, where the latest signs of love were slowly fading. Then why are you leaving? I asked, if he loves you so much? and Ma said, Sometimes love isn't enough, just look at your Grandma DeLuca, and she launched into another installment of family history. According to Ma, my grandma had been what is known as a true beauty. And where did that ever get her? dead that's where, said Ma, so I said, How? so she said, What are you a goddamn Indian? give it a rest, and she reached for the joint Bob held out.

We were headed north, a little detour on our way to Montana. Rather, we were headed Up North, is how Ma put it. She wanted to see the town where she grew up.

"Where the men are men, and the women sell Mary Kay," she said, applying blusher in the rearview mirror.

Ma hadn't been back in fifteen years. She outgrew the place, she said. I'll bet, said Bob, and snorted and looked her up and down. Ma's hand automatically went to her size seven waist. She tried to do 115 situps a day, her motto being, a situp per pound, you'll never be round.

Bob was driving, one hand on the wheel, the other holding a joint carefully like it might need protection. Her third since leaving her brother's. I myself had sort of liked Elroy, but I could tell right off he wasn't Ma's cup of tea. Too quiet, Ma said, like all motorheads, with them it's smooth engines forget smooth talk.

Before Elroy's, back before we'd left the city, Ma had used some of her saved-up tip money for one last trip to Curl Up and Dye. Her idea of a natural disaster was that her roots would start to show when she was miles from nowhere. Which is right where we're headed, she'd said, and a new word entered my life: Elroy lived in a place called the Boonies.

    I could tell right off the Boonies weren't Ma's cup of tea either. Too much space with no bars and restaurants. Too quiet, like Elroy. Elroy wasn't enough for Ma. Not rich enough, mainly. Ma was looking for that pot of gold, she said, Elroy barely had a pot to piss in. Though he did, however, have some pretty good pot, a fact definitely in his favor. So we'd stayed awhile.

    I myself had sort of liked the Boonies, all those dead cars in the yard, and those long wind-y paths through the woods and fields. I could get stoned and pretend I was driving somewhere, or wander for hours without having to worry about getting hit by a bus. But no sooner did Bob announce she was heading out for Montana, Ma started packing.

    Not that we had much to pack. Between our old apartment back in the city and the women's shelter, we'd left most of our stuff behind. A trail, like Hansel and Gretel and the bread crumbs, if anyone had it in mind to come looking for us. For instance my dad, who we hadn't heard from in awhile, but like all dogs, said Ma, he had a good nose, he'd sniff us out once she got back on Welfare. Until then I was to refer to him—if at all—as that A-major asshole.

    We'd been in an A-major hurry when we'd packed up back at the old apartment.

"Don't let anyone tell you you can't take it with you," Ma'd said, and handed me an empty Seagram's box from the nightclub where she worked. She still said "nightclub" like she'd forgotten I'd seen the place. I'd pointed out that she herself had actual suitcases. She told me to shut up and pack, luggage is something a person has to build up to.

"I'm a woman," she said, "I deserve luggage. You're a goddamn kid."

But then my birthday had come around out in the Boonies. To celebrate I'd snuck some Colombian from the Humpty Dumpty cookie jar and spent the afternoon pulling up Indian tobacco—Elroy had showed me how—and following garter snakes around. A snake can lead a person to some pretty cool places if a person is polite enough.

A few days later, during a commercial in "Dallas," I'd informed Ma that, in case she hadn't noticed, which she obviously hadn't because she'd forgotten to give me a present, but never mind all that, the point was, I was a kid no longer.

"I'm in the teens now," I said, and lit a cigarette to prove it.

Ma slit her eyes. "In my book, anyone who walks around with purple hair is a goddamn kid," and she yanked the cigarette out of my black-painted fingernails and started in on it herself. She was always telling me all is fair in love and war, and beauty leads to love, so all's fair in beauty, too. I figured I was just following her advice, with different color schemes.

"Look there," she says, waving smoke at the TV, "that is what a goddamn teenager looks like, like her, like Lucy Ewing. Will you just look at that hair? those clothes? In my book, *that* is a beauty." I wondered which chapter of Ma's book I might be in.

Once I was sick and came out of a fever to find Ma sitting on the coffee table staring at me. I was too weak to get up, so I closed my eyes and pretended I was alone. It was starting to

24   MINIMUM MAINTENANCE

work—the couch had lifted off the rug and was heading for the ceiling where a door had appeared—when I heard Ma's voice in the distance, like she might be standing at the end of a tunnel.

"It's only a matter of time," she said, "before your face comes into its own."

Even if Ma had remembered my birthday, I wouldn't have had room for a present, not in Bob's truck. All our stuff was piled back in the bed under an olive green army tent. The three of us were piled up in front on a half dozen folded-up olive green army blankets. The blankets were necessary to protect us from springs. Bob had scored the tent and the blankets at an Army surplus store, our first stop on our way out of the Boonies.

"War is hell," said Bob, "and to the victor goes the spoils," and she pulled a lighter from one of the pockets of her new olive green army jacket and relit the joint.

In the middle of the dashboard in Bob's truck sat a little wobbly arrow suspended in water inside a glass bubble. The bubble featured tiny black letters in a circle, like a clock: NEWS. Bob had purchased the contraption a few years back at a Navy surplus store, she couldn't remember in what state. The letters stood for the four directions, she said, and a compass, if it's working, only points one way.

"A compass always points true north," said Bob.

"Never mind all that," said Ma, "watch for signs."

We passed a sign which said State 73. I watched as Bob made the turn toward Ma's hometown. Sure enough, the little black arrow in its bubble of water spun right around and wriggled happily at the N. I pointed this out to Bob, who told me actually it was the truck that does the spinning, the arrow itself never moves. I thought about this for awhile, and watched the highway line slide past under the hood of the blue Chevy. I decided maybe Bob should cool it a bit on the hemp.

We passed a sign which said County 37, and Ma got all misty

and started in on more family history, reminding us once again how her mother had been a beauty and her mother's mother and so on. It seems the women in Ma's family had taken all this beauty seriously, refusing to leave the house without eyebrows and always wearing lipstick, even while canning or giving birth. Ma and her two sisters had all gone to beauty school, and the last Ma'd heard, the youngest owned her own shop—the Beauty Barne—one town over. Only we wouldn't be seeing Doris, Ma said, Doris still held a ridiculous grudge over that one boy, Ma couldn't even remember his name, anyway, the poor thing couldn't French kiss to save his soul. Ma had saved her little sister from a fate worse than death, she said, though to hear Doris tell it, you'd think he'd been the second coming.

    I was about to ask Ma if this boy had been any good at hickeys, when we passed a sign featuring the silhouette of a deer. The sign was shot through with bullet holes. The deer was leaping upward, like a ballerina, as if it to escape. I checked the compass. We were right on target, headed for the land of truth: true north and true beauty.

    I lit a cigarette. Then I lit another, and offered it politely to Ma.

Our first stop on our journey through Ma's past was a bowling alley on the outskirts of town. Though town wasn't the right word for where Ma grew up. Ma grew up in a location, she called it. Locations were built away from the towns, right up next to the mines. Like ticks on a dog, is how she put it. Every night Ma and her sisters would fall asleep listening to the ore trains like background music. Like a lullaby? I said, and Ma said, Yeah, like that. In those days, she said, the foundations of the houses, the driveways, the streets, the curbs, the tree trunks and car tires were covered with red ore dust. Location kids learned to take their shoes off at the door so as not to track red footprints on the linoleum.

"For a long time I thought the sunset was red on account of the sun reflecting off the ore dumps," Ma informed us.

Then she said, "After awhile, all that red, it just gets in your blood." I was thinking it must've been like looking at the world through red sunglasses. I was thinking I might have to try that.

On blasting days, Ma said, kids would go flying out of their desks, then pick themselves up and go on reading about Alice and Jerry and Jip as if nothing had happened. Location kids were always covered with black-and-blue marks anyhow, and nobody thought twice. Black-and-blue marks from one thing or another—and nobody's business, either—were a way of life for location kids.

"The teachers worried that if Kruschev came, nobody'd know it was a bomb until too late. Everybody'd just think the mine was opening up a new vein, and we'd all die from fallout."

I was thinking from the looks of things, this place might've gone through a war anyway. No traffic, not many people, only one stoplight so far, which didn't seem to be working. Not a trace of red on any of the tires of the two cars parked outside the bowling alley. Which Ma said was on account of most of the mines were shut down. No more blasting, no more red footprints. Though she herself didn't bother about any of this, what business was it of hers if they filled all the mines back up and hit golf balls off them? She'd made it out of this godforsaken place, that was the whole goddamn point. And she'd made it out as a Kane, to boot, thank god somebody —my grandma, namely—had had the goddamn good sense to do something about that Kanezevich.

She poked my arm, told me I had her and my lucky stars to thank that I hadn't been born a goddamn location brat. She only wanted to check back in, see what the poor old place had done without her all these years. She just wanted to stretch her legs. Maybe the lanes still served lemon Cokes, besides, she used to go out with a boy who set pins here. Who's probably dead or in jail, says Bob, or haven't you heard? lemon Cokes and the counters that served them went out with Eisenhower.

Ma wasn't gone long before she came hurrying back to the truck, shaking her head. Bob was right. The Lucky Strike was now the future site of a chopsticks factory.

"What can they be thinking of?" she said, climbing in, pulling an army blanket around her. "Jesus I forget how goddamn cold it gets up here. And it's only goddamn November."

Our next stop was Big Nick's Bottle Shop. Ma and Bob each picked out bottles with animal themes: Beefeaters for Bob, Wild Turkey for Ma. As if to say, drink this, act like an animal. Though to my mind in most cases this would be an improvement. I could picture Bob as a cow, and Ma did have definite turkey leanings. I wandered the rows until something caught my eye. At the counter I set down a bottle, but Big Nick shakes his head, puts the lime vodka back behind him on a shelf. Sorry sunshine, he says, then hands me a purple sucker.

"So's you're color co-ordinated," he says, eyeing my hair, and he winks under his umbrella eyebrows. Out on the sidewalk I could feel him watching. I spit on the Welcome mat and lit a cigarette.

We drove a few blocks more, past another stoplight stuck on yellow, across one set of railroad tracks then another, past echoey-looking buildings that didn't seem anything like the names Ma kept rattling off between chin exercises—Shop-Rite Meats, Open Pit Lounge, Tuffy's Tavern, Heikenen's One-Stop, DeLuca Liquor.

"DeLuca, wasn't that Grandma Della's name?" I said, and Ma said,

"Stop the presses, we've got a genius on our hands."

Finally Bob parked where Ma pointed, in the middle of a block in front of a place called the Corner Bar.

"Wasn't a genius who named this establishment," said Bob.

"For your information," said Ma, "the Corner used to be on one, in the old days. Only they discovered a new vein of ore, had to move the whole town south, houses and all."

"You're a regular tour guide," said Bob, turning off the ignition. "You missed your calling."

"My calling, you may recall, was beautician," said Ma, ratting her hair with her fingertips. She was trying out a new effect—tiny stars at the tip of each nail. "Five months, Talk o'the Town Beauty College."

"Shouldn't that be Talk o'the Location?" I said.

"If you get any smarter," said Ma, opening the passenger door, "I swear I'm going to dis-locate something," and she picked up the Beefeaters and Wild Turkey and hopped down and marched across the sidewalk.

Just outside the red door she stopped. Shh, she says, listen. I thought I heard a motorcycle revving up inside. Step-in-wolf, she says, this is a sign, and in we stepped as the jukebox blared.

Ma walked into the Corner Bar like she was wearing a crown and trumpets were sounding. She paused just long enough in the open doorway for everyone inside to get a good long look at the vision of beauty which had just entered. Then she tapped in her gold open-toed sling-back wedgies across the red-and-black-speckled linoleum over to the bar and asked the bartender for set-ups in her best Farrah Fawcett voice. Her small high voice, the one featuring breaths between the words.

The bartender moved his cigar to the other side of his face, his belly to the other side of his belt. He looked down over the wide wooden bar at Ma's golden-wedgied feet.

"Pretty risk-ay, wouldn't you say?" he said, "this time of year?" and Ma said,

"Risk-ay (breath), that's my middle (breath) name (breath)."

We parked ourselves front and center at a table by the window, to get a bird's-eye view of the action, Ma said. It was more like Ma wanted the action to get a bird's-eye view of her. I was thinking there was more action waiting in line for a bus than in this particular establishment in this particular town Up North in the land of truth. Then Bob spotted a pool table and called over her shoulder they had Pac Man, and it looked like Space Invaders, too, which Ma had always referred to as her Space-in-Babysitter. In at least four establishments back in the city I'd been unbeaten champion.

I got up to follow Bob and glanced at Ma. She had a cigarette in one hand, a lit match in the other, only they weren't coming together. Instead she was staring straight out between them, her mouth half open, her eyes big as cueballs. I turned in the direction she was staring, and suddenly I was face to face with Destiny.

Only I didn't know this was Destiny. And Ma said later she'd thought it was a ghost. But she gave up the ghost idea when the match burnt down to her fingers and she saw things in a clearer light. Her hands jittered as she moved her cigarette between the ashtray and her lips. Her eyes jittered as she moved them between the barroom and Destiny. She motioned for Destiny to join us.

"It's when something happens," Ma said, "and it's like it happened before, in the exact same way. Or say you see someone, and you swear you've seen them before. I saw Destiny, I had deja view."

Destiny chewed her gum. She twirled her earring, a tiny pink rhinestone. She stared at us through her spidery mascara.

"It's just, you're the spitting image," said Ma. "Same eyes, same mouth. Same expression, for godsakes. It's my sister all over again, it's Doreen. It's Doreen at ..." Ma smiled shyly. "You must be about ... how old?"

Destiny said she was sixteen. She twirled the pink rhinestone ring on her little finger. She had no fingernails to speak of, they were bitten to rags. What she did have she'd painted pink. She said she'd never known her momma. She was wearing a pink rhinestone necklace and a long-sleeved pink sweatshirt featuring a teddy bear. Her white waitress apron was wrapped high up around her stomach, which stuck out like a pink bowling ball. She said she was pregnant.

I thought about this. "We're cousins," I said, and Ma said, "Meet your cousin, the genius."

"I seen pictures though," said Destiny. "Momma was pretty."

"Your mother," Ma said, "was a true beauty." Ma looked down at her hands, then back at Destiny. "And it looks like she might've passed that beauty on."

I was thinking I'd never seen Ma like this, talking all sweet to this hick like she was made out of glass and might break apart at any minute. From the back of the room came the clack of balls on the pool table, followed by a pause, followed by a cheer from Bob. I lit a cigarette, snuffed the match out between my fingers.

"So where's this true beauty these days?" I said, and blew a smoke ring toward the ceiling fan. From the back of Ma's throat came the sound of sucked-in breath, followed by a pause, followed by Destiny saying something which caught my attention.

"In the boneyard," she said, "out at Miner's Memorial."

She tucked her hair behind her ears, and something else caught my attention: the two hickeys spaced close together on her white neck, right above the pink rhinestone necklace. I was thinking maybe this cousin of mine wasn't such a hick after all. I held out a cigarette. But she shook her head, said she better not, Jimmy Carl said if she smoked his son would be born a midget, and no one to blame but a shit-for-brains mother.

I said, "How do you know it's a boy?"

"Jimmy Carl says Cermacks always make boys, it's in their

blood. He says if it ain't a boy, it ain't his."

I looked at Ma, who was looking at my cigarette. I moved it out of reach.

"Well, I'm not sure exactly how those things work," says Ma, "after all, we come from a long line of girls, girls run in our family."

"What do you spose they're running from?" I said. Ma ignored me.

"And every one of them girls is 'D's," said Destiny, leaning closer. Her eyeshadow was dark purple. She wore it in a circle around her eyes, which sat in the middle of her face like two holes. Maybe Up North this was the latest thing. I wondered if it was Mary Kay.

"It started, you know, with the DeLucas," said Destiny, "and them four girls, Daisy, Delores, that Deer one ... "

"Deirdre," said Ma.

"That's her." This subject had perked Destiny right up. "Then comes, you know, Della our grandma, and her three girls. Auntie Doris, your momma, my momma. Then there's me, then ... "

A black eyelash fell onto Destiny's white cheek. "What's your name?" she says.

I snorted. "A person goes into a coma when they're pregnant?"

Destiny shook her head. "I don't mean 'Sugar,' I mean your *real* name."

"That IS my real name," I said, and glared at Ma. I was forever hoping it had all been a joke, a punishment of some sort, that someday when I was old enough or punished enough or one of us was on our death bed, Ma would tell me that my real name was Janie or Susie. Even Lois.

Destiny stared. "Wow," she said.

"So fucking what," I said, "there's weirder names, like, for instance ... " I couldn't think of any just then.

32   MINIMUM MAINTENANCE

"That's not what I mean," she said. "I mean your name, Sugar with a S, not a D. Don't you see? You broke the chain. That's really somethin', you broke it."

A shiver ran up my arm. My chair felt like it was floating above the floor. My hair felt like it was floating above my head. I checked to see if someone had opened the red door. Maybe this was it, deja view. I tried to think. Had this happened before? Would I know what came next? The jukebox started up again. Some fruity guy, I couldn't understand a word he said.

"So, tell me, hon," says Ma, "if you have a girl, what will you name her?"

Destiny twirled her earring. The fruity guy kept at it. "I ain't really thought about it, I'm sure it'll be, you know, a boy ... Danny, or Denny ..."

"Doreen," I said, "your mother Doreen, how did she ... wind up in the boneyard?"

Destiny blinked. The eyelash dropped to her apron. Ma kicked me under the table.

"The meter man found her ..." said Ma.

"She was wearing her prom formal ..." said Destiny.

"It was an accident ..." said Ma.

"She hanged herself ..." said Destiny.

"*Don't think twice, it's all right...*" sang the guy on the jukebox, fruity but clear, finally something I could understand.

◆ ◆ ◆

"How can a person accidentally hang?" I asked.

"Come again?" said Bob.

I was watching the little arrow inside the bubble on Bob's dashboard. It was dancing all around the N, kicking up its little heels, like it was happy to be home. Bob would probably say it was the truck doing the dancing. Either way, we'd be heading for the W again in the morning, for Montana. But for now we were headed out to the location. I was spending the night with Destiny while Ma and Bob painted the town red, Ma said, isn't that goddamn hilarious? they should be painting this particular town blue, for instance, or maybe olive green.

"What I mean is," said Ma, tapping her fingernails on her gold bangle bracelet, "Doreen wasn't in her right mind when she did it (tap tap). She must've jumped the track for a minute (tap tap). What I mean is, if my sister had it to do over again ..."

"Was she wearing a ... a watchamacallit ..." I said, " ... on her head ... to go with the formal?"

"A tiara?" said Ma. "No, she wasn't wearing a goddamn tiara (tap). Jesus (tap tap)."

"How's that?" said Bob.

We flew through a railroad crossing and bounced up off the army blankets like three gigantic balls of silly putty. Two big white X's flashed past in the dark then disappeared Will you goddamn slow down, says Ma, we'll wind up wrapped around a goddamn red pine, Jesus. I was thinking, *Red* pine? the ore dust made it all the way out here, too?

Ma had another hit of Wild Turkey and continued the history lesson. It was cold. Real cold. I crossed my arms and watched the pines pass in the headlights, all straight and tall and disappearing up into the dark like pillars, like the pillars of a long bridge we might be crossing.

Bob kept driving. Ma kept talking, her words coming out in little puffs you could see. I kept listening, and after awhile it was all around me, there in the air, like I was breathing in a story, or maybe a song:

> *Della DeLuca a true beauty most beautiful of all the DeLuca daughters, shocked her family the whole town all within range the whole shocking range, by*

marrying too early too young too quick, a shotgun wedding a bun in the oven, and worse much worse by marrying beneath her, a location boy from a red-stained trailer and the girls jumping rope in the spring on the sidewalk chanted "Della DeLuca Hooked a Palooka."

Eli Kanezevich, location boy, loved his wife and his three baby daughters, each one prettier than the one before, and he worked his shifts and sold his trailer and built him a house a real house for his Della his Della, and he worked his shifts more and more until most of the time he was working or sleeping and it happened like that, his Della went odd.

Odd from the ladies the good catholic ladies who crossed the street when they saw Della coming, from the beauty which faded with every baby, from the blasting which knocked the iron set to cotton out from her hands to the barefoot floor, knocked cups from the railing, pictures from the wall, cracked windows, blew lightbulbs, broke vases, her heart, from the ore dust which settled over all that was Della's, her sheets on the line, her tulips, her eyes ...

"She did WHAT?" said Bob, turning toward Ma.
"LOOK OUT!" I hollered, and grabbed the steering wheel.
Bob jammed on the brake. Me and Ma flew against the dashboard, then back against the seat. Silly putty. The truck stalled out.
"JESUS H. CHRIST! You could've killed us!" screamed Ma, and she reached up and dug her fingernails into my spike and yanked.
Tears squirted into my eyes. I slapped my hand to my scalp. In the light from the dashboard I could see the clump of purple

hair in Ma's fingers. My own fingers curled. I could feel them curling curling, tighter tighter. I bit my tongue and looked away, out through the windshield into the dark.

The deer was still there, in the middle of the road, standing like a statue in the path of light from the truck. One of its ears twitched, one of its black eyes blinked. And this weird thing: it only had one horn.

"They get tranced by the light," Ma said. "They get blinded. You'd think after all these years, they'd have grown some brains. Just look at it," she said, "standing there like a goddamn fool. Might as well be wearing a goddamn target."

I stared at the deer. I was thinking about a book I remembered, back at the women's shelter, just a kid's book, I'd scoped it out when no one was looking. All about a pony with one horn, a unicorn, the book called it.

"Wait a minute," said Bob, punching in the lighter. "What you said back there, I mean about your mother, about Della."

"It was for punishment, is all," said Ma. "And what of it? Old country, is all. What's the difference between her ways and, say, getting hit with a belt? She learned it from a lady down the block," said Ma. "Only Della, she added her own twist. She made us sit at the kitchen table and watch the water heat up and think about our sins."

Ma called her mother by her first name, I noticed. I was thinking I might have to try that sometime. I was thinking I might wait until I got a little taller. The deer lifted one of its front legs, then set it carefully back down.

"I thought a deer had two horns," I said.

"Your sins?" said Bob. "Just how sinful does a little girl have to be to have her fingers HELD IN BOILING WATER?"

"Oh for godsakes," said Ma, "don't be so dramatic. Della was just highstrung, is all. Always needed to know where we were, always poking her head into our rooms, even at night. Like she might find the devil in there, dancing with her daughters in the moonlight. I'd be laying in bed listening to the trains. I'd be ... you know ... relaxing. Suddenly there's this silhouette in the doorway—none of the doors had doorknobs—that curly hair shooting out around her head like a Brillo pad."

Ma caught her breath. She was talking so much the windows had fogged up. I said it again,

"I thought a deer had two horns."

"They're called antlers, for godssake," said Ma. "Usually there's two, but they fall off in winter. Only this one's starting early, looks like. Now where was I?"

"Della in the doorway," said Bob.

"Yeah. So she cut her hair shorter and shorter the older she got. Gave herself a Toni every six weeks. Della didn't trust beauty parlors," said Ma. "She said beauticians were skags," and another new word entered my life.

"But weren't you ..." said Bob.

"So anyway," Ma said, "Della's dead. So that's goddamn that."

The lighter popped out, unlit. Bob fished in her olive green pockets. Ma unrolled the passenger window a few inches and tossed my hair into the ditch. I cleared a circle on the windshield with my hand. I was thinking about Ma's hands, her perfect nails, currently painted off-white with those tiny yellow stars. She always kept her nails long and pointy and smoothed with color. I was thinking about that boiling water.

"I could tell you every detail of your grandmother's kitchen, missy," said Ma, and I realized she was talking to me. She lifted the Wild Turkey. "Only you'll see it for yourself soon enough."

I ignored her and said the new word a few times in my head and stared out through the circle at the deer. When Ma was drinking, if she wasn't in the mood for dancing, her mouth never stopped. As if her throat got oiled up. Though certain subjects she refused to discuss, drunk or sober. My dad was one. Grandma Della's death seemed to be another.

I knew something had happened to my grandma, but I didn't know what. I knew Destiny lived in Della's old house, that she lived there by herself, that the County was none the wiser. According to Ma, whenever folks up here in the land of truth could put one over on the government, they considered it an A-major cause for celebration, meaning break out the animal theme bottles and load up the guns. Which, depending on the time of year, meant shooting whatever moved: birds in the air, animals in the woods, shadows under the yardlight.

I was thinking maybe somebody shot Grandma Della.

Ma told us that her own first official date had been a shooting date, which automatically put you in a higher category: if a boy took you out to shoot something, going steady was next. Ma's date had been with the boy who set pins at the Lucky Strike. He took her and a bottle of Blackberry Brandy in his father's LeMans out to the municipal dump to shoot rats. He shone the LeMans headlights onto the hills of garbage and picked off the rats with a twenty-two and picked off kisses between gulps of Blackberry Brandy and then Ma's hair got caught in her push-up bra. Mookie LeBarge loved me for my hair, says Ma, so long and straight and shining, at which point Bob says, Other than hair and a gun barrel, what else might that describe? at which point Ma says, Never mind all that, your first love's the hardest, and Bob says, I rest my case.

"Okay okay," says Bob, "let's get this show on the road," and she turns off the headlights.

And there we are, the three of us just sitting in the dark listening to each other breathe. I'm still thinking about the tips of Ma's nails and watching the tip of Bob's cigarette, which reminds me of a tiny stoplight.

"So if red means 'Stop' and green means 'Go'," I say, "what does yellow mean?"

And though I wasn't talking to her, Ma answers. "It's a

warning," she says. "You're in the chickenshit zone, better watch your ass."

When Bob turned the lights back on, the deer was gone.

Destiny had a shoebox of tapes by that fruity guy I'd heard on the jukebox at the Corner. She told me the guy had grown up around there, only in those days people just made fun of him. I said maybe they couldn't understand what he was saying. But Destiny said, No, it was on account of he was skinny and had no interest in learning to drive a Euclid.

"So he got pissed off and left town and turned famous," she said. "Now they name bars and sandwiches after him. Only he could care less, he lives in California."

When Destiny first saw me coming through her front door that evening, she'd led me straight to the kitchen and turned on the oven. Don't worry, she said, in no time flat I'd be warm again. I was thinking that might not happen until July. We sat down across from each other at the kitchen table, in front of the open oven door, a couple of Cokes and the ghetto blaster between us.

The guy's voice sort of grew on you, like listening to traffic or somebody vacuuming. After awhile you didn't want it to stop. Destiny said the tapes had belonged to her momma, and along with the prom formal and a collection of stuffed poodles, they were all she had left of her momma in this world.

By this time the kitchen was getting pretty toasty, and Destiny pulled off the pink teddy bear sweatshirt. Underneath she was wearing a pink tank top. I stared at her across the red-and-white-checked table cloth. The floor was covered with red-and-white-checked linoleum, the windows with red-and-white-checked curtains. The walls were covered with red-and-white strawberry wallpaper. Destiny was covered with hickeys.

There were hickeys on her arms and her chest, and in the bright kitchen light, I saw a few more on her neck I hadn't noticed in the bar. Suddenly I had that floaty feeling again, that deja view. Or maybe it was shyness, in the face of all this love. I thought of what Ma had said, that Destiny was beautiful. Maybe I was starting to see it. Maybe something was coming together.

I took a sip of Coke, cleared my throat. "Can I ask you something?" Destiny shrugged. "It's just, well ... what do you think of me?"

"You're okay," she said.

"No, I mean, my face. What do you think of my face?"

She didn't answer right away. So I said,

"I'm just wondering, because a person doesn't really know what they look like, you know?" I said, "When I try to think of my own face, I draw a blank."

"Well, it ain't lopsided or nothin'," said Destiny.

"No, no, what I mean is, do you think someday ... well, do you think ..."

But I just couldn't do it, couldn't ask this girl if she thought maybe someday someone might want to give me hickeys, too. My cheeks felt hot. I looked away. I didn't mean to, I looked straight at her big pink bowling ball stomach.

Destiny giggled. "Well, you know, you gotta get a boyfriend first."

I said, "I know that, what do you think, I'm a moron?"

Actually I was trying to figure a way around the boyfriend bit. Mostly I thought boys were crybabies. They could dish it out, but they couldn't take it. I'd never met one who didn't go looking for his mommy the first time I did my eye trick, or threatened to hypnotize him without him knowing. My dad taught me the eye trick on one of his last visits, though Ma absolutely forbid me to do it in her presence, she said, or she wouldn't be held responsible for what she might do. The hypnotizing bit was a plain lie, but most boys bought it hook, line and sinker.

40   MINIMUM MAINTENANCE

The closest I'd ever come to a real boyfriend—not counting that friend of Ma's who used to come into my room—was back at the shelter, the kid with three earrings who used to sneak up to the roof with me to smoke. Terrell was between foster homes, he didn't even have a mommy to run to. He bumped me with his face once, maybe on purpose, only he was so short he just smeared snot on my T-shirt. If I'd've known about arm hickeys at the time, I could've probably got Terrell to do the job for a couple extra Kools.

I just wanted the hickeys, forget the boyfriend. I just wanted people to see me coming and say to themselves, Will you look at that girl, that lucky girl.

I said, "Ma says it's a sign somebody loves you."

Now Destiny's cheeks turned red. She rested a hand on her stomach. "That's just what Jimmy Carl says."

I lit a cigarette. "So does it hurt? Or what?"

Destiny looked at me. "Only at first. You get used to it."

"How long does it take?"

"Well, you know, not long."

"How long does it last? I mean, until you need to do it again?"

Destiny stared. "Well, I suppose it depends on how many you want..."

"What if I wanted, say, a few significant ones, but not as many as you have?"

Destiny blinked. "Wait a sec," she said. "You're talkin' about babies, right?"

"Fuckenay!" I said, and choked out smoke. "I was talking about hickeys, for godssake. All your hickeys. Jesus."

Destiny's eyes grew. "Hickeys? What hickeys?"

I shook my head. This girl was something else. "It's coma time again," I said, and pointed to her bare arm laying on the table. "*Those* hickeys." Then I said, "And while we're on the subject, and don't take this wrong, but I was wondering, d'ya think that maybe next time, you know, you might not have so many done?"

Destiny looked at her arm, then back at me. "But these aren't..."

Her face kept that wide-open look for a few seconds more. Then it just closed down, like somebody turned some lights off. She pulled her arm back, felt for her sweatshirt. When the phone rang, she jumped. When she reached to turn down the ghetto blaster, her hand was shaking. I was thinking being pregnant was the absolute pits, you'd have to be nuts to do it. While Destiny tried to maneuver out of her chair, I got up, walked over, picked up the phone.

"Hickey haven," I answered. Nobody said anything. So I said,

"Nothing too tricky 'bout giving a hickey." Then a guy's voice said,

"What the fuck kinda shit is this?"

"Excuse me?" I said.

"That's how you answer the fuckin' horn?" said the voice. "You think you're so cute, 'cuz you're knocked up? Huh? You are one stupid..."

"Jimmy Carl?" I said. "Is that you? We haven't met yet..."

But Destiny grabbed the receiver. The cord was long and stretched out and she pulled it into the back hall and closed the door. I shrugged. Suit yourself, I said to no one, and rooted around for the bottle Destiny told me Jimmy Carl kept in the cupboard over the sink. I walked back to the table, poured some in my glass, turned the ghetto blaster back up. I was beginning to understand this sandwich-named guy better and better. I started singing along,

"Leave at your own chosen speed..."

I sang and circled Della DeLuca's red-and-white kitchen and sipped my Coke-and-Old Crow and tried to come up with the

42 MINIMUM MAINTENANCE

best boy-less way of going about getting some hickeys.

◆ ◆ ◆

Ma's idea of punishment had always been this: she'd ignore me.

Say I was being bad, as in the usual day-to-day stuff. She'd stop looking at me or talking to me for a few hours until she needed someone to give her a neck rub or go down to the Seven-Eleven with a note for cigarettes or three-two beer. Say I was being unusually bad. She'd lock me *in* the apartment and leave and she might not come back until after dark and usually not alone.

But say I was being A-major evil. She'd lock me *out* of the apartment and play the stereo real loud so she couldn't hear me kicking the door. A couple times she left me out in the hallway all night. Once she sent me out there with some clothes packed in my Barbie overnight case. I left the building and walked over to the People's Park and slept behind a Satellite. I figured no one would bother me there. I figured Ma would think I'd been kidnapped and call the cops. When I went back to the apartment next morning some guy answered the door, asked me who I was and why did I stink. He wasn't a cop. Ma was still sleeping.

Like the time I cut off my hair to one inch and dyed it black. This was on account of that friend of Ma's who was always sneaking into my room. I'd be asleep, suddenly there he'd be, standing over me, just wanted to smooth my hair, he'd say, please let him smooth my beautiful angel hair. I was tired all the time. I tried explaining things to Ma, only she'd have none of it, told me I'd been without a father so long I'd forgotten how to act, now just look what I'd gone and done, I'd gone and forced her to think about that A-major asshole and ruined her day. Then she ignored me. When she left the apartment, I headed for the bathroom. I was going through a Joan Jett phase, that was the look I went for. A few days later when I started ripping holes in my T-shirts and using black Magic Marker on my lips, Ma came up with a new angle: she'd lock me in the broom closet before she left.

Mostly, though, Ma told me I was *her* punishment on this green earth. I'd ask her what was it she'd done to deserve me, and she'd say she hadn't the foggiest, the lord works in mysterious ways, she'd always tried her goddamn best, look where it got her. I was thinking at least it didn't get her accidentally hanged.

When I finally felt warm again, Destiny took me on a tour of the house. She started with the root cellar where Grandma Della used to keep her potatoes, then the bedrooms where she used to keep her daughters, and ended with the front room, where I found myself staring up at a shelf, at a row of stuffed poodles. The poodles were made out of netting, poofy like clouds, in various pastel colors. They had long curly eyelashes and big staring eyes with a sequin in the middle and black velvet collars and tiny pink tongues. Destiny said her momma had gotten them with Green Stamps, they'd been all the rage.

"A week later," said Destiny, "I mean, after the meter man found her, Green Stamps calls. Doreen Kane's twelfth poodle come in, they says, she can stop on over and pick it up."

I counted. "There's only eleven."

"Nobody picked the twelfth one up," said Destiny. "Her being dead and all."

I looked at the dogs. They looked back, eyes bright and flat with that silver sequin, tongues hanging down like they might be dying of thirst. The netting looked stiff and scratchy. I thought of the prom dress Destiny had showed me in an upstairs closet. She'd pulled a photo album off the closet shelf, pictures of the old days, black-and-white with those little triangles at the corners. One in particular caught my eye: a group of girls lined up like bowling pins on the edge of a gigantic hole. The hole took up most of the picture. Then a few pages over, another group of girls sitting in the back of a gigantic truck. Slow down, I said, who *are* they all? But Destiny was flipping to the last page, to a girl standing in Grandma Della's front room in a long dress, holding a bouquet of flowers. The girl was looking off to the side, but I could tell she was pretty. Real pretty. Behind her along a shelf a row of stuffed poodles stared back at the camera.

Now here were those poodles in real life. I cleared my throat.

"Your mom," I said, "Aunt Doreen . . . why did she do it? Why did she . . ."

"On account of me," said Destiny. "Momma wasn't married, she'd went to the unwed mother's home. Grandma Della was gonna give me to the next door neighbors. She was gonna let some other lady raise me, make Momma watch, not be able to say nothin'."

I thought about this. "But why didn't your momma just, you know, grab you and run? Head for the hills?"

Destiny put her hand on her stomach, leaned against the recliner. "It was different in them days. A girl like that, not married with a little baby, that girl was branded."

"Branded?" I was thinking that'd be right up Grandma Della's alley, going after her daughter with a red hot poker.

"You know, like a bad rep," said Destiny. "Like a slut."

"A skag?" I said, and Destiny said, Yeah, like that.

"Anyways," she said, "she did it in her prom formal because . . ." she lowered her voice, as if somebody—the dogs, for instance—might be listening, " . . . well, because she *did it* in her prom formal."

We looked at each other, and we started to giggle. Then we started to laugh. We laughed harder and harder, we couldn't help it, until we started to cry. And that's how we were, Destiny trying to catch her breath, me trying to wipe my tears, when the doorbell started to ring. That's what it did. The doorbell just kept on ringing, just one long ring. I wiped my cheeks. Destiny smoothed her sweatshirt.

"Jimmy Carl," she whispered. "He likes to lay on it."

I looked at her and she looked at me and we started in again. Then suddenly the ringing stopped. Destiny slapped her hand over her mouth, raised her finger to shush me. She took a deep breath, walked over, opened the door, and in walks her boyfriend.

"Cat got your tongue?" says Jimmy Carl. He winks at me, scoops Destiny up against him with one arm. He kisses her on the mouth, puts a big hand on her stomach.

"How's Jimmy Junior tonight?" he says, then he looks at me. "And how's ...?"

I don't know what I expected, but Jimmy Carl wasn't it. It wasn't his Jack Daniels hat, or his red-stained workboots, or the belt buckle which said Sit On This. It wasn't even his sideburns and mustache. It was that his sideburns and mustache were striped with gray, there were wrinkles around his gray eyes. Jimmy Carl was ancient. I thought of that friend of Ma's. I thought of my spike, ran my fingers through it.

"That's Sugar," says Destiny, and Jimmy Carl moves his eyes.

"That's for her to know and me to find out," he says.

"I was just showing Sugar the poodles," says Destiny.

"Well, ain't that a fuckin' riot," says Jimmy Carl, and twirls his keys. "Youse gals sure know how to have yourself a party. Now move your asses, the truck's runnin'. And dress for it, the heater ain't workin' so good."

Destiny handed me a jacket from a hook in the hallway and started toward the door. I was thinking of something. I pulled the jacket around my shoulders.

"Do they still have Green Stamps?" I asked.

They both looked at me.

I said, "The store, the Green Stamps store." I looked at Destiny. "Maybe it's in the back, in a box or something."

"What're you yappin' about?" said Jimmy Carl, and pushed open the door.

"I was just thinking," I said, "maybe it's still around somewhere. The last poodle."

Jimmy Carl was still cackling about that last poodle when we saw the first deer. His truck was old and cold, with two big orange fire decals pasted on the hood like they might actually help. Destiny sat in the middle between us, her knees on either side of the long gear shaft. Every time her boyfriend shifted, she giggled. When he made a sharp left and downshifted, she laughed out loud.

"Shut the fuck up!" he barked, just as his headlights picked out the deer standing in the ditch up ahead. He hit the brakes and the tires sprayed gravel. The deer jumped away into the woods.

It happened so fast, I wasn't sure there had even been a deer. And when Jimmy Carl's hand flew off the gear shift onto Destiny's face, I wasn't sure that happened, either. I'd already figured this out: driving these location roads at night, with the woods packed in on either side, shadows appearing and disappearing, a person could start seeing all sorts of things.

Destiny made a noise, then she was quiet. Jimmy Carl let out his breath real slow.

"Now, baby," he says, "one more time. What're we doin' here?"

"Moonlighting deer," says Destiny.

"And what two things does that call for?"

"Patience and silence," says Destiny.

Jimmy Carl pulled carefully at a piece of her hair. "You know I don't like it tucked behind your ears, baby."

He reached under the seat, pulled out a bottle of Old Crow, had a few swallows. He rested his head against the gun hanging on the rack behind him. The gun was long and dark and shiny. The rack was two deer feet pointing upward. He put the bottle back under the seat, and started along the road again. Destiny moved against him and stared straight ahead. I watched the shadows at the edge of the woods.

The second deer stood in the ditch staring into the headlights exactly long enough for Jimmy Carl to stop the truck, open the door, step down onto the gravel. The whole procedure must've taken ten minutes, the only sounds being the wind and the squeak of Jimmy Carl's jeans. But just as his boot touched down, the deer snapped out of it, snorted, and was gone in a flash. I let out a little cheer under my breath. Destiny jabbed me with her elbow.

"Don't be a idiot," she whispered.

"Don't call me any of your family names," I whispered back, and we smothered our giggling.

Meanwhile Jimmy Carl swore and walked across the road and pissed in the ditch.

"I swear them sons of bitches got a sixth sense," he said, climbing back in, reaching for the Old Crow. He took a swallow, then held the bottle toward me. I took a swallow. My toes shook. I took another. My hair got pins and needles.

Jimmy Carl grinned. "Ha!" he says. "Have enough of that there shit, lil' Sugarcube, you'll be seein' poodles everywhere. Ha!"

I had one more swallow and waited for the little warm river to find its way to my stomach. I passed the bottle back.

"I've been wondering," I said, "why don't you have a ... watchamacallit ... a compass on your dashboard?"

Jimmy Carl snorted. "Don't fuckin' need one," he said. "Live in a place long enough, you sure as hell better know where the fuck you're goin'."

Destiny leaned back, half asleep, her hands twitching in her lap. I sat forward, away from the gun rack. Jimmy Carl drove through the dark. One road led to another, each one skinnier than the one before. The woods changed, other trees mixing with the pines, naked and nervous in the wind.

Jimmy Carl had just announced, What the fuck, no luck, he was calling it a night, when suddenly, there in the middle of the road stood another deer. Its eyes were black in the headlights, with a circle of light in the middle. This deer was taller than the others, stronger-looking, and this: it had one antler spiked out above its head like it might be having an idea. The unicorn deer. My hair got pins and needles.

"Well, I'll be fucked," whispered Jimmy Carl. "I been hearin' about this bastard."

The truck slowed, then stopped. Jimmy Carl put his hand over Destiny's mouth and nudged her awake. Her eyes flew open. He reached around for the gun, lifted the door handle, pushed the door slowly outward. He swung one boot onto the gravel, then the other. When he stepped out, his gun bumped against the open door. The deer blinked, and blinked again. But it didn't move. Jimmy Carl took another step, then one more, then he raised his gun.

What happened next was like those dreams you forget as soon as you wake up, though you can remember being somewhere else a split second ago. The last thing I remember was that deer, that gun barrel, how I wanted more than anything to do something, to reach out, to stop this. The next thing I knew the headlights were off, then the blast of a car horn, then a rifle explosion. And then finally just darkness, with all those echoes clanging around.

And this I remember, too: afterward, Jimmy Carl was silent. Patient and silent. As soon as he realized the deer had hightailed it, he carefully put his gun back on the rack and had himself another belt, though he didn't offer me any. He kissed

Destiny's cheek and patted her knee, then put his truck in gear and started back. One road led to another, each one wider than the one before. Until we were back on blacktop bumping along in fourth, crossing that piney bridge with all those broken highway lines slipping away beneath us.

Destiny stopped shaking. My ears stopped ringing. Jimmy Carl drove. Our breaths appeared then disappeared like smoke. But all those roads and miles back to the house, no one said a word.

At last we pulled into Grandma Della's sideyard. Jimmy Carl reached across and opened the passenger door. On its way back his hand brushed my jacket. Then it curled tight around Destiny's arm. He kissed her on the mouth. He kissed her again. He laid his hand over her big stomach.

"Baby, I'll leave youse two to your slumber party," he said. "But tomorrow night, we'll have us another get-together. We'll show lil' cuz over there just how things are done up here in god's country. Ha! I'll bring the pizza ..." and he whispered this next part, but I heard, " ... and a friend."

Then he said, "Now, tell me baby, who d'ya love?"

But I didn't hear Destiny's answer. I was gone, hurrying through the cold toward the back porch light.

◆ ◆ ◆

Bob's brother Elroy had his ways, being a motorhead from the Boonies and all. He and Ma met on the job, Ma being up on stage dancing with the other girls, Elroy being down at a table drinking with the other guys. But Elroy was never Ma's type. Eventually Ma just left him in her wake, is how Bob put it. And now here we were, on our way to Montana, all three of us caught up in the making of Ma's wake.

Only sometimes I wished they'd left me in the Boonies with Elroy.

It's hard to explain. Elroy never said much, just went about his business, messing with his junk cars, selling parts to other motorheads. Though he was a good cook, peanut butter and potato chip sandwiches being his specialty. He was easy to be around, sort of like being with no one. Like being with yourself. He never went anywhere, which drove Ma up a tree. Come on, she'd say, get your butt in gear, she and Bob were in the mood, the town was in dire need of painting. But Elroy would just shake his head and reach for the TV Guide. When I went to bed he'd be watching the late movie. The last thing I'd remember was the stars in the window and the smell of reefer. The first thing next morning, it was the sun and the smell of coffee.

Elroy had a saying, and this saying stuck with me like glue since first I heard it. Like those ordinary times, out of all the other possible times, that for some reason a person remembers, as if somebody took a picture. Maybe it's your ma laughing by an open car window. Or the first time you ever saw a duck. Maybe it's the time you dreamed you were a dutchgirl, standing in tulips in wooden shoes.

Elroy said: "I may be ignorant, but I ain't stupid."

Not that I know what this means exactly. Only sometimes I find myself saying it over and over, like a chant, or a song you just can't get out of your head even though it's driving you mental, for instance anything by K.C. and the Sunshine Band.

What I mean is this: Jimmy Carl believed I was the one who turned off the lights and blew the horn in his truck. Well, I may be ignorant, but I ain't stupid. It wasn't me who saved the unicorn deer. It was Destiny.

Later, after her boyfriend had dropped us off and we'd locked the door and turned out the lights and Destiny had gone up to her room, I was lying on the sofa bed in Grandma Della's front room, watching the little window of fire in the oil heater, thinking about that deer. And the more I thought about him, moving around somewhere out in the dark safe woods, the more I felt those poodles on that shelf with their wide-awake eyes watching me. I thought of my aunt in her long scratchy dress, with a long scratchy rope around her neck, and I thought of her daughter Destiny.

By the time I felt the first dream coming on—something about a bowling alley which kept turning into a beauty parlor with trees for customers with hair instead of leaves—the dark was already fading to gray. But I had a plan. Now more than ever I was determined to get myself some hickeys. In honor of my cousin, the deer-saver. And I'd finally figured out how.

In the morning I stayed on the sofa bed, rolled in my blankets like a plaid mummy, and watched Destiny get ready for her GED class. A girl from class was coming to pick her up. Afterward she had her shift at the Corner, and by the time she got home, I'd be long gone on the road to Montana. I told her to tell Jimmy Carl sorry about the party, maybe next time.

It was a little after nine. Ma and Bob would be swinging by around noon. I curled tighter and yawned. I could see Destiny through the archway, watched her turn down the flame so the coffee wouldn't boil over.

"Is it ever warm here?" I asked.

Destiny poked her head around the corner. She was pouring coffee into a thermos.

"I was just wondering if there's such thing as summer Up North," I said. "I'm fucking freezing."

"This ain't nothin'," said Destiny. "I seen it cold enough to freeze spit. Just blows apart into little bitsy pieces before it hits the ground." She moved her hand in a half circle, the shape of a rainbow. "Like, you know, a magic wand? Like stardust, like that." She reached for her jacket.

"That's a thing everybody oughta see," she said.

I thought I could see where her hand had made the rainbow,

as if she'd left something behind in the air, something glittery. I rubbed my eyes.

"Any coffee?" I said, swinging my stocking feet to the cold floor. This would be a first, but I needed something warm.

"Half a pot, burner's on," said Destiny. "Oven door's open, too. Just remember turn 'em both off."

We heard a car in the driveway, and looked at each other. All my life before, I didn't even know Destiny existed. Now I was leaving, things would go back the way they'd been. Like throwing a rock into a lake, and all those circles appear. Before the water smooths over again.

"Hey," I said, "a penny for your thoughts," which is something Ma always used to say until the time I said, Make that a quarter, and she never said it again. So now I said,

"Make that fifty cents."

Destiny tried to pull the jacket closed, which didn't work. "It's nothin'," she said. "It's just ... well, I was wondering if you might like something, you know, to take with? A souvenir or something. To remember me by."

She glanced up at the shelf. "One of the poodles, maybe?"

I looked. The poodles looked back. I shivered, not from cold. A car horn honked. It was now or never.

"Hey, Destiny," I said, "I've been wanting to ask you something. It's just, well, how did Grandma Della die exactly?"

Destiny blinked.

"My ma won't talk about it," I said. "I was just wondering if somebody shot her, or something." I looked toward the window. "Or, I don't know, maybe she froze to death."

"Who said she died?" said Destiny.

"Well, Ma," I said.

"Well, she ain't dead," said Destiny, in that same way she'd told me about Aunt Doreen. As if a teacher had called on her and for once she knew the right answer.

"Well, maybe in a way she is," said Destiny. "She's over at

Moose Lake. Last time I visited she wouldn't even talk, not one word, didn't even look at me. Just wanted to be wheeled around the halls in her wheelchair. Just kept wavin' slow and smilin' at everybody, even the nurses, like she was a queen on a float in a parade." Destiny's face lit up. "I seen a guy over there, he just lays under his bed all day. Thinks he's fixin' his car."

I said, "Moose Lake ..."

"The loony bin," says Destiny. "Jimmy Carl says that's where I'll end up, if I ain't careful. He says it runs in families."

"But how ..."

"Well, for one thing, I'm always wantin' to move somewheres else," said Destiny. "The Cities, maybe. He says it's a sign of a weak mind, when a person can't make do in their own back yard. He says ..."

"I mean how did she wind up in the loony bin?"

"I don't know, she's there is all. One day I wake up, she's gone. Next thing I know, she's got shocked."

"She got hit by lightning?"

"Shock treatments," said Destiny. "They electrocute your memory, so you can be calm and watch TV. So I moved in with the neighbors, which is weird, that's where I'd've been if Momma wasn't hanged. Anyways, they moved away, so I moved back here. I don't know, maybe I have a weak mind from all that movin'. But I do think about it, you know, about leavin'. I'm tired of bein' so ... bein' so ... only Jimmy Carl ..."

Destiny moved her books to her other arm. "So what d'ya think?" she said. "About the poodle?"

I glanced at the shelf again. The poodles stared, like they'd been doing all night, like they would all day and for the nights and days to come, like they'd done since the days when they'd been all the rage and Doreen Kane had lined them up there, since all the times they watched her leave through that door, and then that one special night in her long scratchy dress, through the months when she was gone and the day when she came back, until the afternoon the meter man came, and when Green Stamps called. And all that time those same sequin eyes, those lashes and tongues and toenails.

The horn honked again.

"Listen," I said, "about the poodle. I mean, I'm not sure that's such a good idea, on account of, well, there's not much room in Bob's truck. Besides, you don't want to, you know, break up the collection or anything . . ."

"Forget it," said Destiny, looking away, moving her books again. "I shouldn't've brang it up." She turned toward the door.

"But wait a sec," I said, "I'll keep my eye out. If I ever come across another one. You know, like the twelfth one, the one nobody picked up. The last poodle."

I was thinking about the night before, how her boyfriend had gotten such a kick out of this. It worked. My cousin grinned.

"That Jimmy Carl, ain't he the one though? If he ain't the one."

"And if he ain't the one," I said, "who is?"

We looked at each other. Then we started to giggle. Then we started to laugh. Then out on the driveway an engine gunned and Destiny jumped.

And I was thinking, what's so hard? You just get in a car, or on a bus or a plane, or you stick out your thumb, and you leave. Ma left—her family, this town, she was always leaving something—now here she was, leaving again. I was thinking I only wanted to ask her if maybe on our way out we could swing by Moose Lake. I only wanted to get a look at this grandma, who wasn't dead, who'd found her own way of leaving. I'd tell Ma Della wouldn't even know us, all she did was watch "Hollywood Squares" and cruise around in her wheelchair. I'd be sure to mention the guy under the bed, if nothing else, he'd be worth checking out.

"At least," I said, waving my hand at Destiny's stomach, "whatever it is, don't have it start with a D."

She didn't say anything. Then she said, "I'll think about it."

"See ya," I said. Then I said, "Skag."

"See ya," she said, and we both smiled, exactly together, like we might be looking in a mirror. Then the door closed with a whoosh of cold and Destiny was gone.

I heard the car spin out and drive away. I checked the time, pulled on my hightops and ran upstairs. I hurried back down, pulled a chair up to the open oven door, poured myself a cup of coffee. I spread everything out on the counter—ashtray, cigarettes, photo album, hand mirror, and six of the pink plastic clothespins Destiny used to hang up her L'eggs—and got to work.

Halfway through the photo album I stopped at a picture of a girl standing next to a snowbank. The girl was young and her hair was long and the snowbank was gigantic. Mostly it was a picture of white. I was wondering if this was Grandma Della, if a person's hair changed once they'd been shocked, when I heard the front door open and close and footsteps move down the hall. I heard the footsteps stop at the kitchen archway, I heard a voice.

"What in god's name . . ."

I turned, careful not to jiggle the clothespins. I'd already learned how much it hurt to do that. There stood Ma, mouth open, hand clutching her neck, with Bob right behind, both of them stark still, square in the middle of the archway, like you could put little black triangles around this and slap it on a page.

One of the clothespins caught against my shoulder. I lifted it carefully, touched each of the other five. They still held. I'd tried to place them unevenly on my neck, so as to look natural. I'd tested one after about fifteen minutes, unpinching it to see if it'd taken. The skin had just started to turn blue, so I put it back. I figured it would take about an hour to get the look I wanted.

"Ma," I said, holding the album open, "look what I found. I think it's your ... I think it might be Grandma Della." I took a breath. "Now listen, Ma, don't get mad, but, well, Destiny told me ... what I mean is, I wanted to ask you ..."

"WHAT IN GOD'S NAME ..." Ma said again.

And then Bob did something that turned out to be the wrong thing. She started to laugh. In fact, she started to snort. Which didn't bother me so much. But Ma was a different matter. She snapped out of it real quick, and came marching across the red-and-white-checked linoleum in those clackety wedgies. Before I knew what was happening, she'd yanked off one of the clothespins. My mouth fell open, my breath fell out. Then she yanked off another and a sound came out of my mouth. She managed to pull off one more before I stood up and stepped back, knocking into the chair, my eyes fogging over.

"FUCKENAY!" I hollered.

But the oven door was open and I lost my balance, then I was falling against the stove and all that coffee from the pot on the stove that hot hot coffee was slow motion falling for a split second nothing no falling no feeling and then everything speeded up all at once onto my arm.

As far as pain goes, clothespins are nothing compared to coffee. I almost didn't notice the truck turning onto Destiny's road as we drove off, but then I saw the fire decals. I was thinking, But this is too early, did somebody get it wrong about the party? I was about to ask Bob to turn around, go back, only my arm started screaming again and I lost track of things.

If this had been night, I might've rolled up my sleeve to

find my skin glowing in the dark like a night light or radiation. But this was noon, and there we were, bumping along in Bob's truck, heading in to cruise the main drag one last time on our way out of town. Ma told me to quit crabbing, it was only a butter burn, lucky for me I'd been wearing a long-sleeved shirt, to which Bob replied, Actually long sleeves make it worse, to which Ma replied, Whatever, and held out the tub of Promise she'd copped from Destiny's fridge. So far the Promise didn't seem to be working.

Then Ma started in. She thought she'd been fucking dreaming when she came around the corner into that kitchen, she'll say it again, I surely am her punishment on this green earth, what had she ever done to deserve such a re-tard, Jesus H. Christ in a Cadillac. I'd pretty much decided I'd save any questions about Moose Lake until some later date, I was in enough hot water. Maybe someday, when I was old enough to drive, I'd come back Up North. If Destiny was still around, I'd take her and her baby with me out to the loony bin. People in shock might get a real bang out of a baby. We could hang around, help the nurses, watch TV. We could even join Della's parade, I'd never ridden in a wheelchair.

I looked out the passenger window, trying to remember what all these buildings had been, trying to remember if Ma had said any of them had been a Green Stamps store. I watched the streets pass and pretended I could hear music to drown out the sound of Ma's voice. We passed the Corner Bar and I swore I could hear it, clear as a bell in my head, over and over like background music, like those trains at night,

"*chosen speed chosen speed chosen speed . . .*"

"I gotta find a goddamn Rexall's," said Ma, studying her roots in the rearview mirror. "My luck we'll be in the middle of No Mans Land, I'll need a touch-up." She squinted up the street. "Seems there used to be one right around . . . there!"

We passed a drug store. The sign still hung over the sidewalk, but the door was boarded up. "COMM. PROP. FOR SALE" painted across the window in bright red. We passed what used to be a Woolworth's, and further down, what used to be a Monkey Ward's, Ma said, with an attached beauty bar. She was starting to sweat it, I could tell. We passed Big Nick's. We passed DeLuca Liquor.

At the far end of town Bob stopped for gas. Three guys were standing around a pickup over by the air pump, smoking and watching the vehicles come and go. The pickup was painted camo. The guys could've won a Jimmy Carl look-alike. They smoked and watched us get out of the truck. They watched Bob start the pump. They smoked. They watched me and Ma cross the street to the Seven-Eleven.

We were on our way back when one of the guys lowered the rear of the camo truck, and I saw: a deer was laying in the truck bed. A big deer. I could only see its back, I couldn't see its head, couldn't see if . . .

In the middle of the street I stopped. I couldn't move. Couldn't breathe. A sound was banging in my ears. Ma yanked my arm just as a car swerved around us and laid on its horn. It was my burned arm, I barely noticed.

"Have you lost your goddamn mind?" she said. "Your brain must be goddamn frozen solid. Now get a move on."

I looked down, followed the backs of her knees to Bob's truck. I got in. I didn't look up.

In the truck Ma settled herself between me and Bob, pulled a box out of the bag she was carrying. Thank christ for Loving Care, she says, after all a blond's a blond, what do these goddamn rednecks know anyway? She pulls out two King Cans of three-two beer, a Coke, a giant-sized box of Fiddle Faddle, and a People magazine. Then she holds the bag towards me and tips it. A pair of sunglasses with silver frames and red metallic lenses falls onto my lap. Snowplowers, the girl at the Seven-Eleven called them, best things ever for winter glare. I put them on. The world changed.

Bob pulled out onto the pink street, let out the clutch, laid down a long pink patch right there on County Road 37.

"Yee-ha!" says Bob.

"Montana here we come!" says Ma. I look up, one of the pink Jimmy Carls flips us the bird. I flip it right back.

Then we drove. The pink trees slipped by. The pink signs passed. I sipped my Coke. Ma and Bob sipped their beers. After awhile Ma lowered her magazine, turned toward me with her beery breath. I could feel her studying me.

"I hate to admit it," she said, "but they do look like the real thing. If I don't say so myself." I realized she was talking about my hickeys. I sat up straighter.

"You are something else, Sugarpuss, you know that?" She was using her new sweet voice, the one she'd used with Destiny. "How did you ever come up with such an idea? How did you know it would work?"

I decided to chance it. "I'm a genius," I said.

"She's a genius," said Bob.

"I'll say it again," said Ma, smoothing back her pink bangs, "in that regard, she takes after her old lady."

"Why," I said, "because you figured out a way to get out of this town?" and Ma said,

"No, because you understand about beauty. That beauty is just delusion."

"That's 'illusion'," said Bob.

"Whatever," said Ma, and raised her pink King Can.

I had no idea what they were talking about. But I took advantage of the friendly atmosphere and lit a cigarette. Ma didn't seem to notice. She patted my knee and smiled, and after awhile turned back to her People. I turned back to the road, to the pink woods streaming past, and continued to watch for deer. I saw one, finally, but only for a split second, and only as it jumped away, its tail like a pink flag waving.

Then I didn't see any more, and after awhile I stopped watching. Instead I watched the little arrow inside its little bubble wobble slowly away from the N. Instead I started thinking about all the strangers who would see me in the days to come, who would see me and say, Look at that girl, that lucky girl. My hickeys would last for a week and a half. About as long as it would take for Ma's roots to start showing again.

3

Still Life

After he left, my dad would drop back in once in awhile to check up on things. Somehow he always found us. One day there'd be a knock on the door of our latest apartment. He'd be leaning on a cue stick in the hallway, a six pack under his arm, a smile so wide it had to hook itself onto his dimples to keep from falling. A shit-eater grin, Ma called it.

"What's the news from the front?" he'd say, and pat my head and open a beer, and if Ma was there, she'd start in. Where the fuck had he been, who the fuck did he think he was, why the fuck didn't he send her any money, was he aware his kid was turning into a fucking nutcase? I tried to warn Ma all she did was bitch every time he came around. She said, Butt out. Once I asked her how they ever got together and made me in the first place. She said not that it was any of my beeswax, but he could always make her laugh. He did this by reciting the names of his relatives, at which point Ma would recite the names of her former boyfriends, and before you knew it, there they'd be, rolling on the floor howling.

I glared at her. I said, "You must've been fucking hysterical when you named me," and lit a cigarette right in front of her, and she said,

"Sugar, I really wish you wouldn't swear so goddamn much."

The times my dad did come around, though, he had it in his mind to turn me into a catholic. He wanted me to experience faith, he said. He called this faith his legacy to me. Only Ma said she'd rather have cash or how about that 100-year-old stamp collection he was always fucking yapping about, meanwhile his wife and kid collecting food stamps.

"Ex-wife," my dad would say, and spit into the nearest ashtray. Then he'd tell me how people need to believe in something, how faith is believing in something you can't see, then Ma would say,

"Sounds like a good description of *you*," and then he'd say, That's it, I can't fucking take any more, believe in this, and he'd grab his cue and slam out the door.

Here's what I know about catholics: they don't sing as well as lutherans. They have sins on a scale of one to ten, from saying "dickhead" to murdering your neighbor or his wife. If you have faith, don't be surprised if one morning you look in the mirror and your hair is on fire. The fire will have been put there by a ghost. And there's this place called purgatory, a sort of pit stop on the way to heaven. Like "last call" before the eternal lights come up.

It didn't take me long to figure out Montana was purgatory. My dad would've been proud. I turned into a catholic in Montana.

I got to Montana in a blue Chevy pickup. The first time Ma saw the pickup, she'd run her fingers slowly along the blue fender. Now here's something a girl could get used to, she'd said, and Bob had winked at her.

We were headed for a place belonging to one of Bob's friends, some sort of dude ranch, Bob called it. It was winter. We'd been driving for days surrounded on all sides by white nothingness, Bob at the wheel, me riding shotgun, Ma in between. All of a sudden there's this sign:

WELCOME TO MONTANA!

"Yo! We're here!" says Bob, and lights another joint.

The sign passed. I looked around. Everything was the same as it had been. No houses, no trees, no hills, nothing but sky and land as far as you could see until they turned into each other. If I stared without blinking, after awhile I could get the land to turn into the ocean, even though I'd never seen the ocean. Or at night, into the universe, which everybody has seen.

I guess it was those times at night, staring out at the universe from the hole I'd scratched in the frost on the passenger side window of the Chevy, started me thinking about my dad. Maybe if I stared without blinking, I could get my dad to appear. Ma'd heard he was somewhere in Montana, a cosmic coincidence, she called it.

The last time I'd talked to my dad he'd called from a phone booth, traffic in the background, that echoey sound like he might be talking in a can. Meanwhile on my end, there's Ma in the background, mouthing instructions across the room. So I ask him, In exactly what state might this phone booth be located? so he says, Never mind that, are you a practicing catholic? so I say, Not exactly, mostly I'm practicing smoke rings, so he says, Remember purgatory lasts a long time, is there ANYfuckingthing you believe in? so I say, Yeah, ghosts, so he says, Well, that's a fucking start, don't forget to cross yourself. Then an ambulance goes by on his end and he hangs up.

That was the last we'd heard from him. Still, thinking about my dad just naturally led to thinking about god. Not that I believe in god. I didn't think much about god one way or the other. Until I saw Montana.

The idea that we were heading for a dude ranch gave Ma hopes. In fact it got her through North Dakota, she started plucking her eyebrows again.

But by the time we arrived at the ranch, there wasn't a dude in sight. The place had been abandoned as a tourist spot long ago. Bob's friend had inherited the ranch from her father, one of the original owners. On the side of the barn—which was turquoise—two fancy Ps had been painted brighter turquoise, then outlined in black. Below the Ps a turquoise tractor poked out of the snow.

Bob pulled up in the blue Chevy. "Welcome to 'P-Paradise'," she stuttered.

"Two Ps?" said Ma.

"In a pod," said Bob, and winked. She patted the Chevy's blue dashboard. "Thank god we're color coordinated."

That's my point. Bob wasn't thanking god, she was thanking some guy on the line in Detroit for working on a Monday because that was blue paint day. That guy changed Bob's life, he didn't even know it. I picture him eating pizza with his wife and four kids or bowling or looking through the Sears catalog, and not knowing, at that very moment, some truck he sprayed blue once on a Monday was dropping some green-haired 13-year-old at an abandoned dude ranch in the middle of winter in the middle of Montana. What would that guy have said about my safety pin earring, my homemade tattoo? Maybe, "Thank god my kids have sense," and there you'd be. Some guy in Detroit thanking god again, when he was really thanking some belt hanging on a hook behind his back door.

Or when Ma said, "I've got some business to take care of, Sugar, I'll be back before you know it," and left me at the Double P and drove off with Bob, why couldn't she have said, "I'm going looking for your dickhead of a father, I'll be back by spring, see if you can grow your hair out by then"?

We were standing together on the long turquoise porch, watching the blue Chevy pickup disappear off down the road, when

Still Life 67

Bob's friend clued me in. The Double P. Paradise on the Prairie.

"And really, in the end," she said, "it's never the way you picture it, is it?"

I had no idea what she was talking about.

But I can still picture Nova like she was standing in front of me. In a way she looked like everybody. She might've been an Indian or a gypsy, a cowgirl or an Egyptian. She might've been from Jupiter or Kansas City. When I met her she was in the last throes of a creative rebirth, she called it, "Specializing in sociological wallpaper and theme rooms."

Once I asked her what was the most exciting thing she'd ever done? First she said it was when she'd appeared in a potato chip commercial. Then she said it was when she'd been accepted into the astronaut training program. I asked if she'd ever gone up in a rocket, and she said no, she'd quit after deciding she didn't think she'd like the sensation of weightlessness.

Nova was anything but weightless. She weighed about as much as a buffalo, I guess. Her chairs were permanently caved in. Her bed folded over on itself, like a trench. I saw a picture of a trench once, in a book on World War I. A guy was holding a bible and looking at the camera. The guy's face was dark except for his eyes. Behind him were other white-eyed guys. I tried to imagine it, lying with your buddies in the dark and mud, thinking about god while bullets flew past your head. Meanwhile across the way some other guy and his buddies were doing the same, in another language. Maybe they were all catholics. In between was No Man's Land, the book called it. A good description.

A good description of the Double P would start square. Square yard, square barn, square house, like that cardboard dollhouse I made then left in the middle of the apartment we left in the middle of the night before Ma's friend got back, before Jack got back, and Ma saying, Hurry it up now Sugar shake a leg there girl, and I never said goodbye to my friend Lucille. Then after square, big. Big rooms, big ceilings, big hallways, and because Nova lived there alone, I thought, big echoes, until I heard about Judith, big secrets. And after big, turquoise. Nova had painted everything turquoise—the barn, the shed, the old airplane hangar, the old airplane, an abandoned plow, a jeep, a windmill and the ranchhouse itself, including the rocks which held up the long front porch—not for any particular reason, she said, except for a going-out-of-business sale at a paint store in Butte.

In the beginning Paradise on the Prairie had been a real hot spot, a jumping joint. The owners—Nova's father was one—used to fly the tourists in, right onto the runway beside the barn. When the plane still worked, before it was turquoise. I thought of the great white fields stretching into forever on every side.

"What would they do, once they got here?" I asked.

"Relax, play cards, shoot things," said Nova.

Inside the ranchhouse every room had a theme, reflected in ads Nova cut from newspapers and magazines and pasted on the walls. The kitchen was the Nike room. The front hallway was the Japanese car room. I was staying in the cigarette room. The only room which didn't have a theme was the room with the big stone fireplace at the front of the house. I wandered into that room exactly once, and never again.

I'd been studying the fireplace from the doorway, some of the rocks seemed to spell a word. I stepped in, walked over, read it plain as day: "PARADISE." Suddenly I got that feeling when you think somebody's watching. I turned, expecting to find Nova standing in the doorway. Only nothing. So I turned back around, and I saw: the walls were covered from top to bottom with animal heads. Some I recognized, some I didn't. But one thing was certain, they were all dead. I moved closer. The heads stared out with those fake shiny eyes that are scarier than anything because they're nothing. If I looked close enough into those eyes, all I saw was my own fishface self.

There I was, in the middle of the rug in the middle of that room, when it happened. I swear to god one of the deerheads moved. To get a better look at me, I figure. Then another head across the room, a buffalo to be exact, took a moment to readjust itself, and that was that. I hightailed it out of there and didn't look back. In the doorway I almost tripped on something, a lavender scarf.

When I told her what had happened, Nova listened and nodded, let me finish. Then she said one of these days she was going to clean that room out once and for all, give those heads a proper burial. Maybe she'd turn the place into a coffeehouse, she said, serve cornbread and espresso. She'd turn the fireplace into a stage, hang plants in front of the windows, wallpaper the walls with National Geographic cutouts.

"Elephants, gazelles, wildebeests, zebras," said Nova, "the usual." She hadn't said anything about what I'd told her.

"But who'd come to this ... coffeehouse?" I was picturing all that Montana nothingness.

Nova smiled. "The usual," she said. When I asked what that was supposed to mean, Nova said don't think too much, just use your imagination.

"But use it wisely," she said, "you wouldn't want to run out."

I was thinking, here we go again, what on earth is she talking about? A person can't run out of imagination like she can run out of cigarettes, say, or hair dye. Then I remembered.

"Here," I said, "you dropped this," and pulled the lavender scarf out of my back pocket. Nova's eyes flickered. But she shook her head, said it wasn't hers, couldn't be hers, she never wore that particular shade.

But I can picture Judith in lavender.

70   MINIMUM MAINTENANCE

Judith was an Artist with a capital A, said Nova, her work made Nova's theme rooms look like bathroom graffiti. I learned about Judith after I'd been at the Double P long enough to leave a shadow, is how Nova put it. Judith lived in a room of her own up on the third floor. She slept during the day and came out at night, a routine she'd fallen into when she used to work as a musician, but she'd finally quit the Life with a capital L, said Nova, when she realized she'd seen enough bars to rebuild Alcatraz. At first after she'd quit the Life, she'd still pick up her guitar every so often. But after awhile, for a number of reasons, Judith became what is known as pathologically shy, Nova called it. Now she just wanted to be left alone to paint.

"So don't expect to see much of her," said Nova.

The fact is, I didn't see any of her. Ever.

I'd lie in bed at night obsessed by the idea of some pathologically shy skin-and-bones Artist—Nova said Judith weighed next to nothing—wandering the halls outside my door. I'd strain to hear her footsteps, but she didn't make a sound, that's how skinny she must've been. Like an Indian or a ghost. I told Nova I wanted to meet Judith, I really did, but Nova said, Absolutely not, Judith has her ways, she needs her space, such a thing is out of the question.

Still, one night, I couldn't help it. I got out of bed, tiptoed across the room, opened my bedroom door. The moon was bright and big, as if the lights were on. I moved along the hallway to the stairs, up the stairs to the third floor. At the end of the third floor hallway there was a door, closed tight. A light came through the crack at the bottom. I moved up to the door, listened. I raised my hand, then lowered it. I stood and waited for a few minutes. When I turned to leave, I caught it: the smell of paint and something else—cigarette smoke—coming from the room behind the door.

I didn't know what to make of Judith at first, but after awhile I relaxed. Because every few days I'd show up for breakfast, there'd be a freshly-painted canvas, Judith's latest inspiration, propped against the kitchen table. With that smell of still-wet oil paint, like you wanted to eat it or breathe it or somehow mess around in it, make it a part of you always.

Judith favored bright yellow in her paintings, also silver and white, with streaks of gold and occasionally a few sequins. Her pictures were big, four or five feet. They featured strange beings, with wings and hooves and human arms and long hair, who hung out in amazing places, with trees and planets and highways and waterfalls. And even though you'd never seen anything like it, something about those paintings seemed familiar. Like seeing your face in a store window and going,

"Who the hell's that?", then going, "Shit, it's me."

To my mind, if Judith's paintings were anything on this earth, they were holy.

◆ ◆ ◆

When my dad came back from overseas and met me for the first time, he gave me a handful of holy cards. I was just a baby. Unlike Ma, I never thought my dad was a dickhead. Actually, he was a jarhead. I learned that from Nova.

We were sitting at the kitchen table at the Double P one morning. The table was made from the lane of a torn-down bowling alley. I was helping cut underwear ads. The ads in the lingerie room—the bathroom—kept peeling off and had to be reapplied. Judith's newest painting, in which she'd used more sequins than usual, leaned against the table beside us.

I kept glancing toward the doorway. That feeling again, like we were being watched. Maybe it was Judith, checking out our reaction to her picture. It made me nervous. I reached into my shirt pocket for a cigarette.

Nova looked over. "Sorry, hon, house rule. No smoking." I put the pack back. I was thinking of something.

"But Judith ..." I said.

"What about Judith?" Nova said quickly. I couldn't very well tell her I'd gone up to the third floor, up to the closed door, that I'd smelled smoke. Maybe Judith didn't like the rule either. Maybe she snuck a cigarette now and then.

"What about her?" Nova said again, so I said,

"It's just, I mean, I wish I could ... you know, hear her ... play guitar."

"Now why would she let you do that?" asked Nova.

"Well, because ..." I thought for a minute. "Because maybe she could play at the Paradise Coffeehouse. And maybe I ... I could be like her audience. To practice on. Ma always says when it comes to dancing, talent only gets you halfway, the other half is audience. Ma always says it's the story of her life, trying to connect with the audience."

Nova seemed to think about this. We cut ads. Then she smiled, patted my hand across the table.

"So tell me the story of *your* life," she says.

So I do.

I tell how my dad finally showed up one day, out of the blue, bald and tan, when I was a year old.

"Like he just dropped out of the sky," Ma always said, "like a meteorite, or a plane crash."

He told Ma he'd been in Okinawa, no not Nam, yeah he'd thought about her, how was she anyway? still looking foxy, did she still have that red dress? maybe a loose brewskie rolling around? there was this particular episode involving a graveyard he wanted to recount, by the way she sure was looking foxy. Then he saw me sitting in the high chair quietly dropping peas onto the linoleum. He shoved his hands into his camo pockets and shut right up.

They never quite figured this out for themselves, my dad and Ma, but they must've been meant for each other. Because when my dad got around to asking what she'd named me, and Ma told him "Sugar," he didn't say, That's the cheesiest name I ever heard what the fuck were you thinking of? Of course my dad had a cousin named Sharky Fraboni.

"So what about the graveyard?" says Nova.

So I tell how my dad was on guard duty one night, over in Okinawa, making rounds with his dog, and he stops by this old marines' cemetery and hears this whistling, like a person whistling, coming from the graves. The whistling gets closer and closer and any minute he expects a whistling man to walk on out of the shadows, past where he's sitting in his jeep. Only what happens is this whistling gets closer and closer then it's right in front of him then it passes him and all the while no whistler in sight. Finally the whistling just fades away off down the road.

"And," I tell her, "his dog? First he barks, then he whimpers, then he tries to hide under the seat. Only it's too small." I carefully cut around two happy women in slips. "Once I asked my dad, did he think it could've been the holy ghost in that graveyard? He slapped me, hard, said 'Quick, say a hail mary'."

That's when Nova called my dad a jarhead. I told her, no, he's a catholic. She laughed so hard she got the hiccups. Then she explained it was a military term.

I thought for a minute. "My dad tried to take it with him, but the jarheads wouldn't let him."

Nova looked at me and hiccuped.

"The dog, back home, to Toledo," I said, reaching for a Life. "But they made him leave Duke behind. He said it was the hardest thing he ever did, walking away from Duke."

"Is that so?" said Nova, and she said something else I

couldn't make out. Then she said, "Well, jarhead or not, maybe that dog was his familiar."

I said, "I guess they knew each other pretty good by then."

"That's not what I mean," said Nova. "A familiar is like ... well, it's ... an old term. Been around for awhile. It means like a spirit, usually an animal, who sort of guards a person, keeps them safe."

"You mean like the holy spirit?" I said, and Nova said,

"Well, not exactly, that is, have you ever *seen* the holy spirit?" So I said, No, not that I can remember, but I don't think I've seen a familiar either, and Nova just smiled and hiccuped and told me to think again, honey, think again.

What I was thinking right then was that talking to Nova was like going in circles. You believe you're getting somewhere, then the first thing you know—or the last—you're back where you started. But even though you never got anywhere, I was thinking, at least in the end, it didn't feel like you'd been standing still.

In the end, after he'd finished with the graveyard episode and satisfied himself that I'd inherited his dimples—"a real heartbreaker, like her old man"—my dad took off again, leaving behind a half dozen empty beer cans and those holy cards. Ma kicked the door closed behind him and smoked the rest of her cigarettes. She put the cards in the secret compartment of her Timeless Treasures jewelry box for safe-keeping. I was one.

When I was eight or nine, I found the cards. I'd been rooting around in Timeless Treasures one day, studying all the great antique jewelry—the pop-it beads, the edible earrings, the circle pin, the My Merry poison ring, the rhinestone sweater guard. My favorite was the friendship charm bracelet. Ma had stolen the charms from the Woolworths in the town where she grew up, then made up a girl, Trudy June Eskola, to be the friend.

The bracelet had over a dozen charms—a pair of ice skates,

a pair of roller skates, a pair of praying hands, a tennis racket, a heart with an arrow through it, a basket of flowers, a crown. Ma said she told everybody Trudy June Eskola was dying of leukemia and had a tutor and couldn't come out of the house, that's why no one ever saw her.

Trudy June also gave Ma a transistor radio, an eyelash curler, a new forty-five every few days, and a truckload of Yardley makeup. Then Eli, Ma's dad, went out to get a pack of Pall Malls one evening and never came back, and Trudy June suddenly started giving Ma a whole lot of new clothes.

"Trudy June feels sorry for me," Ma told her mother, "even though she's dying. It's in her religion, to give things away on your death bed."

"And what religion might that be?" asks Della, and Ma says, "The kind where they roll around and say things in a foreign language they can't remember the next day."

By then Trudy June had given Ma a dozen pairs of nylons, a red plaid kilt, three poorboy shirts, a madras wraparound, two mohair sweaters and a pair of Kickerinos.

As Trudy June grew nearer her death bed, she started asking if Ma could sleep over. Ma told Della leukemia wasn't catching, and Della says, Well, all right, but don't sit directly on the toilet seat. So Ma started staying at Trudy June's at least once a week.

When Della finally got around to asking her daughter some *real* questions—it took her long enough, you ask me—Trudy June Eskola had a sudden miraculous recovery and swore to dedicate her life to god. She moved to Florida and joined a convent where they only let you speak (letter-writing counted as speaking) during odd-numbered years. It was 1964.

Soon afterward Della got a call from the Dean of Girls at Greenhaven Junior High School. Not only had Ma been skipping school ("Does Mrs. Kane know a boy by the name of Mookie LaBarge?"), she'd also been caught shoplifting ("Was

76 MINIMUM MAINTENANCE

Mrs. Kane aware that Mookie just got out of Reform School?"), a frosted-blonde pixie wig and a push-up bra from Vera's Smart Shop. Vera ("And her sister Bunny Feldman, who really owns the shop, but can't work most days on account of, well, you know about the husband . . . ") had decided not to press charges ("But could Mrs. Kane please come and collect her daughter?").

When they got home, Della rounded up Ma's two sisters and ordered everybody into the basement, where she ordered Ma to take off all her clothes, even her underwear. Then she tied Ma's hands to the overhead pipes and shaved off all the hair on her body with the electric Norelco Eli had left behind. Ma said the hair on her head had been almost to her waist, she'd been ironing it every morning. Della told her other daughters to have a real good look, then ordered them back upstairs. According to Ma she stayed tied to the pipes all night, although one sister snuck down around midnight with a stool.

Eventually Della relented and let Ma buy a wig—frosted-blonde, in a pixie style—which Ma wore for the rest of that year, then saved for special. She saved the original hair, too, which didn't need ironing any more because nobody slept on it. She wore that hair as a fall, she called it, for the rest of high school, whenever her regular hair was dirty.

I've tried to remember the first time I heard the Story. I've tried to picture the top of Ma's head in the lamp by my crib, the smoke from her cigarette snaking into the dark. Sometimes when I listened I was one of the sisters, in the basement, watching. Or I was Ma, hanging from the pipes. Sometimes I was Grandma Della. And sometimes . . . But the point is, the Story was mine. Ma gave it to me. Like a legacy. Like my dad and the holy cards.

By the time I was eight or nine, when I found the holy cards, I knew the Story by heart. I'd been looking at Ma's old charm bracelet in the Timeless Treasures jewelry box, wondering whatever became of that original hair, the hair Della had shaved off Ma's head so long ago. I could've used that hair. I was going through this phase where I'd drape a towel over my head, tie it under my chin, let it hang down my back like I had long hair. Ma was refusing to take me anywhere until I snapped out of it.

"I can't have people at K-Mart thinking I gave birth to a re-tard," she'd say, before locking me in the apartment and leaving. "Errands," she'd say, and sometimes she'd be gone until dark and I could wear the towel all afternoon without listening to somebody squawk about it.

Every morning I'd wake up and promise god over and over, "I won't wear the towel today, I won't wear the towel," and for awhile the promise would take. Then sometime between cartoons and the mailman, I'd start getting that feeling again. Like something was going to happen, something really bad, like an earthquake or an explosion or something. Only it might not happen if I had long hair.

Then one day there I am, messing with the charms on Ma's old bracelet, a ratty brown towel hanging down my back, when one of the charms gets stuck. I pull at the bracelet, up comes the floor of the Timeless Treasures jewelry box. And there they are, the holy cards. Five of them, all ladies.

"Now that's significant," says Nova.
"Which part?" I said.
It was just after noon. We'd finished with the lingerie ads, and were sitting back drinking tea, admiring Judith's painting. The sun on the sequins was so bright we were wearing sunglasses.
"Which part's significant?" I said again.
"The cards, of course," said Nova, with a wave of her hand. "All women, five of them." She counted on her fat fingers, pinched with a half dozen turquoise rings. "One, two, three

sisters, your grandmother, you. Five. It's a sign."

She folded her hands. "So what happened to the cards?" she says. "You still have them?"

So I told her.

A couple of apartments later, after I'd found the cards, I used to play with this kid Lucille. One day Lucille finds the cards. I used to keep them in my room, in a box by my mattress. Lucille had a bike. Next thing I know, there's Lucille roaring up and down in front of our building on her bike, and there's my holy cards, clothes-pinned to the spokes.

"Good lord," says Nova.

"Don't worry," I said, "I beat her up good. But the cards were wrecked. I buried them over in People's Park on the next block, by a fake pond." I looked at Nova over the top of my sunglasses. "I saw a duck in that pond, a couple days later. My first duck."

"Yeah?" said Nova. "Well, that's good, a duck's good." She thought for a minute. She looked at me over the top of her sunglasses. "Can you remember what color this duck was?"

I thought for a minute. "One of those ducks with a green shiny head."

"A mallard," said Nova. She stared at Judith's painting. "Now, your favorite holy card. Can you remember what that lady was wearing?"

I knew right off. "A long robe, with a long hood draped over her head, hanging down her back."

"And what color was this robe?" said Nova. We were having one of those conversations again.

"Green," I said, "the whole shebang was green."

Suddenly my hair got pins and needles. I could see her again, the lady in the green hooded robe, standing on a cloud, her hands stretched out against a blue blue sky. I turned to look at Judith's painting, and I must've caught it just right, the sun blasting off a sequin, because all the air exploded in

Still Life 79

light. I stared into the blown-apart light until I couldn't see any more. But I kept staring.

One of the ways I tried to see god was by looking at something for a long time without blinking, say a car or a couch, all the while thinking holy thoughts and asking for a sign. But it never happened. Not one parked car or piece of furniture ever budged an inch for me. Not that this is the best way to experience faith. Because, like my dad said, faith isn't something you can see or touch, it's something you just know. And not even in your head, where your brain is. But in your heart, where, well, where your blood is.

 I'll admit it, faith was my biggest problem, the reason I stayed a catholic just long enough to get out of Montana. In Montana, a person needed something to keep them going. Besides, it was one thing to stare at a table and wait for it to move across the room. But it was a whole other thing to stare out at the prairie and wait for something to appear. Sooner or later, something usually did. Sometimes it was a hallucination, Nova called it. Like the time the deerhead moved.

 Or the time I saw the buffalos.

 The temperature that day had reached twenty-five degrees below zero. When we walked out to the mailbox, my nose stuck to itself like velcro. The lower half of my face stopped working altogether. I was thinking hell might be hot, but to my mind, purgatory is fucking freezing. Though I kept this thought to myself due to another of Nova's rules: no swearing.

 At the mailbox Nova handed me a National Geographic and a postcard. The National Geographic featured a couple of gorillas, one of them holding a red flower. I pictured the gorillas on the wall of the Paradise Coffeehouse, maybe up by the stage, which would have curtains to match the flower. The postcard featured a truck the size of a small building. It was from Ma, from Butte: Bob had a job driving for the Berkley Pit, she herself was waiting tables at the M & M Bar, they never did locate my dickhead of a father, she'd be coming back soon to get me, how did I like the sound of Nevada?

I tried saying it, "Nevada," only nothing came out.

Later, after my face had thawed and we'd eaten a few times and talked some more about the Paradise Coffeehouse ("How about an Everglades theme in the bathroom?"), Nova announced it was after midnight, time for bed, and she went up to her room and shut the door.

And there I was, sitting at the window in my own room, just staring out. The way I used to, from the passenger side of the blue Chevy. At the universe, all stretched across the sky like a black cape. At Montana lying underneath, white and quiet and endless, like a satin lining. Or one of Judith's canvases before it became something. Or No Man's Land. As if everything was waiting.

And so was I, waiting. For sleep, for Ma, for Judith. I was thinking I'd be gone and never get to meet Judith. I wanted to offer her a cigarette, tell her not to be so shy, that in spite of my hair I was okay. I was getting an idea to go up to the third floor, and I started to stand. But then I stopped. Because I thought I saw a river, dark and moving, out there on the snow where there couldn't be. I blinked and looked again.

Then I saw the buffalos.

Slowly, from where the sky and land turned into each other, a long line of buffalos came walking across the snow. Tiny at first, they grew bigger, closer, and always in a line, dark and slow and walking. They got to the middle of the field, about halfway to the Double P, and stopped. Like maybe they were waiting, too—for morning, for spring, for Paradise. There they stood, in that still dark line, against the white. I watched through the window, holding my breath to keep the glass from fogging. Then I had to breathe, and they were gone.

But I saw them.

Call it what you will. Sometimes what appeared when you stared out at the prairie was not what you'd expected. And sometimes it was exactly that. For instance Ma, in a yellow Buick, the windows rolled down and the radio blaring, in a cloud of dust at high noon on a Saturday. In the spring. My time in purgatory had ended.

◆ ◆ ◆

One thing I've never understood, people who manage to hang onto things. I mean *real* things—dolls, toys, clothes, jewelry, furniture, cars, and can you imagine, houses.

"But you know, Sugar," Ma always said, "it's not things that matter, it's people." Though you ask me, we never managed to hang onto any people either.

Like Ma saying to Nova, while we loaded up the yellow Buick getting ready to hit the road, "I'll be sure to write and let you know where we are."

And Nova saying back, "I'll come visit, soon as you're settled. Judith can hold down the fort."

None of it happened. No letter, no visit. Ever.

Though I'll say one thing for Ma, she kept her mouth shut about Judith. She kept her mouth shut that morning, the morning of the day we left. We all came down to breakfast to find another canvas, smaller than usual, a towel draped over the top, propped against the bowling alley table.

"What have we here?" Ma asked, and yawned, and reached for the towel.

Nova stopped Ma's hand mid-air. "It's a present, for Sugar. Judith told me to give it to her."

Ma looked at Nova, opened her mouth, then shut it. They both looked at me.

"Go ahead," said Nova. "It's for you."

So I pulled off the towel.

There, staring back at me, her hands held out against a silver sky with gold sequin stars and a bright yellow moon, was the most beautiful lady I'd ever seen. A green shawl draped over her head, and like a shadow behind a shadow, the shawl became the bright green head of a duck. The lady's green gown became the land where she stood, with trees and mountains, rivers and flowers, and a thin line of buffalos along the horizon, where the land became a sea stretching into forever until the sea became the sky. Like one big circle, it all kept turning back into itself.

After awhile Ma said, "Does this picture have a name or something?"

And Nova smiled. " 'Still Life with Duck and Buffalo'."

But Ma kept her mouth shut. Even when I excused myself to go to the third floor and slip a note under Judith's door:

"Thank you for the beautiful picture. Did you see the buffalos too? S. Kane." Then, "P.S. I smoke." Then, "P.S.S. I used to stutter."

Ma kept her mouth shut, until we'd loaded up the yellow Buick, waved good-by to Nova, were well on our way down the black highway. Until the Double P was only a cardboard speck in the rearview mirror. Then she lit a cigarette.

"That broad's crazy as a coot, Sugar. You know that, don't you?"

I glanced at the towel draped over the painting in the back seat. "Well, she's pathologically shy, but she sure can paint. Though I wish I could've heard her play."

Ma laughed out loud. "Shy? What are you talking about? Man, I'm getting you out of this goddamn state in the nick of time." She waved her cigarette at the windshield. "A person could go goddamn crazy themselves, looking out at all this nothing all day."

I thought of the buffalos. "Yeah, well, you're the one who

fucking left me here," I said. Now that I was leaving Montana and would no longer be a catholic, my natural swearing ability seemed to be returning.

"Besides," I said, picking a cigarette off the dash, punching in the lighter, "Nova's cool. I wouldn't have got to meet her, otherwise. And Judith, I never did meet her, but if it wasn't for Judith, I wouldn't have this cool picture."

Ma actually stopped the Buick in the middle of the road. There wasn't any other traffic, but still. She pushed her sunglasses up on her forehead, bugged her eyes at me. Mascara was smeared under her left eye.

"Don't you know?" she said. Her sunglasses slipped, she pushed them back up. "That's the whole goddamn point. There IS no Judith, I mean, there WAS, but she's DEAD. She goddamn died, a couple years ago. Bob told me the whole story. Judith and Nova were ... well, never mind. But the point is, Judith's dead."

I stared at her. I didn't know what I was thinking. I said, "But how ..."

"A fire, some sort of fire. Back in the city. She fell asleep smoking, or something. I don't know the details." Ma twisted the mirror around, wiped at the mascara.

I shook my head, hard. "No! I mean, if she's dead, how did she paint all those pictures? How could she know about the green lady? Or the buffalos? How could she fucking know?" I leaned away from her. My voice was getting louder.

(a fire? some sort of fire?)

"For chrissake, calm down," said Ma. "Use your imagination. Who do you think painted those things? Huh? See what I mean? She's crazy as a goddamn coot. If I'd known that, I'd never have left you there. Jesus."

She pushed hard on the gas, the Buick took off with a jerk. She flicked on the radio, flicked it off.

"Goddamn it, I'll be glad to get away from this goddamn

country western shit." She lowered her sunglasses back onto her nose, started tapping the steering wheel and humming.

I moved closer to the door. I rolled the window down as far as it would go. I tossed my cigarette, closed my eyes tight, stuck my head out. The air pushed my lips open, roared past my ears. I was thinking it sounded like fire. I was thinking it sounded like the ocean. I was wondering if there was an ocean in Nevada. I was thinking of all the cars we'd ever known, me and Ma, so many cars they blended into each other. Until they all became one car, the same car, an Oldsmobile became a Chevy became a Buick.

I was thinking there I was, alive for thirteen years already, let alone Ma, alive for who knows how long, and all either of us had in this world was in the trunk of this latest car. What had happened to all our former stuff, from two, three, four cars back? The cardboard dollhouse? the Timeless Treasures jewelry box? that red dress Ma had loved so much? I was thinking about Judith's painting in the backseat—or whose was it?—wondering how long before she was gone, too, the beautiful green lady. Just like the pop-it beads and the friendship charm bracelet and the holy cards. Because I knew she would be—a garage sale, a pawn shop, a robbery, a fire. Eventually.

And right then, right there—screaming along in the yellow Buick, my hair standing out behind me while what was left of Montana slammed against my face—I figured something out. Right then I knew, it's not things that matter. But it's not people, either, like Ma said.

"IT'S SOMETHING ELSE!" I hollered into the wind, and Ma hollered back,

"WHAT DID YOU SAY?"

"SOMETHING ELSE!!"

"I CAN'T GODDAMN HEAR YOU!"

It didn't matter. I was thinking the catholics would call it faith. But it didn't matter. Call it what you will. Because

Nova saw Judith, I swear she did. And I never saw Judith, but I saw the buffalos. And I never saw god, but I saw Trudy June Eskola.

I never told anyone, I was just a kid. But it must've been after I'd heard the Story enough times—the push-up bra, the blond pixie wig, Ma hanging from the pipes, her sisters watching.

What I remember is this: one day, this girl started to show up in my life. I'd wake up in the middle of the night, there she'd be, standing at the foot of my mattress. I'd be out drawing on the sidewalk, I'd look up, she'd be sitting on the curb across the street. If me and Ma took a bus downtown, the girl might be there, in the seat across the aisle. If Ma took me out with her at night, warned me not to leave the barstool for fear of my life, I'd look around, there'd be the girl, a few stools away.

She never did anything, this girl. Only watched me with her gray eyes, and blinked, a little straight look on her face. And because she was silent, and pale, and wore pajamas, it didn't take me long to figure out who she was. It got so that all I had to do was think of her, Trudy June Eskola would appear. She'd come walking through a door into a room, or suddenly be in the back seat of a car, or waiting around a street corner beside a parking meter.

The times I got locked in the closet, Trudy June stayed locked in with me. If I wet my bed or threw up on the floor, if I hit my head against the wall or bit my wrist until it bled, Trudy June would be there. When I pulled out my eyelashes in second grade and put them in a pile on my desk, Trudy June stood by the blackboard, blinking and watching. The day I started stuttering, I remember, because Trudy June was there. The day I finally stopped, three years later, she was there that day, too. And when I started wearing the towel, and when I stopped.

And then came that night in our last apartment, the apartment of the cardboard dollhouse. The night Jack shot a hole in the living room ceiling. It was summertime, and hot. I couldn't sleep. I'd been lying in my room on my mattress, listening to the traffic. In between cars, I could hear voices out in the living room. I hadn't even been thinking about her, when all of a sudden, Trudy June appeared. Right in front of the bedroom door, standing in the shadows, blinking and watching. I stayed very still, held my breath, stared back. Finally she sort of raised her hand toward me, then her other hand, and then she blinked her gray eyes, and Trudy June Eskola disappeared. A split second later, the gun went off.

That was the last time I saw her.

Which doesn't mean I won't ever see her again. But maybe now I'll see animals for awhile. Then, in the years to come, something altogether different. So that toward the end of my life, say when I'm forty-five, I might actually see god.

But until then, until some couch moves across a room toward me or my hair catches on fire or I suddenly find myself back in Montana, I'm not going to worry about god. Let the catholics worry about all of that. Or the lutherans. In fact, let the jarheads worry about it. People need something to believe in —invisible whistlers, pale girls in pajamas. Artists who only come out at night. Because maybe god is something a person has to build up to. Not that I believe in god.

4

Here Comes the Sun

I'm never going to have a baby. The meanest thing I can think of is to bring a baby into this world, knowing what I know. About the way the world really is. Once a person knows about the world, suddenly nothing else matters except the truth. And once a person knows the truth, how could she for one second consider bringing a baby into the bargain?

I'm talking about the fact that one day the sun is just going to explode. Out of nowhere it's going to smash to smithereens. And that will be that. One minute the earth and all the planets will be booking along, spinning in space, and the next minute KA-BAM! That's all she wrote.

I asked Ma if she'd known about the sun when she decided to have me, and she said first of all, decision wasn't exactly the right word for it, like I'd been part of a divine plan or anything, and secondly, if I didn't quit watching the educational channel, she was going to start staying in motels without television.

"Didn't you ever hear the saying," she said, "a little learning is a dangerous thing?" She took a sip of coffee and set the mug back on the table, leaving a bright pink kiss on the mug's thick white lip. "What that means is, watch out what you learn, it can ruin your life. You'll never have any fun any more."

"But what about the sun?" I asked, and Ma said,

"What on earth does the sun have to do with anything? Mind your own goddamn business." She thought for a minute. "Besides, stuff like that doesn't happen in real life. Even if the sun does explode, it won't be for a long time."

I said, "And how long is that?" and Ma said,

"Eight hundred years, at least. By then you'll be long gone."

I thought for a minute. "But what if I have a baby, and that baby has a baby, and so on. Won't I be setting up the last baby in a long line of babies?"

"You make me dizzy," said Ma, "finish your pop."

Then she said, "Why don't you worry about something worthwhile for a change, like how are we going to pay for this pie?"

She glanced around the restaurant, at the cardboard cutout of a giant Easter bunny beside the cash register. She glanced over my shoulder at the next booth. One of her eyebrows moved, her voice lowered.

"Listen," she whispered, "I'll get a refill on this coffee, you nurse that Coke. We'll take our time. That one behind you looks like a big tipper. When she gets up to leave, I'll make my move."

I'd seen Ma in action. She was smooth. Eyes drifting dreamily while long fingers brushed across some tabletop, as if by accident, as if they had nothing whatsoever to do with that long arm.

I whispered, "So what's a big tipper look like?"

Ma smoothed her hair behind her ears, adjusted her gaze slightly to the left of my shoulder.

"Hair streaked gray, pulled up in a bun, earrings down to here made of feathers. Smile wrinkles around the eyes, no makeup. Big yellow teeth. Says 'thank you' every time the waitress pours coffee in her cup."

Ma shifted her eyes back to mine and smiled, her small teeth gleaming and white as the sheets at the Motel Six.

"A real goddamn bleeding heart, that one," she said. "She doesn't know it, but that broad's going to buy us Easter pie."

◆ ◆ ◆

Actually, first the sun is going to sort of cave in on itself, then explode. But all this will happen so fast, nobody will notice. A part of me wishes I could be there.

I like to think it'll be like one of those rides, those big rides, the Skydiver or the Wild Mouse. Because my idea of heaven is the Midway at the State Fair. I'm one who'll go on those rides, over and over, while everyone else stands around on the ground, shifting in their shoes, staring upward. At me, going round and round at the speed of light, while some guy hollers into a loudspeaker,

"DO YOU WANT TO GO FASTER? I CAN'T HEAR YOU!"

Maybe at that final moment, when the sun flies apart, the voice of god will be heard hollering similar things.

I learned about the sun while listening to call-in radio in the cab of Delta Dave Wilson's 18-wheel Peterbilt. Ma and Delta were off drinking gut bombers and doing the two-step in some roadhouse off Interstate 35. I was waiting out in the parking lot with the other 18-wheelers, perched high in the cab of Delta's rig like the Queen of Sheba, just spinning that radio dial.

I'd tuned in a show called "You Asked For It," which featured a couple of guys sitting around discussing various topics, "Tonight's being 'The State of the Universe,' call 1-800-YOU-TALK with your comments." The guys were going on and on about comets and black holes and super novas, when some caller mentioned the bit about the sun. By the time Ma and Delta stumbled back out to the Peterbilt, laughing and banging on the driver's side door, I'd learned enough to put two and two together: we were headed for oblivion.

92   MINIMUM MAINTENANCE

Actually, we were headed for Oklahoma.

At first Ma was worried about the tornado factor. When I think of Oklahoma I think of tornados, she said, at which point Delta said, Well, start thinking fair weather, there's the fair weather factor, I aim to change your mind. Which perked Ma right up. She was goddamn sick and tired of the windchill factor, she said, she could use some fair weather for a change, maybe work on her tan.

In honor of this weather-to-be, she was playing a particular song over and over on the Peterbilt's tape deck. No sooner did the song finish, Ma'd press REWIND, then PLAY, then George Harrison would take over once again with Ma right behind,

"Little darlin', it's been a long cold lonely winter ..."

Delta Dave had a sister who lived in Oklahoma. This sister raced stock cars. When she wasn't racing, she worked odd jobs. Currently she was running rides at the Tri-County Carnival, biding her time between Saturday night races, keeping an eye out for flying vomit and falling change. Pennies from heaven, Delta called it. When I heard about the rides, I perked right up. Even started humming along with George and Ma.

"My sister," says Delta, "she ain't married or nothin', so's she's got room. Lives in a mo-bile home. Lets me stay ..." and he winked at Ma, " ... when I ain't staying somewheres else. You ask me, that's what a home oughta be, mo-bile." He patted Ma's leg. "Now, me and you, we can stay in the chrome and velvet bedroom. And Miss Muffet, here," and he glanced over at me, "she can stay out back, in the bomb shelter."

Ma's chin snapped forward, her eyes grew round in the dashboard light. Her concentrating look. She stared at me, hiccuped, shifted her eyes to Delta.

"'Scuse me, Del," she says, in her piney voice, and hiccups again, "did I hear you say velvet?"

Here's how it happened: me and Ma hitched a ride with Delta

Dave out of Missoula after our yellow Buick convertible converted to a pile of scrap metal. Which had nothing to do with letting go the steering wheel for a teeny second to fix her eyeliner, Ma said. Anytime Auto gave us a hundred bucks for the Buick's steering wheel, hood ornament and hubcaps. And there we were, me and Ma, sitting in the waiting room waiting for what came next.

What came was Mr. M. David Wilson, whistling through the swinging doors in his slicked-back hair and slippery vest, looking to pick out a new set of mud flaps for his rig. He picked out Ma real quick, sitting there in her high heel fake fur boots and matching earmuffs. Ma stuck a cigarette between her lips, the guy looking for wheel protection leapt across the room like he was being chased by wildfire.

"Need a light?" he says, and Ma says,

"Always."

By the time the cash register was ringing up the guy's sale, it was obvious: me and Ma would be leaving Montana. Ma disappeared into the Ladies. I smoked a Winston and watched from the window of Anytime Auto as Mr. M. David Wilson bolted the new flaps onto his rig. When the last one was in place, he pulled out a red bandana hankie and rubbed them until they shone like mirrors.

Ma emerged from the Ladies with a new lease on life, she whispered, and winked at me, and dropped the ear muffs in a magazine rack. Then Mr. M. David Wilson helped us up into the cab of his Peterbilt, having stored all our worldly possessions back in the long echoey trailer, which was empty on this trip, he said, what with him being between runs just then, weren't we the lucky ones though? and he grinned and reached for the gearshift.

Out on the frontage road Delta worked on getting up a head of steam. Ma worked on background music. I worked on adjusting the passenger side mirror to get a better look at the new mud flaps. The quadruplets, Delta called them, and I kept picturing those silver girls bumping happily along underneath us, mile after mile, beside those eighteen whirling wheels.

We hit the interstate heading south and Delta lit a cigarette. Ma hit REWIND, then PLAY. George Harrison promised for the umpteenth time that the ice was slowly melting. I squinted through the windowshield into the growing sun and had to agree.

When she wasn't tearing up a speedway in her baby blue stock car or turning people upside down at the Tri-County Carnival, Wednesday Alice Wilson lived alone in a light green trailer with a matching add-on sunporch. The trailer was parked just off Interstate 35 on the site of a former Mobil gas station, one exit removed from the Nation's Ultimate Truckstop. The NUThouse, the locals called it. The NUThouse had everything—a couple of motels, a few bars and restaurants, a couple of clothing stores, a beauty parlor, a barber shop, a wedding chapel, a Piggly Wiggly, a movie theater and an emergency clinic. And everything the NUThouse had, stayed open all night.

Wednesday's trailer also had everything—bathroom, combination living/dining room, kitchen, and three bedrooms, the one in back done up in gold chrome and red velvet, as mentioned. All the rooms in the trailer lined up behind one another, like a convoy, Wednesday called it. What more could a gal want, she said, it's all right here, in a nice straight line, let me tell you it's heaven.

Although Wednesday's mother had had her own ideas about heaven. Mrs. Wilson had been a Jehovah's Witness, Wednesday told me, and named her kids after the seven days of creation. Delta Dave was the first born, his real name being Monday, middle name David. After that came a baby born dead, no need to ask what name appeared on its little gravestone. Then along came Wednesday.

Only Mrs. Wilson got halfway through the week and stopped. Nobody knows why. One day Mr. Wilson comes home from his garbage route, his wife hands over the six quart jars of money she's been saving since their wedding. She puts the seventh jar in her shoulder bag, walks the two miles over to Route 66, sticks out her thumb. She wasn't there more than five minutes, along comes a cucumber truck and hits her broadside. Mrs. Wilson was killed instantly, the seventh jar broke all over the road.

"And you wanna hear somethin spooky?" says Wednesday. "The road where she got run over? That old road's got another name to it." Wednesday's green eyes glittered. "Chicago to the ocean, I swear to god, another friggin' name. Lookee here."

She pulls her wallet from her back pocket, an old folded postcard from the wallet. Just a picture of a road with a faded white line down the middle, headed straight for the horizon toward a faded rainbow. The rainbow looks fake. Down in the corner of the postcard is a white sign, "Route 66," and across the top, three words:

"THE MOTHER ROAD"

My hair got pins and needles.

"What d'ya think of them apples?" says Wednesday, and carefully folds the postcard back up.

When I told Ma about Mrs. Wilson getting run over like that, even before I got to the part about the road's other name, Ma snorted.

"I'll tell you something about J.W.s," she says, and lights a cigarette. "J.W.s are goddamn crazy. They believe, when the world ends, only a certain number of people will get into heaven. Around two thousand, I think."

I thought for a minute. I asked her what it took exactly to become one of the two thousand, and how would a person know if another person, Mrs. Wilson, for instance, made it in? At which point Ma says, Will you give it a rest, you make me tired, why don't you go grab me another Fresca, the sun seems hotter than usual today.

In Oklahoma, as I saw it, the sun spent the morning hours working its way up the sky. Ma and Delta spent the morning hours closed up in the velvet bedroom. Wednesday worked on Margaret, her stock car, and I worked on keeping cool. Margaret stayed parked out back of the light green trailer. Wednesday would scoot around underneath her on a little flat cart with wheels, banging on various metal items and swearing. I'd sit in the dust in the shade nearby and watch the ants building their little bridges and roads and houses like there was no tomorrow.

    Once I asked Wednesday if she thought those ants were aware of us looming over them, like god, accidentally stepping on their little cities and ruining their little plans and families. Wednesday sniffed, moved the toe of her boot around in the dirt, uncovered a chunk of glass. She held the glass over an ant house. After a minute a couple of ants went up in smoke. A couple more came out to see what was going on, they got fried to a crisp also. When Wednesday moved the glass to the house next door, I pulled her hand away.

    "What's with you?" she says. "It ain't like they can feel it or nothin'." I was about to ask her how did she know, but she tossed the glass into an empty barrel where it clanged like a bell, and scooted on her cart back under Margaret.

    Around two in the afternoon, when it was hot enough outside to fry rubber, as Wednesday put it, Ma would emerge from the back bedroom in her yellow bikini, leaving Delta snoring away behind the closed door. She'd grab a Fresca and a Ladies' Home Journal and haul her lawn chair and reflector panels around to the south side of the trailer. For the next few hours she'd continue her search for the ultimate tan. Like a perfectly roasted marshmallow, she said, and sip pop and do her stomach exercises and study "Can This Marriage Be Saved?"

Delta usually emerged in that between time of day, just after supper. He'd sit there smoking and drinking coffee by the phone in the kitchen, staring at the refrigerator magnets and waiting for a call. A call about a job, any job, so long as it involved driving. The call of the open road, Wednesday said, like a priest gets the call, only with her brother it was another job, another road trip. Like something was beckoning to him out there on the highway, she said, out there on the Mother Road, might could even be the voice of their poor dead momma, who'd gone looking for something and never found it, now it's the son's turn.

"They say every mother wants a son," said Wednesday, "maybe our poor momma just wants hers back."

While Wednesday's brother smoked and stared at magnets and waited for the call, the rest of us spent the evening out in the add-on sunporch—Wednesday checking her watch to see if it was time for her Midway shift, Ma admiring her newest layer of tan, me sneaking sips from the bottle on the floor beside Ma's chair. We'd listen to the kitchen stool squeak and watch the fields around the light green trailer fade to lavender where, at the horizon, the lights of the NUThouse shot toward the sky like a crown.

The NUThouse, as we were constantly reminded, was Ma's idea of heaven.

"If I'd've stayed in beauty school, I'd have a job right there, right now," Ma said, reaching for the bottle, tilting it at her glass. "I'd be getting my hair done for nothing, living in one of the weekly rentals, hanging out at 'Keep on Truckin'. Anyways ..." Ma was starting to talk like Wednesday. She took another sip of her drink. "Anyways, I wouldn't need any goddamn car ever again. I could put my feet up, get my fair share of the American Pie."

"You mean American Dream, don't ya, hon?" says Wednesday, and checks her watch, but Ma says no, she means the song about driving the Chevy into the levee. Which is where every car she's ever had the misfortune to own belonged, she says. According to Ma, cars have been her major downfall.

"Many a time has opportunity knocked on my door," says Ma, "but I didn't have the proper vehicle to get me there."

Wednesday moved her eyes toward me, I shrugged. Then she moved her eyes up and down Ma stretched out in the lavender light, long and tan on the lawn chair.

"Car or no car," says Wednesday, "looks like opportunity might've friggin' knocked again," she flicked her thumb toward the trailer, "on that there door back there. Tell me, hon, does Mr. Right know yet? He have any idea?"

"Ex-cuse me," says Ma, "but I just might have a few ideas of my own." She stayed quiet for a minute.

Then she said, "For instance, how about Davidson ... or Dellwood ... or ..."

She glanced at me. She reached for her drink, then seemed to change her mind. Instead she smoothed her hot pink tank top over her stomach, folded her fingers there. She gazed out through the screen at the horizon, shot with the lights of the Ultimate Truckstop. Ma had a look in her eyes, like someone had carefully drawn them in, then changed their mind and erased them slightly.

"Or," says Ma, "how about Thursday?" and Wednesday says,

"For what?" and Ma says,

"For a ..." and she glances at me again, "for a change, I mean."

"A change of plans, is what you mean," said Wednesday, and looked toward the kitchen. I got a whiff of Delta's cigarette, I could see his shadow on the stool by the phone. "And I gotta tell ya, hon, that one's a tumbleweed. Don't have no roots, don't friggin' want 'em."

Ma's fingers tightened on her hot pink stomach. "Well," she said, in her pouty voice, "sometimes things have a way of coming back around on a person. Maybe ..." she said, looking out through the screen again, "maybe we'd ... all of us ... like to stop tumbling. Maybe stay put for a change, grow geraniums, join a bowling league."

Ma turned to me and smiled. The smile looked fake. "Wouldn't you, Sugarpuss?"

"Wouldn't I what?" I said, and took a long swallow of pop.

Ma says, "Wouldn't you like to, you know, put down roots, for a change?"

And I couldn't help it, I laughed right out loud, spitting ginned-up Dr. Pepper all over the fake grass carpeting in Wednesday Wilson's add-on sunporch. I wasn't too sure what Ma was talking about, but I thought I knew one thing: I thought I knew what it felt like to put down roots. Because ever since stepping foot in Oklahoma, I'd been living in a bomb shelter.

In the beginning, the Mobil station had been owned by a guy who was deathly afraid of communists. So this guy builds himself a bomb shelter, out back behind the station garage, where the fields start. He fills it with cans of food and soup and bottles of water, matches and candles, paperbacks and comics and cards, and games like Monopoly and Parcheesi and Barbie Goes to the Prom. Once a month he has his family practice driving to the bomb shelter in a calm and orderly fashion from their home a half mile away. Whenever they make the trip in under four minutes—that is if they haven't been chased there by nuclear fallout—they celebrate with Dr. Peppers and shoestring potato chips in the shadow of the red-winged flying horse which towers above the four fuel pumps.

The years pass. Russia never attacks, the Nation's Ultimate Truckstop springs up, business at the station comes to a standstill. Finally the guy closes up shop and sells, to Wednesday

Wilson, who parks her light green trailer in the shadow of the flying horse. The bomb shelter becomes a guest house/home entertainment center, except Wednesday keeps a few of the original furnishings, like the shag carpet and the bean bag chairs, for historical interest, she calls it.

Now, most days I couldn't think straight from the Oklahoma heat. So the bomb shelter, which was always cool, became my home away from home, Ma said. At which point I said, Just where exactly is this original home you're referring to? and Ma says, Don't get goddamn smart with me, and pinches the back of my arm in that place where it'll show for a week or two.

Wednesday sometimes joined me underground on those rubber-fried afternoons. We'd play games and watch TV with the sound turned off and listen to the radio. I'd found a station which played "You Asked For It." I'd tune in, hoping they'd mention the sun again. Sometimes I'd call the 800 number. Some voice would ask what input did I have toward the discussion, so I'd answer, Who gives a shit about the wheat crop when the whole shebang is going to explode some day, you brought it up in the first place, let's talk about *that*. Not you again, the voice would say, and hang up.

I don't know why I kept calling, except it had become a routine. Or maybe I wanted to know exactly how much time we had left before oblivion hit.

◆ ◆ ◆

Oklahoma was situated in Tornado Alley, Wednesday called it. I pictured the world as an apartment complex, Oklahoma as somewhere out back behind the garages.

"See them clouds, look like egg cartons?" she said, shading her eyes. "Each one of them little dips might could be a twister."

It was a Saturday afternoon. The next day was Palm Sunday. We were headed for the bomb shelter to escape the air, which sat over the earth like an army blanket. Wednesday glanced out at the fields, so bright and flat it hurt my eyes to look there.

"Might could be in for a real ride," she said, pulling open the door of the bomb shelter. "And just in time for Sunday services." She flicked the light switch and walked over to the TV. "I'll check the weather, you go ahead try the radio."

But "You Asked For It" wouldn't come in. I was thinking maybe it was those egg cartons, messing with the airwaves, when I heard a siren. Only this was like no siren I'd ever heard. And I'd heard plenty back at the old apartment, where for a long time I believed it was the sound the stars made when they came out each night somewhere up above the lights of Lake Street.

Then I realized this particular siren was coming from the TV. Something was moving there across the screen, something tall and dark and rubbery. *A tornado!* I couldn't help it, I fell on my knees on the shag carpet.

"Don't get your fur in a bundle," says Wednesday, and lights a cigarette. "This ain't real life, it's a friggin' news video."

I straightened up, moved to a folding chair by the card table. My cheeks felt hot.

"I know that," I said. "It's just, you know, I never *heard* one before."

Wednesday raised her eyes at me, started to say something, then stopped. She took a drag of her cigarette, exhaled slowly. The smoke sat in the air for a few seconds, then fell apart.

"Course, everybody knows a tornado sounds like a friggin' *freight train*," she said, looking at me sideways with her green eyes. "I just wanted you to hear what a tornado *warning* sounds like, so's you'd know, just in case."

(a warning, a friggin' warning)

"So now you know," she said, and waved her cigarette around the room. "Anyways, bombs, tornados, the friggin' heat—what's the difference? This here little hacienda is the ultimate escape, the ultimate shelter. Hon, you couldn't be in a better place. Am I right?"

On the TV a blonde appeared in front of the tornado and pointed at it with a stick. Wednesday swore and turned the volume down. The siren stopped. The blonde continued to smile and point. Wednesday walked over, sat down across from me, picked up the cards, started to shuffle.

"Big doin's tonight," she said, "gotta relax."

Wednesday was racing Margaret in the Powderpuff Derby at the Tri-County Carnival Speedway. We were all going to watch and check out the Midway afterward. Everyone, that is, except Wednesday's brother. Mr. M. David Wilson had finally gotten the call he'd been waiting for. I was there in the kitchen, getting a Dr. Pepper, when the call came in. He'd hung up the phone and glanced toward the add-on sunporch. Then he saw me standing there in the refrigerator light.

"Well, Miss Muffet," he says, and bows slightly. "I must say, it's been a pleasure, it surely has. But you know what they say about all good things." So I say, "No, I don't, and nobody ever accused me of being good." So he says, "Well, ain't you somethin'. But y'all take care, y'hear? Both of you gals, y'all take good care."

And that was basically that. Now Mr. M. David Wilson was back on the road. He'd been gone three weeks. Nobody had heard from him.

"Yup, gotta relax," said Wednesday, and moved her piece. "Cuz after tonight we'll be bidin' our time 'til the Good News and life's back to friggin' normal." I looked at her.

"Church talk for Easter," she says. "I'm talkin' a whole friggin' week, saloons slow, Midway's slow, people walkin' slow, drivin' slow. You ask me, the true good news is all this slowness is finally over. Hally-loo-ya, christ is risen, drinks on the house."

I was thinking my idea of Easter meant Ma got me a two-pound chocolate rabbit and herself a new pastel outfit to parade around in. I was wondering if J.W.s had Easter, which started me thinking about poor Mrs. Wilson again, wondering if she'd made it into heaven or what. I asked Wednesday what exactly it took to become one of the two thousand.

"Get your tickets in advance," she said, "before the big day."

I lowered my card, the one which said Barbie has a run in her nylon, lose one turn. Through Wednesday's tall spidery hair I could see the shelves along the back wall, all those books and records and tapes and cans of Spaghetti Os and Spam. On the wall next to the shelves I could see the painting of the black velvet girl crying one gigantic velvet tear, and next to her, the painting of the Green Lady. A few sequins had fallen out of the sky from riding in the back of Delta Dave's Peterbilt, but otherwise she was still beautiful, a real hoot, as Wednesday put it. I'd hung her up there for something to look at while I escaped the heat, it isn't every day a person lives in a windowless bomb shelter. Besides, you could only stare for so long at that huge velvet tear in the other painting before you wanted to scream, What's the friggin' problem? So after awhile, studying the Green Lady up there day after day, I'd started to get inspired. Like maybe I myself might want to try my hand at this artist routine. After all, I'd spent that time doing theme rooms with Nova, oohing and aahing over Judith's other paintings... you never know, something might've rubbed off.

Beside us the lava lamp dropped a sizeable glob.

I looked at Wednesday. "Did you just say something about buying a ticket to heaven?"

She laughed. "Some folks might call it that, hon, but around these parts, it's the Wreck-'em-Rodeo." She tossed the dice.

104 MINIMUM MAINTENANCE

"'Ken asks to go steady, take extra turn'."

I let out my breath. We weren't discussing the end of the world, just the Demolition Derby at the Tri-County Carnival. Wednesday had given me the scoop: guys in souped-up cars with advertisements for "Valvoline" and "Piggy LaVake's Parts and Salvage" drove around backwards crashing into each other. Eventually all the cars were wrecked except one, which was declared winner. Every so often some car would blow up and some guy would be hauled away on a stretcher while the crowd waited for him to raise his hand. Any guy worth his salt usually waited with the hand-raising bit until just before they slid him into the rear end of an ambulance. For dramatic effect, Wednesday said, to give the people their money's worth.

Females, on the other hand, weren't allowed to drive backwards and crash into each other. On account of their parts, she said, nobody wants to jeopardize the future of mankind. Females could only drive one way: straight ahead, in circles. The Powderpuff Derby was an all-female race. In honor of the Powderpuff, Margaret now featured a wreath of pink flowers on her hood, surrounding an advertisement for "Helene's Hilton Hairtel" at the NUThouse, and a big purple "53," Wednesday's number, on her passenger door.

Wednesday picked up the dice again. She had a thin line of dirt, like a tiny brown moon, under each fingernail.

"So what's your ride tonight?" I asked.

The lava lamp had developed another formation and was dropping it slowly, like a gigantic tear, toward the bottom. I glanced at the sad velvet girl.

"The Bullet," said Wednesday, and tossed the dice. "THE ride, in its day, but not no more. Though yours truly can give you an experience on the Bullet you won't soon forget." She moved her piece up seven squares. "Other night some guy says 'Gimme a real good ride, toots, go for broke,' so I oblige. Ride's over, guy gets off, walks a ways, lays right down on the ground."

The glob in the lava lamp finally let go.

"Stayed there five minutes," says Wednesday. "I seen it with my own two eyes. I'm wonderin' what's next, when the guy gets up, shakes his head, walks off kind of crooked." She holds up her card and grins. "Queen of the friggin' Prom, yours truly."

I could see the blank space where one of her teeth used to be. I'd seen her stick a lit cigarette into the space so she could work on Margaret with both hands. She started setting up the board again. When everything was in place she leaned back, ran a matchbook cover along the underside of her thumbnail.

"That guy might've seen the lord on that ride," said Wednesday Wilson, "the friggin' lord."

I glanced at the beautiful Green Lady.

Ma, on the other hand, looked like she might've seen the devil. We'd gone back up to ground level to check on the weather in person. Ma was sitting in the add-on sunporch, chasing after flies with a rolled up newspaper, a look on her face I would have to call gray. I tried to remember the last time I'd seen her haul out the reflector panels. Her tan was fading fast, replaced by this new gray look. To match the clouds that kept gathering like an army.

I opened the screen door, flopped into the chair next to hers, just as she brought the newspaper down on another fly. The fly bounced up like a beebee, landed neat as can be in Ma's half-empty glass. I glanced through the screen at the egg carton sky.

"Looks like it's breaking up," I said. "Looks like a person could get some tanning in after all." This wasn't true exactly, but it didn't matter. Ma wasn't paying attention to anything but those flies.

I tried again. "Ma, we still going tonight? Watch Wednesday race? Check out the rides?"

Ma, however, had never been much for rides.

When I was a kid my dad would show up, like clockwork, at State Fair time. We might not've seen him for months, and for awhile Ma would try to be a sport about it. Come on be a sport, he'd say. But in the end she always looked for a sunny table in the Beer Gardens. She'd settle in with her sunglasses and cigarettes, a sandal dangling from her glittery toenails. Just watching the world go by, she'd say. Meanwhile me and my dad would circle the Midway and eat. Then we'd go on rides. We'd circle back to Ma periodically to report how many times we'd spun a particular cab, or how long we'd held another one upside down, or whether or not we'd thrown up. My dad had taught me the age-old technique of going on rides with a full stomach, To see what you're made of, he'd say.

Now I said, "Ma, remember that time the Zipper stuck? How long did we hang there? A half hour?"

Ma lowered her newspaper.

"That's it," she said, "that's what I've been trying to remember." She ignored the fly perched on her toenail, busily washing its little face. Her toenail polish was half chipped off.

"You and your dad," she said, "and that one ride. What was the name of it? You were so little, I was scared shitless you'd be killed. But you loved that ride. You'd holler and carry on, you wanted to go again and again."

I knew exactly.

I could see my dad, grin as big as the moon, taking my hand, walking up the ramp, strapping us in. I could hear the music start up, that screaming rock and roll so big and loud it was like silence. I couldn't hear my dad's voice, I could only see his mouth stretch, his dimples kick in. I could feel us start to move, slowly at first, then faster and faster, until it was like we'd left something behind, like we'd lost track of something. Until all that mattered was my dad's tight arm and his smoky breath and my wide-open unheard laughing mouth and all that circling circling through the screaming guitars and the world.

But all that happened in the Stone Age, Ma would say, if I've told you once I've told you a million times, don't mention his goddamn name in my presence, and she'd light another cigarette. So usually I was careful not to mention anyone in particular, just to wonder out loud if one of these years we might not run into Someone again somewhere, and then to myself, what if there was a Midway nearby, wouldn't that be fucking heaven?

After taking a breather, the fly on Ma's toenail had started up again.

"The Himalaya," I said, "the ride you mean. It's the Himalaya."

Ma actually looked at me.

"Do you want to go faster?" she said, and I said,

"I can't hear you!"

"DO YOU WANT TO GO FASTER ...?"

"I CAN'T HEAR YOU ...!"

We said it again and again, louder then louder. Then we accidentally grinned at each other, me and Ma. Our lips stayed stretched out like that for maybe fifteen seconds. Something in my fingers wanted to move, something behind my eyes wanted to come together. Then Ma's mouth just dropped slowly back in on itself, like a glob from the lava lamp, her face faded back to gray. She turned her head and blinked, and then she raised the newspaper and faster than the speed of light brought it down THWACK! on her red-chipped toenail. A tiny smudge dropped onto the fake grass carpeting.

Sometimes on the Midway my dad would suddenly haul me up onto his shoulders, and there I'd be, high above the crowd, looking down from my perch like the Queen of Sheba. We'd go circling like that, me and my dad, around and around, through the smells and the music and the dizzy lights, with all my fingers locked in my dad's black hair and all his locked around my lavender jelly shoes.

On our way to the Tri-County Carnival and Speedway Races, I rode in Margaret, flat-towed behind Wednesday's regular vehicle, a light green three-quarter-ton Dodge. Wednesday warned me to keep my head down or Smokey would get her ass for sure. I could see the back of her mile-high hair up in the Dodge, Ma's flatter version over by the passenger door. Helene's Hilton Hair-Tel had offered a free session in honor of the Powderpuff, and Wednesday had taken advantage. Ma, however, hadn't even bothered to wash her hair, let alone try out a new look.

I looked at the sky again, wondering if that might not be the tip of a funnel cloud poking down from the egg cartons, and if it was, could we make it back to the bomb shelter in time? In say, less than four minutes? Wednesday had told me her mother once described a tornado as the finger of god poking down at the world, searching for bad little girls.

"So when the big one come," Wednesday said, "the summer I turned ten, and everybody piled into the root cellar, yours truly run out and stood in the bean field. I seen that twister come dancin' over the earth at me, kickin' up turf and beans, with that sound like a locomotive. Only I just stood there in my little white sandals, singin' 'Jesus Loves the Little Children' over and over. I'll be damned if that old tornado didn't doe-si-doe around me, polite as pie, and head on over to County Road 50 and blow Hadley Malacker's Bar and Girl to kingdom come."

I said, "Bar and Girl?" and Wednesday said,

"Old Hadley was drunk when he painted it. Anyways, looks like I proved once and for all jesus loved this lil' gal. Not long afterwards, I start gettin' me an allowance."

I look up again, and now I'm sure of it. That's got to be a

tornado snaking down from those clouds like the finger of god. Then I start thinking about the sun exploding, wondering if that might not set off the rest of the tornados who've been patiently waiting, so they'd all come down on the world at once, like the fingers of god and jesus and all the angels, like all those hands clapping clapping because it's finally over the evil old world is finally finished a standing ovation that's all she wrote.

Only I was wrong. We made it to the carnival in one piece.

I got my first glimpse of the Tri-County Carnival when Wednesday pulled into the parking lot behind the speedway. I squeezed through Margaret's window, jumped to the dirt. The Midway bloomed up out of the Oklahoma fields like a bouquet of neon flowers. In the other direction, the NUThouse looked like the pile of crates the flowers came in. There was no doubt, the Nation's Ultimate Truckstop looked better from a distance.

Wednesday jumped out of the Dodge, lit a cigarette, poked it into the space between her teeth. She walked to the rear of the flat trailer, pulled out the ramp, laid it in the dirt. Then she walked up the ramp, crawled through Margaret's driver's side window, took a minute to settle herself and cranked the ignition. Nothing. She cranked it again. A few more tries, a small BANG!, and Margaret jumped awake. The sound filled the parking lot, rattled the ground. Two workers sitting behind a Midway tent looked over.

Wednesday said something I couldn't hear, I could only see her cigarette bob, smoke disappear up into her hair like it knew the route. She looked over her shoulder and backed down the ramp. Once she had all four tires in the dirt, she squealed off toward the rear entrance of the speedway, trailing all that sound and dust behind her like a tail.

Meanwhile Ma stood in the dirt beside the Dodge, her hand on the open door, staring out over the car roofs toward the

NUThouse. Someone passing by wouldn't know if she was getting in or out. The men behind the tent glanced at her, then turned back to whatever they'd been doing.

That's when I got the queerest feeling.

Men never, ever glanced at Ma. They stared, they watched, they bumped into other men, they stepped off curbs into traffic. They touched their belts, they moved their hats, they spun their rings, they cleared their throats. They lit cigarettes. Now this feeling, like that time I saw a kitten walking by the side of the freeway, or the time that friend of Ma's handcuffed me to the steering wheel so I'd be safe while they went shopping. This feeling like something was going to happen, right some very minute, only there was nothing I could do about it, one way or the other. Just like TV, I could only watch.

"Ma!" I said, and her shoulders jumped under her sweatshirt.

(a sweatshirt?)

"Come on," I said, walking up, closing the door of the Dodge, "before the grandstand fills."

Ma stared off toward the NUThouse. She cleared her throat.

"Twenty-four hours," she says, in this scratchy voice, like it hasn't been used in awhile. "Everything's twenty-four hours a day over there. Three in the morning, you can get your hair done, cleats put on, teeth cleaned ..."

"Ma ..." I said, and started toward the grandstand.

"Three in the morning," she says again, "you might can go to a goddamn tanning booth. Everything you need. Don't even need the goddamn sun."

The first speedway event was the Demolition Derby. One of the cars flipped over a few times, but the driver walked away on his own two feet.

This was followed by a lull in the action while they cleared away dead cars. People bought more beer and hot dogs and watched the crowning of Miss Spark Plug, which took place on the flagman's platform. The crowd cheered the loudest for contestant number five, who was declared winner and got to ride around the track in the raised bucket of a Case loader accompanied by a few firecrackers. Beauty contests usually got Ma going on her "lost opportunities" routine, how events always conspired to keep her forever in the wings of life, while less talented girls wore crowns and rode around in convertibles and got in the paper. If they ever made a movie about Ma, if anyone ever asked me, "Wings of Life" should be the title.

I watched Miss Spark Plug circle the track. I commented on her too-long teeth, her too-short neck, her doughy knees. Only Ma didn't seem to hear. I drank half Ma's beer, she didn't notice. She appeared to snap out of it for a second or two at the start of the Powderpuff Derby, even got to her feet with the rest of the crowd to cheer the lineup of cars chugging around the track in formation.

The cars circled once, twice. Like a herd of pastel horses chomping at the bit, just waiting to be let loose. Then the flagman flew into a frenzy, whipping his flag back and forth, the white flag which said, Drive like hell ladies, go for broke and don't look back. I knew all about the colors, how they lead up to the last flag, the checkered flag, the one waiting behind all the others. The one which said, Race is over, ladies, tend to your hair. Wednesday told me you lost track of the colors, of the number of times you'd circled. You just kept watching for the cars around you, watching for some flaky bitch to cut you off, watching for those blessed frigging checkers.

I'd lost track of the colors, too, and the flags. And I couldn't tell what was louder, the cars roaring around the track or the humans in the grandstand hollering. The sky got darker, the grandstand lights came on. I couldn't see beyond the lights. Like the night was some big upside-down mixing bowl, and any minute it might mix up a batch of tornado.

Then something caught my eye: a checkered blur waving madly, and streaming past underneath it, a baby blue car with a big purple "53" on the passenger side door. And there was Ma, the only person in the whole grandstand sitting down, staring quietly ahead at the "LEE" on the ass of the guy in front of her.

"Ma!" I hollered at the side of her face. "She won! Wednesday won!"

A breeze split Ma's bangs in the middle. Usually her hair was so sprayed up it moved in one piece like a plate.

"Wednesday won, Ma!" I hollered again.

"That's nice," she said.

"But, Ma ..." I tried again, then gave up.

I looked back at the track. Margaret was taking her victory lap, Wednesday's arm sticking out the window waving a bouquet of pink flowers with green ribbons trailing. Donna Summer was belting out over the loud speaker, and from what I could tell, I had to agree: Wednesday Alice Wilson worked frigging hard for her money.

By the time Margaret finished her lap, the crowd in the grandstand had started to leave. The music and the cheering had stopped, sounds from the Midway were drifting in. I turned to Ma. I couldn't wait any longer. I needed to ask for money. I got ready for the big sigh, the big You-have-no-idea-what-I've-goddamn-had-to-go-through-for-you routine. But instead, there she was, rooting in her clutch bag.

"Take this," she says, "have yourself a ball."

I stared at the bills in her hand, then at her. She seemed to have perked up a bit.

"You know I don't like rides," she said, in her half-perky voice. "So we can all of us meet up later on, at the parking lot. Around midnight?" She looked at me as if she only just realized I was there.

"Maybe they have the Himalaya," she said, and started in,

" ... Do you want to go faster ... ?"

But before I could answer, she did the queerest thing. She reached over, tucked a piece of hair behind my ear, adjusted one of my safety pins.

When I'd first started wearing the pins, she'd thrown an orange brush at me and threatened to send me to a foster home. This was awhile back, during the Stone Age, the last time we'd had our own apartment. This apartment had featured its own bathroom, as opposed to down-the-hall, plus a couple other rooms and a fire escape. After she threw the brush, I locked myself in the bathroom and came out two hours later with orange hair. At which point Ma looked me up and down, then walked calmly over to the phone and picked it up to call a foster home. Only the line was dead, we hadn't paid the bill. So she walked calmly over to the back door, opened it, and when I was outside, locked it behind me and pulled the shade. I spent the night on the fire escape for the first time, biting off orange split ends and listening to cars cruise the alley.

When Ma reached toward my other ear, I was ready.

"Okay, thanks," I said, taking the money, stepping back. "Parking lot, midnight," and I started climbing the seats toward the exit.

"DO YOU WANT TO GO FASTER ... ?" Ma called out behind me. A guy looked around. I started through the cement archway.

"I CAN'T HEAR YOU ... " she called louder.

And she might've said it all again. But I was gone.

I started with a few low-key rides, to get the feel of the place before any serious eating. The double Ferris wheel, the Scrambler, the Octopus. I was building confidence. After awhile I felt so confident I blew two bucks on Fool the Guesser, who guessed my age in less than ten seconds. I asked if it was the leftover purple in my hair that fucking clued him in, and he whispered back, Funny you should mention it, actually it was the camo fucking hightops. I could feel him watching behind his sunglasses as I walked away.

I checked out Little Irvy the Whale and Secrets of the Amazon. I checked out the two-thousand-year-old mummy. I wandered through the Glass House and Dracula's Dungeon. I checked out the Freak Show—Popeye and Rubber Man and Spider Woman and the Two-headed Girl—though my favorite was the Alligator Lady, and for a dollar extra I bought a photo of her ten normal children. At Spin Painting the lady let me paint on the photo. When I was finished, the ten normal children appeared to be up in a tornado.

Then I started to eat. Cotton candy, Teeny Weeny Donuts, corn-on-a-stick, apple-on-a-stick, potato-on-a-stick, deep-fried cheese curds, peanut butter pie, peanut butter pancakes, "All The Milk You Can Drink For A Quarter For The Daughters Of The American Revolution." I was finishing off a banana-on-a-stick, feeling almost ready, starting to look around for the Himalaya. I'm chanting to myself, *"You can't get in, you can't get out, can't get out of the Glass House, the Glass House,"* when I look up and there's a rainbow of lights flashing:

"BULLET ... BULLET ... BULLET ..."

A pretty lame-looking ride, but a crowd had formed in front of it. People kept coming, joining the crowd, watching with the people already there, all those eyes following the Bullet as it moved through the air WHICK WHICK WHICK.

I moved closer. I could see Wednesday's hair. I could see her shoulders move under her blue satin Powderpuff shirt, her jaws move under her skin. A line of sweat moved along her cheek, her hands held tight to the controls. The Bullet circled. The air whistled. The people looked around, at Wednesday, at each other, back at the Bullet, which hurled toward the ground then up toward the sky.

(you can't get in, you can't get out)

Finally the Bullet began to slow ... WHICK ... WHICK ... Wednesday's knees unlocked, her fingers relaxed, the Bullet came to a stop ... WHOOSH. We watched Wednesday walk in her dusty boots and skyscraper hair up the exit ramp, unlatch the door of the cab, swing it upward like a wing. We watched her reach in, take hold of a hand.

(you can't get out)

We watched a foot with red-chipped toenails appear, and down out of the Bullet stepped Ma.

Her hair stuck straight up. The rainbow of lights flashed across her face, which was no longer gray. Her face was white, white as the towels at the Thrifty Scot, as the broken line in the middle of the highway, as the flag which says, Drive like hell, ladies, go for broke and don't look back.

Now Ma looked back, at the silver cab, at Wednesday. I thought I saw her mouth move, she might've said "thank you." Wednesday nodded, and Ma turned around and took two steps and fell over. I pushed through the people and ran up the wooden planks of the exit ramp. Ma's eyes flickered open.

"Sh-Sugar ..." she said, "where'd you come from ..." she said, and her eyes flickered closed.

Then I saw the blood.

(can't get out)

It covered her jeans, it covered her legs, between her legs. It was spreading onto the exit ramp. I was thinking it looked like a spin painting. I was thinking of the ten normal children, wondering if their children would be normal or alligator. I was thinking it didn't matter anyways, the sun is going to frigging explode some day, nothing frigging matters except that. Except Ma, I was thinking, and I looked down at her white skin red blood and that's when I heard the siren just like on TV.

A tornado!

◆ ◆ ◆

Only I was wrong.

And Ma was right. The lady behind us at the Korner Kafe was a big tipper. The lady finished her coffee, applied Chapstick, adjusted her feathered earrings, and laid a five spot on the table underneath the salt. She maneuvered out of the booth and smoothed her madras tent dress. Ma kept me informed of these developments in a low whisper, her eyes sliding sideways, lips barely moving. Someone passing by wouldn't know if she was listening to someone, me for instance, or daydreaming. Maybe they'd think she was praying, seeing it was Easter Sunday and all.

The lady of the big tip passed our table and smiled with her yellow teeth. And I couldn't help it, I smiled back. Ma sniffed.

"Horse teeth," she said, when the lady was out of earshot. "Hair like a hail storm, butt like a buckboard."

I was wondering just how long it would take Ma to quit talking like Wednesday Wilson. Maybe as long as it took us to get out of Oklahoma. We were at the Korner Kafe, sharing a piece of apple pie, waiting for the 5:15 to start loading passengers next door. We're just going to head west, said Ma, just going to follow the sun, plus there's nothing like a good long bus ride to get a person's priorities straight. I'd already checked out the laminated road map on the wall of the bus station and had to agree: Route 66 looked pretty straight to me.

"So, do you know about the Mother Road?" I asked.

Ma narrowed her eyes. "What are you talking about?" she said, staring hard at me, not blinking. "What are you goddamn up to now?" Two can play at this game, I was thinking, and stared right back.

I won. Ma fluffed her bangs and looked away. Here it was, Easter Sunday, a whole week after her famous Bullet ride, and she still looked pretty peaked. The nurses at all-night Emergency at the NUThouse hadn't wanted to let her out until some color came back to her cheeks. But after three days, when she discovered they also weren't letting the photographers in, the ones from the paper who wanted to interview her, Ma escaped. Straight to Helene's Hilton Hair-Tel, where she asked for the works, then straight to the newspaper offices, where she was politely told she was old news, and when she demanded to see the goddamn owner, politely asked to leave.

Ma was considering adding nurses to her list of major downfalls, right behind cars. Nurses just get my goat, she said in her Wednesday way, my goddamn goat.

Now she whispered, "Watch this," and picked up her clutch bag and slid out of the booth like she was moving through water.

I lit a cigarette. A guy at a table over by the window glared at me. I blew a smoke ring and watched him through it. Then I blew a long line of smoke into the middle of the ring, and watched as everything broke apart. I was thinking it looked like a tornado.

The siren I'd heard at the Tri-County Carnival had been an ambulance. I guess they didn't sound the same in Oklahoma. I was thinking I should consider myself lucky it hadn't been a tornado warning. Lucky as Lucifer, Wednesday would say, to be getting my priorities straight and hightailing it out of Tornado Alley before learning what the fuss was all about. Before learning what it might feel like to have the finger of god poking down from the clouds, rooting around in the dust, looking for yours truly.

I was thinking maybe there are some things a person is better off not knowing. Because once a person knows about a thing—the sun, for instance—a person can't not know it.

"Because learning can be a dangerous thing," I said out loud. The guy over by the window looked away.

"I'm gone two minutes," says Ma, sliding back into her side

of the booth, "you're goddamn talking to yourself."

She checks her watch, signals the waitress, pulls her sunglasses out of her clutch bag. In the Ladies she put on fresh lipstick, her hair is a few inches higher. When the waitress comes, Ma squints at her name tag and holds out a five spot. She winks at me.

"Keep the change, Arnette," says Ma, and smiles with all her small white teeth. Arnette smiles back with all hers and tucks the bill into her apron pocket.

"That's real nice of y'all," says Arnette, then lowers her voice. "'Specially after that there booth behind you stiffed me. And her so polite and all. Y'all just never know."

"Y'all never do," says Ma, and shakes her head. Then she smiles and clicks her clutch bag shut. "Anyways, Happy Easter."

"Likewise, I'm sure," says Arnette.

Ma puts on her sunglasses, the white rhinestone wraparounds Wednesday gave her for a going-away. And then we're really going away, me and Ma, out through the swinging glass doors of the Korner Kafe, to a bus headed straight for the Mother Road headed straight for the sun.

5
Drawing from Life

I started drawing dinosaurs when Nesta Hernandez, who cleaned our room at the Starlite Motel, told me they never existed.

"They weren't in the Bible," she said. "That proves it. Look anywhere you want, you won't find a dinosaur in the Bible."

"But what about the scientists?" I said.

"Men make mischief," said Nesta, "not God."

I thought about this for awhile. But I just couldn't help it, I started to doubt. Then I started to draw. I figured if I could draw them, they must've existed.

I drew dinosaurs everywhere, on anything. Bar napkins, waiting for Ma to decide to leave. Restaurant menus, waiting for Ma to decide to stay. Used kleenex boxes, turned upside down to the flat white part. The spaces around the edges of newspapers, the plain white covers that came with Ma's Playboys.

"Just wanna keep track of the competition," Ma said about the Playboys, which she kept in four piles under her bed in the motel. Nesta refused to clean under the bed "as long as that blasphemy remains there."

The piles corresponded with the four seasons, the magazines arranged according to month. All the girls looked happy but blurry, like you might need glasses to see them. Nobody had zits, or looked tired. Airbrushing, Ma called it. My favorite was a particular August, featuring a girl in various poses in the desert, with a snake. It made me think of dinosaurs.

Then I discovered the stationery shoved to the back of the desk drawer at the Starlite, behind Ma's makeup and matchbook collection. I'd been rooting around looking for the matches from the M&M Bar in Butte, Ma's last job. The matches came in a tiny silver box. Their tips were silver, too, and a tiny silver flame jumped up when you lit one.

I pushed my hand further into the drawer, searching for the match box, and felt the smooth sheets of the notepad, the little pile of envelopes alongside. I pulled them out, saw the three spiky stars in the top corner of each sheet, the spiky writing at the bottom, "Dreams Come True at the Starlite." With Ma's nail scissors I carefully cut the bottoms off, threw them in the wastebasket and settled back to draw.

Nesta tapped at the door and let herself in.

"See," I said to her, "how would I know to draw them this way unless they were proven?" I showed her a pile of sheets, a dinosaur on each one.

"What's all them black lines everywhere?" said Nesta. She smelled like Lemon Pledge, which she kept in her apron pocket. Once I snuck the can of Pledge from where she'd set it on the dressertop, sprayed my neck and wrists. It beat Ma's perfumes, with names like Midnight Mystique or Secret Scentsation. Like something mysterious was going on and Ma had the answer.

"That's shading," I said, pushing the best dinosaur a little apart from the others on the desktop. "I figured it's night on account of the stars, and that's the darkness."

Nesta clucked. "You'll spend eternity in darkness, drawing that blasphemy." Nesta was big on blasphemy.

She picked up the bible. It came with the room, along with

Drawing from Life 123

the TV and all the toilet paper you could use.

"Now look here," she said, and held the bible out in front of her with her eyes closed. She'd told me that you could open the bible to anywhere, at any time, and the passage you opened to would be like a message from God, meant just for you. Like a miracle.

After a minute, she opened her eyes, then the bible, and read, "'Then two harlots came before the king and ...'"

She glanced at me, her cheeks red.

"Wrong side," she said, "probably the other side," and she looked across the page and read, "' ... Ten fat oxen, and twenty pasture-fed cattle, a hundred sheep, besides harts, gazelles, roebucks, and fatted fowl'."

She closed the bible.

"There," she said, laying it back on the nightstand. "Did you hear any mention of dinosaurs?"

She whipped her lemony dustrag around with a snap, started wiping down the television. The big silver cross she wore around her neck knocked against the screen. Crew-so-fix, she called it. Like something bad was going on and Nesta had the answer: call a crew to fix it.

"But Nesta," I said, grabbing the drawings out of her way, "why would the scientists make something like that up?"

"You have no idea, the plans they have," said Nesta. "They make this stuff up to throw us off the trail."

"The trail of what?" I said, and Nesta said,

"UFOs. They're everywhere, watching us. The goverment don't want us to know. They're afraid we might get some idea to go up in one of them UFOs, take off someplace, not pay taxes."

I thought for a minute. "But Nesta, UFOs aren't in the bible."

Nesta rolled her eyes. "Honey, the Bible is nothing but UFOs, every time you turn around, just chock full of 'em."

She picked up the bible again, opened it, moved her eyes up and down the page. "'Then he brought me into the inner court, and behold, there were two chambers and ...'"

She kept reading silently to herself.

I said, "And ...?"

"And what?" said Nesta, closing the bible, looking up.

I said, "What's that supposed to prove?", and Nesta said,

"It goes on from there, it's a description of a spaceship, anyone can see that."

So I started drawing flying saucers and spaceships up by the stars on the Starlite stationery, hovering over the dinosaurs below. The combination seemed to calm Nesta. After awhile I used up the pad of stationery, she gave me three more. I kept drawing. Sometimes I added more stars. Sometimes little faces looked out of the spaceship windows. Sometimes the dinosaurs looked up, sometimes down, sometimes straight out of the page at me, drawing them.

I drew in the afternoons, after Ma left for her job at the casino. Her job was to walk around with a glass on a string hanging around her neck. Men would pour tequila in the glass, then drink it, then give her a dollar. Sometimes more, depending on how short the string was.

Ma had hopes of making it to daytime dancer, then evening dancer, then maybe even dealer. Though to be dealer you had to go through training, and Ma said she'd never been much for school.

"I've always sort of figured things out as I went along," she said. "Never had a manual."

By the time I'd reached the second pad of Starlite stationery, the dinosaurs seemed to be drawing themselves. Between Ma swishing back and forth in a cloud of Rumors of Romance and finally pulling the big metal door of room twenty-six shut behind her, and Nesta showing up awhile later to clean, there I'd be at the shiny blond desk with my Starlite notepad, dinosaurs just pouring onto the page. Like they'd been waiting in that black-and-white Starlite pencil for a chance to escape and run around on their own.

The dinosaurs appeared in all shapes and sizes, some posing dramatically, some just standing there thinking. I started to draw little trees and hills, which the dinosaurs towered over, and together with the stars and flying saucers, the pictures looked complete. Like a world.

The first time I showed them to her, Ma flipped through a couple of the drawings, looked up, studied me for a minute.

"When are you going to do something about your hair?" she said, and I said,

"Ma, the drawings ..."

She sighed, flipped through a few more. Then she said,

"Are you sure these are real?"

I stared at her. "What? You too? Since when do *you* read the bible?"

She stared at me.

I said, "So what if they're not in the bible?"

Ma shook her head. "There is no doubt, I have raised a re-tard." She tossed the drawings onto the bed. "What I mean is, they don't look quite right. What did you use for a model?"

"Who needs a model?" I said. "Everyone knows what a dinosaur looks like."

I picked through the pictures, chose one in particular, in which a dinosaur with a long neck and wings stood peacefully munching a treetop. "This is a prontosaurus." I picked out another, with Ws along its back, and three legs. "A trilegotops," I said. "And these ..."

"You've been watching that educational channel again," said Ma, rooting around in her purse. "All I ask is you keep track of my daytime stories, but no, that's too much to ask." She pulled out a Playboy, tossed it onto the bed, then pulled out one of those miniature bottles of tequila left over from her last shift at the casino. "I have no clue as to whether Lucia came out of her goddamn coma or not. It's all I goddamn ask." She twisted the cap of the little bottle, put the bottle to her lips and drank. Her cheeks caved in, a dribble appeared along her chin.

"You gotta leave an airhole," I said, "else everything sort of sucks in on itself."

"Nobody goddamn asked you," said Ma, and wiped her chin, and threw the little bottle into the wastebasket. She walked into the bathroom and shut the door loud. Ma always got crabby when the new Playboy came out.

I sat on the bed and paged through this latest issue, which featured a girl tied to a tree with ribbons. The ribbons were tied in bows. A couple of cavemen stood around in the background. I wondered if there were any cavemen in the Bible.

◆ ◆ ◆

Ma claimed to be able to spot men with money. She said it was a certain way they had about them, quiet and relaxed, no matter what they were wearing. Deadbeats and losers, Ma said, were louder and dressed in brighter colors. Many of them looked like Elvis.

"They try so hard, they make me tired," Ma told me. "But a man with money, he doesn't need to lift a finger. He just *is*."

Ma said she'd paid her dues with Elvis lookalikes. Now all she wanted this side of heaven was a man with money. He could look like Elvis's horse for all she cared. All she wanted was some peace and quiet and a few Gold Cards, was that too much to ask?

Still, every guy Ma brought back to the Starlite was suspect—slicked hair, flarey pants, white shoes. I asked why she didn't just cool her jets, wait around for Mr. Money to turn up, and Ma said that wasn't the point, she needed to keep in practice, there were some things I just couldn't understand. A couple of the guys were even prettier than Ma—a sure sign. They all smoked and wore rings on their little fingers. They all owned steel-belted sunglasses. They called Ma darlin', and me, lil' darlin'.

"Here's a dollar, lil' darlin'," they'd say, "go on, take a walk, get yourself a Coke."

They never seemed to notice that it was usually three in the morning when they said this, that Ma'd had to shake me awake beforehand, hand me my jeans. I took to sleeping in my clothes. I'd take the dollar from the latest Elvis, go ask for change at the Nite Owl across the street, stop by the cigarette machine at the end of the first floor hallway. Then I'd sit in the lobby of the Starlite, smoking and drawing, until it was time to go back to room twenty-six.

I'd graduated from dinosaurs to dogs. In the desk drawer back in the room, I'd come across a book of matches with a test on it. "Can You Draw Me?" it said next to a picture of a happy dog. You were supposed to draw the dog, then send it in. Then, if you were good enough, you could go to the Famous Artists' School, where they'd teach you to draw other animals, and eventually people and buildings.

I spent my nights in the lobby drawing the dog over and over. When I finally got it right, I sent the drawing in a Starlite envelope to the address on the matchbook cover, and threw in a few dinosaurs for good measure. Then I kept drawing, to keep in practice.

Nesta's brother's grandson, Manuel Jones, was the night clerk at the Starlite. He was old, maybe twenty.

"What's the little artist got goin' tonight?" he'd say, and come around behind my chair and lean down and look over my shoulder. Whenever he did that, my hand would suddenly go haywire and some dog or dinosaur would have a little line shooting off of it somewhere. Like an antenna.

"Fuckenay," I'd say, and turn the sheet over and light a cigarette. Manuel Jones would laugh, lay his hand on my shoulder, then go back to his desk. His hand was warm and smelled like soap.

After awhile room twenty-six would light up on the switchboard—Ma's signal. "Coast is clear," Manny'd say, and if I happened to glance in his direction, he'd wink.

Back at the room, Ma would be alone, stretched out under the faded sheet, smoking, one of her pastel scarves drooped over the lamp beside the bed. The air would have an Elvis smell, I called it. Ma called it brute. I'd pull off my jeans and crawl into bed. Then, as if she thought the situation called for it, Ma'd start talking.

Mostly she'd talk about herself, her dreams of landing a rich man, not having to work any more. She'd been working her whole life, she said, ever since she'd been asked to leave beauty school, and she was goddamn sick and tired of it. Her legs hurt all the time, her hair didn't grow as fast as it used to, she was starting to think she needed glasses.

"Jesus, glasses," she'd say, and light another cigarette.

Ma told me it was never too early to set a goal for yourself, she wished someone had given her the scoop when she was my age. She might've taken things more seriously, not wasted so much time.

"I could've become a stewardess," she said, "married a goddamn pilot. We could be heading somewhere, right this very minute."

I myself had never been up in a plane. Ma said she'd been up in one once, a long time ago, at a party. It'd been a very big party and a very small plane, and eventually the plane had landed on a lake. She said it felt like the Tilt-A-Whirl at the State Fair, and she'd thrown up. I wondered if it felt the same as going up in a UFO.

Pretty soon the drapes in room twenty-six would start growing light with morning, and Ma would grow quiet, thinking her own thoughts, maybe of flying. I'd watch the smoke from her last cigarette curl through the room like it was making pictures, thinking my own thoughts—of dinosaurs and dogs, UFOs and Elvis. I had it in my mind to learn to draw Elvis. I'd graduate to people and be that much further ahead when the Famous Artists' School called.

Manuel Jones told me he'd be my model. He came up behind me one night in the lobby before I had time to turn the notepad over.

"I see where you're comin' from," he said. I could feel him breathing on my hair.

"What do you want, a medal?" I said, and covered the drawing with my hand.

He lifted my hand. "No, but maybe *you* want a model," he said, studying my drawing. I'd been at work on the sideburns.

"What for?" I said. "Everyone knows what Elvis looks like."

"For proportion," said Manny. "You gotta draw from life."

I said, "Yeah, well, who died and made you expert?" And Manny said,

"Mechanical drawing. Night school."

I looked at him out of the corner of my eye. I noticed he wore a ring on his little finger. His hair was black, with sideburns.

I said, "Do you have sunglasses?"

Manny winked and patted my shoulder. "Tomorrow night," he said, "I'll be ready. You'll be amazed."

So that's how I learned Elvis.

The first night as my model, Manny showed up in a white blouse he borrowed from his sister, he said, white patent leather loafers he borrowed from his cousin in jail, white bell bottom jeans and a pair of tinted sunglasses with silver frames. He even brought a guitar with a cactus painted on it and a long red tassel hanging from the neck.

"From my grandfather's old-timey band," said Manny.

He slicked back his hair, arranged his mouth in a pout, and stood across the room from me, for perspective, he called it. He struck various poses while I drew. He timed the poses to be ten minutes, when he'd stop and we'd each have a cigarette, then he'd strike another pose and I'd draw some more. Sometimes I drew the whole shebang, sometimes only from the blouse up, sometimes just the head.

If I was working on a portrait, Manny called it, he'd sit in a chair facing me and look to the left at the men's room door, or to the right out the window at the Nite Owl, or straight ahead at me. Then, as if he thought the situation called for it, he'd start talking. Mostly he talked about himself. He told me the most important thing in life, besides a car and properly spiced food, was to seek your heart's desire. I asked him what that meant, and he said the thing you want more than anything else. So I asked Manuel Jones what it was he wanted more than anything else, and he said,

"To join the Air Force and see a volcano."

I stopped drawing and looked at him. "You've been up in a plane?"

"Hell, yes," said Manny and pouted some more. Then he said, "Well, a helicopter, when they took my grandfather to the heart hospital. But it's the same thing." He looked at me looking at him. "The eyes are the windows of the soul," said Manuel Jones. His eyelashes were long and curly, his eyes so black you couldn't see the pupils.

I said, "Elvis had blue eyes," and turned back to my drawing.

"Then don't fill 'em in," said Manny. "Leave 'em blank. They'll look blue."

So I left the eyes blank and concentrated on the eyebrows

and eyelashes and added sparkles and rhinestones to the blouse and bell bottoms. I left the cactus and tassel off the guitar, added a few more rings to the fingers. Mostly I liked doing the hair, which I shaded dramatically, with a few rays shooting off.

After I'd been practicing him for awhile, I showed a few of the Elvises to Nesta. She laid her dustrag across her shoulder, looked at each one, then at each one again, then handed them back. Muy bonito, she told me, especially the eyes, god rest his soul in heaven. I started to tell her that I had a model, that my model was Manuel Jones, her brother's grandson, but I changed my mind. Instead I asked her if any cavemen were mentioned in the bible, and Nesta said, Absolutely not, it's those blasphemous scientists again, cavemen never existed, and she rolled her eyes and snapped her lemony rag.

One night Manuel Jones asked to see the drawings.

"You gotta take the plunge sometime," he said.

"And what plunge would that be?" I said.

But Manny only winked, laid his guitar against the coffee table, picked up the Starlite notepad. He looked carefully, for a long time, at every Elvis.

"I'd say you got the hang of it," said Manuel Jones. Then he said, "Check this out," and picked up the pen and added a bunch of little musical notes along the edge of one of the drawings. The notes looked easy, like grapes, or little Ms and Fs with feet.

"I wish faces were so easy," I said, and that's when Nesta Hernandez's brother's grandson did an amazing thing.

Before I knew what he was about, Manuel Jones bent over and kissed me flat on the mouth, all light and hard and long and short, and smelling like soap and perfume from the blouse and tasting like smoke. Then the hand on my shoulder slid down and the fingers pushed inside the neck of my T-shirt and moved down down then up, the fingers moved back up, and then Manuel Jones straightened himself and winked at me and walked on over to the men's room door. I watched him walk through the door and then I sat in my chair in the lobby of the Starlite Motel, blinking and breathing and thinking my thoughts—of volcanos and sideburns and cavemen and planes.

◆ ◆ ◆

Then Manuel Jones was gone.

One night he was there in his Elvis outfit, posing and kissing and moving his hands, and the next time I found myself in the lobby of the Starlite Motel at three in the morning, a fat girl in a man's sweater and numbered shoes waddled out from behind the desk.

"You can't be here," she said. "Go on, vamoose, or I'll call the cops."

I stared at her. "Who are you?" I said. "And where's Manny?"

Her eyes sat in her face like ping pong balls, one of her numbered shoes moved. I looked down at her feet.

I said, "And what the fuck kind of shoes are those?"

"Bowling shoes," said the girl, pushing at her stringy bangs. "My feet are swollen."

"You're telling me." I snorted and lit a cigarette.

The girl straightened, took a step forward, waved her hand at the smoke. "I told you, you can't be here, there's laws."

I said, "Yeah, well, there oughta be a law against *you*." I blew smoke in her direction. "I asked you, where's Manny?"

The girl stared at me. She might've been pretty if you could find her face. Finally she said, "Do you belong here?"

I blew a smoke ring, took my time. "For your information," I said, "me and my Ma are the occupants of room twenty-six."

The girl's cheeks turned red, her hands fluttered down the sweater. "Oh I'm sorry ... I thought you ... well, I thought you ... well, I didn't know ..."

"So who are *you*?" I said, and she said,
"I'm Ritalee Jones. I'm Manuel's wife. I'm sorry."
I blinked. I said, "Well, you shouldn't be."
Ritalee Jones blinked.
I said, "Sorry about it, I mean." My throat felt funny.
Ritalee Jones put her hands on her stomach. "I'm not really this fat. I'm going to have a baby. Two babies, in fact." She looked down at her hands. "One of them's kicking. You wanna feel?"

I felt like I wanted to throw up. I got out of my chair, walked across the lobby, put my hand on Ritalee Jones's stomach. The stomach was hard, like a car tire. She moved my hand over, I felt a little ripple, like maybe the tire was getting ready to blow. Then something poked out at me from the other side.

"Fuckenay!" I said, and jerked my hand away.

Ritalee Jones giggled. I guess she was pretty. "That's what I said, when the doctor told me." She eyed my cigarette. "Sure wish I could have one."

I started to reach into my pocket when the switchboard buzzed. Ritalee waddled back behind the desk, lifted the receiver.

"Your room, twenty-six," she said. "Only nobody's sayin' nothin'."

Ma's signal. I went over and picked up my pencil and notepad, shoved them into my backpack.

Ritalee cleared her throat. "He got a new job. Manuel. Driving cab." Her eyes were so black, you couldn't see the pupils. "In answer to your question."

I looked over at her looking at me. My hand was on the swinging door leading to the rooms. "No," I said, "in answer to yours. I really don't belong here."

I stood outside room twenty-six, feeling in my pockets for the key, wondering about that sound coming from the other side of the door. I shifted my backpack, turned the key in the lock. The room was dark. I was hit by a blast of cold air. The air conditioner had been turned up, that was the sound I'd been hearing. The light from the hallway made a path into the room.

"Ma?" I said, squinting into the darkness.

"Ma?" I said it louder, trying to be heard over the air conditioner. "I got your signal. Can I come in?"

Even in that short time, I'd started to shiver. I followed the path of light over to the window, feeling in front of me through the hurricane of icy air. When I found the dial, I cranked it hard. In an instant the hurricane stopped. But the room seemed even colder, the quiet all of a sudden too loud. I shivered again.

"Ma?" I whispered, and listened.

Then I heard it, that swishy sound of someone moving around in bed. Jesus, I thought, I gotta hightail it, Elvis is still here. I turned back toward the doorway when Ma said my name.

"Sugar?" Her voice sounded funny, like she might be talking with her mouth full.

"Yeah? Ma?"

There was a pause. Then,

"Could you come around here ... turn on the lamp? I think ... it's on the floor ... by the bed ..."

I was stuck. I couldn't move. My feet wouldn't move.

(don't belong here)

She said, "Don't be scared. You gotta help me ... find the light ..."

(really don't belong here don't)

She made a noise, sucked her breath. "Sugarpie please ..."

Then suddenly I wasn't stuck. My arm reached out and my hand felt the edge of the bed and my hightops moved along the carpet. My fingers felt, found the lamp, the switch, then they clicked the switch, then the light came on.

After a minute, Ma said, "Can you ... start by untying me?"

Ma wouldn't let me call anybody. Not the police, not the hospital, not Ritalee Jones. She even made me put out the Do Not Disturb sign, so Nesta would pass by our door.

It took all morning. I had to run to the Nite Owl for things we kept forgetting—aspirin, Kotex, Ben-Gay. The last time, I asked the girl behind the checkout if they carried any of that special makeup.

"And what kind would that be?" said the girl, and she snapped her gum.

I said, "Airbrushing makeup. My Ma's looking kind of tired."

The girl looked at me like I'd just stepped out of a cave. She said, "Airbrushing makeup?"

I said, "Yeah, you know, the kind they use in ..." I looked at her looking at me. "Forget it," I said, and told her to ring up the rest of my stuff. When she wasn't looking, I pocketed a handful of miniature tequilas from the display beside the cash register.

When Ma saw the little bottles, she accidentally smiled, and her lip started bleeding again. By the time I heard Nesta down at the end of the hallway, there were three little empty tequila bottles lined up on the nightstand, Ma was in bed with her eyes closed, the TV was on with no sound. The air conditioner was turned to low, to drown out the sound of traffic and Nesta's vacuuming. I glanced at Ma. Her face was too big, there was dried blood in her hair, one of her hands looked like a foot. But she seemed to be asleep.

I reached over and picked up the last little bottle, twisted the cap, took a breath. Then I took a long swallow, making sure to keep my lips partly open for an airhole. When I finally lowered the bottle, a long shiver raced through me, from my hair to my hightops. Like it had a life of its own, like I was just along for the ride. Like the Tilt-A-Whirl.

I glanced at the TV. Mister Clean was walking out of a wall with his arms folded. A woman stood off to the side, holding a mop, with a look on her face like maybe she just got off a ride, too. Mr. Clean had an earring. I'd never noticed this. I flipped to another channel. Two people, a man and a woman, stood beside a hospital bed, where another woman lay sleeping. The sleeping woman's hair was spread across the pillow like a scarf. Suddenly the sleeping woman began to mew, her eyelids began to flutter.

"Ma!" I said. "I think it's Lucia! I think she's finally snapping out of it!" Lucia's eyes, which were blue, were now wide open. I turned toward Ma, but she turned her head ever so slightly and kept sleeping.

I set the bottle on the nightstand beside the other little bottles, and my eye fell on the bible. When we first moved into room twenty-six, Ma'd put the lamp on top of the bible to make more room. Nesta'd called this a blasphemy and put the bible back.

Now I picked the bible up, and opened it. Nothing but words, and tiny words at that. I flipped through the pages, then stopped.

"'O Lord, my heart is not lifted up, my eyes are not raised too high ...'" I glanced over at Ma. "You're telling me," I said, and turned to another page.

"'When I heard this, I rent my garments and my mantle, and pulled the hair from my head, and sat appalled.'"

I wasn't too sure what this was all about. Seems somebody got a bit of news—maybe they came into some money or something—then rented out their clothes and fireplace. Like maybe they didn't need them any more, now they had better ones. For some reason it reminded me of Mister Clean, who was certainly bald, and probably appalled, too, whatever that meant. I decided Mister Clean should be my next drawing project—that was the message the bible had meant to give me.

Just then I heard Nesta's cart squeak to a stop outside our door. There was a light tap. I started to get up. I needed a new Starlite notepad, maybe another pencil. But then I sat down again, and waited. I thought I smelled Lemon Pledge. Another light tap, another wait, and Nesta moved on. I thought I heard her crew-so-fix knock against something, maybe the vacuum cleaner. Maybe I'd catch Nesta later, when I went to check the mail to see if I'd heard from the Famous Artists' School. Maybe I'd ask her how Manuel Jones was doing, and throw Ritalee in for good measure, so she wouldn't think it was blasphemy.

I closed the bible and put it back on the nightstand. A nice word, I thought, and said it out loud.

"Appalled."

I liked the sound of it, so I said it again.

"Appalled."

It came from the bible, so it must be okay. I was going to have to try to use it sometime. Nesta, for one, would be impressed.

6
Homestudy

I learned to gamble the summer I lived with Earlene in Nevada. Ma wasn't around. We were between things, is how she put it. She'd started to get nervous, the way she always does, when she'd lived in a motel too long and put on a couple of pounds. One morning she decides she's going on ahead to California to pave the way. Like the Yellow Brick Road, she says, and leaves me in the care of one of the dealers at the casino where she'd been waiting tables.

Ma instructed Earlene to keep her eye out, gave her permission to use a belt or lock me in the closet if I tried anything fancy. Then she got on the Greyhound. I watched her white face and red lips in the back window until she turned around, then I watched her beige hair. I didn't see her again for three months. Though I got a postcard every week from various interesting California tourist spots.

The first postcard featured a big shiny bus with mountains in the background. "*Next stop Hollywood and Vine!*" she wrote. The bottom half was filled with Xs and Os. The next postcard featured a pink motel with a palm tree and alot of sun. "*My new pad! Hollywood just around the bend! Keep smiling!*" She never once used a period. I stuck the postcards in the edge of the mirror in my room at Earlene's.

Ma left for California just after school was out. Not that I'd been in *real* school. That spring the truant officer had tracked me down, part of a general roundup at Voodoo Video. Ma managed to convince him I wasn't public school material, I was more the artistic type, she told him, I took after her. She also told him my dad was a Hollywood producer suffering from amnesia after being hit by a sound boom. We were just passing through on our way to California, she said, which should explain our confusion over minor things like school attendance, our being stretched to the emotional limit and all. There was some truth to this story: when it came to me and Ma, my dad acted like he had amnesia.

Between Ma and the T.O.—and the six pack they killed in his van out behind the motel—they arranged for a lady to come by and tutor me. It was a law, Home Study, and the lady, Ms. Alvarez-Brown, made Ma watch TV with the sound down or leave the room whenever she was there. We did workbooks, where I'd read a story then turn the page and answer various interesting questions such as, "How many miles did Jeremy travel?" or "When did women win the right to vote?" The workbooks went by color. When you got to green you were done. I got to blue, then it was summer.

"It's only summer once!" Ma says, and puts my workbooks in the bottom dresser drawer at the motel. Seems I'd won the right to screw off.

When I unpacked at Earlene's the workbooks were nowhere to be found. Earlene had cleared a space in her second bedroom. Boxes were stacked along a wall, clothes pushed to one side of the closet. All my things—jeans, T-shirts, underwear—were spread across the open sofa bed. But no workbooks.

"So much for homework," I said, throwing my backpack on the sofa bed. The camo looked funny against the shiny white spread. "I'll forget everything. I'll have to start over with brown in California."

Earlene was busy poking hangers into my T-shirts, now and then glancing out the window. She was thinking it might rain, Though in Nevada, she said, that was like thinking you might see jesus shooting craps in a leisure suit, still, hope springs eternal, she said. Rain meant rainbows, or as Earlene put it, the possibility there-of.

It was Earlene's belief that if a person stood in the place where a rainbow began—or ended, depending on how you looked at it—that person would have their fondest wish come true. She herself had one wish in particular she'd been saving for eleven maybe twelve years. She told me I should think of one for myself, so as to be prepared. Give it your best shot, she said, blow your wad.

"Now y'all listen," she said, reaching for a hanger. "I know a thing or two about the three Rs. If it's readin' you're worried about, we'll get the newspapers. Writin', well, y'all can keep a diary ..."

"There's math," I said. "What about math?"

Which automatically made me think of my dad, who, if I remember, basically wanted two things for me: to be a good catholic and be good at math. No kid of mine is gonna be math anxious, he'd say, that's for fuckin' sure, and he'd start in again trying to explain the bank shot. Pool, he said, is pure mathematics, any halfwit knows that. Mathematically speaking, I figured I'd last seen my dad two-thirds of my life ago.

Earlene shook her head. "Y'all are worried about math? My stars, girl, ain't you ever played cards?"

"Like I'm sure," I said, "Crazy Eights, Go Fish ..."

Earlene laughed. "Lands, hon, that is most cer-tainly not what I had in mind. Now give us a shirt."

I tossed her another T-shirt. "So what's yours?" I said. She looked at me. "Your wish?" I said.

"Now y'all know you can't say a wish out loud," said Earlene. "Sayin' it cancels it out, breaks the spell. Y'all know that."

Earlene was from Texas, and stretched her name out when she said it like it was longer than it had to be. She was tall, with green eyes and, this week, red hair. And, being a dealer, she could divide and multiply in her head, something my dad would drink to. She'd been married three times, she'd been in a movie and in jail. She was also superstitious—she said tall females generally are—and kept fourleaf clovers and threw salt over her shoulder and was always studying the tea leaves left over in the bottom of her cup. Generally she hated tea, she said, but she drank it for the information there-in. And she believed in rainbows. She'd been looking for the rainbow with her name on it her whole life.

But the main thing about Earlene was this: she was a man.

"I just don't see why y'all think that's so interesting," she'd drawl. "Will y'all just quit yammerin' about it?"

"But tell me one thing more interesting than that?" I'd say.

She'd try changing the subject. "Well, your name, for instance. What kind of a name is Sugar, anyway?"

I'd ignore her, ask her again to tell me about when she was a little boy. "Did you like baseball? Could you run fast? When's the last time you felt like running?" I'd say.

"Girl, you are the livin' end," she'd say, and shake her head and light a cigarette and look around to see where she'd left her tea cup.

Earlene lived alone, her preferred M.O., she called it. No roommate, no pets, not even a plastic plant. She had her phone hooked up to an answering machine. If the phone rang while we were home, she'd stop whatever she was doing and listen to see who it was. If the caller didn't leave a message, she'd get the jitters. If she came home to find the little red message light blinking, she'd light a cigarette and take a long jittery drag and walk over and press PLAYBACK. Usually it was someone from the casino, or a pool-cleaning service, or someone selling Avon or insurance. If she happened to like a particular message, she'd save it and play it back again and again. Like a record. For instance when the Fireman's Fund called, she liked the fireman's voice. Listen to this, she'd say, and walk over and press PLAYBACK, and a deep slow voice would fill the room, saying there were heroes among us, walking among us, even today, heroes.

Far as I could tell, Earlene never returned any of the calls. When I asked her why, she said phones were dangerous, folks back in Texas were always getting hit by lightning over the phone. I thought of that endless Nevada sky stretching above, told her to try again, I wasn't buying. So she said it's a girl's best de-fense, a sense of mystery, best to keep 'em guessing.

My guess was Earlene was expecting a call.

The walls inside Earlene's house were gray. She kept the windows closed, the drapes pulled, the air conditioner going full tilt. Didn't I ever have a grandma who put up pre-serves? she said, so I said, Not that I know of, so she said, Well, never mind, that there was pre-cisely what she was up to, self-preservation.

The neighborhood had rules about color, so the outside of the house was pink. There was a silver fence around the yard, with a sign on the gate, "Beware of Dog."

"This here is what you call a cy-clone fence," she told me.

"What about the dog?" I asked.

"That's what you call a de-terrent."

Most of the backyard of the pink house was taken up by a turquoise swimming pool. White plastic chairs sat on the orange bricks around the edge of the pool. There was an orange flower pot at one corner with a tired-looking cactus poking out of it.

"She came with the house," said Earlene.

"How do you know it's a she?" I asked.

"It takes one to know one," said Earlene.

Every so often the cactus would bloom tiny pink or white blossoms. After a few days they'd fall off, as if the plant was exhausted from all that effort. It made me sad, seeing all those tiny flowers lying around on the hot bricks or floating on the turquoise water.

"Stayin' pretty sure takes it out of you," said Earlene. She picked up a blossom with her long nails and dropped it in her drink. "For luck," she said.

Earlene's nails were fake, also her hair color, and she often added a fake mole just above her lip. Though I couldn't decide about her eyelashes. I knew you could have ones put on that lasted six to eight weeks. Earlene's stayed in place every time she came up from the bottom of the pool. Something else stayed in place, too, so I figured they must've been attached directly to the inside of her swimming suit top.

We'd developed this game where we'd throw a spoon into the water and watch as it drifted down through the sunlight like a silver fish. When the fish hit bottom, one of us would count seconds while the other dove in and retrieved. We played the game first thing in the afternoon, when Earlene woke up. There was nothing like immersing yourself in water, she said, immediately upon rising.

"Like bein' bap-tized," she said, "like startin' over."

I always seemed to win the game, probably because of the way Earlene talked.

"One one thou-sand, two-oo one thou-sand, three-ee ..." she'd drawl, and there I'd be in the air again, baptized, a spoon in my mouth.

In my bedroom at Earlene's, the mirror where I stuck Ma's postcards was attached to the top of a dresser. The mirror was old with little speckly patches here and there like fog. The dresser was old, too, with those little glass knobs. Earlene had hauled the entire get-up—mirror still attached—all the way from Texas. Heavy as a coffin, she said, but this was one mirror destined never to break and bring her bad luck. One minute I could be spraying my spike, looking at a pink motel or a red sports car or a bunch of sailboats packed into a tiny blue bay. And the next, if I moved my eyes the slightest bit, the rest of the room suddenly popped up behind me, only wavy around the edges because of that mirror, like the room might fade off into oblivion at any minute.

Like that "Twilight Zone" where a door to the fourth dimension showed up on the girl's bedroom wall. Of course the girl fell in, they always do.

"The point is, she was saved by a dog," I said to Earlene during the credits. "Everybody has a dog."

I was trying to talk Earlene into a pet, for protection. But she said between the cyclone fence and the de-terrent she had all the protection she could handle. Okay then for luck, I said. She said the only lucky one would be the pet, having someone to follow around behind it and clean up its shit. Now that there is luck, she said. What I was really thinking was Earlene liked having somebody there, whether she admitted it or not. She was going to be lonely after I left. No one to talk to, or drink tea with. I was even helping her around the house.

Once a year she painted her walls a whiter shade of gray, she called it. We were watching "Twilight Zone" while we painted the living room. A local TV station was having a "Twilight Zone" Festival that summer, four episodes back to back every afternoon until they'd showed all one-hundred-and-fifty-six. We'd finished with one wall of the living room and had slid the sheets and paint cans over to another. We were trying to finish the whole room before it came time to go to the casino.

I said it again. "Everybody has a dog."

"Not ev-ery-body," said Earlene, "for instance *you*, darlin'."

"But it's the rules," I said. "Motels don't allow pets. But you're different. Living in the privacy of your own home. You make the rules."

"And the rules is, No Pets. Now give us a light." I held out the lighter. She smoked straights. "Besides, we had dogs, my second marriage, a whole pack of 'em. And cats, too. We lived out from town, people always drivin' by, droppin' leftover critters off in the night. Next mornin' there'd be a box of newly-hatched kittens under the mailbox, special de-livery."

Earlene blew gray smoke into the room. I reached for the pack.

I said, "Were you a husband, or a wife, in that one?"

"That's for me to know and you to find out," said Earlene.

"Next stop, the 'Twilight Zone'," said Rod Serling, and we all three exhaled at the same time.

We'd pulled the couch away from the wall and were taking down a large picture—of, what else, a rainbow, though this particular rainbow had faded practically to nothing—when the phone rang. Earlene put her finger to her lips, turned down the TV. The next thing we heard was her voice on the machine, "Thank y'all for phonin', pull-ease leave a mess-age." Then a woman's voice said Miss Earlene Dock's dry cleaning is ready for pickup at her earliest convenience, have a nice day.

"Speaking of which," I said, as we leaned the faded rainbow against the couch, "what kind of a name is Dock, anyway?"

"Those who live in glass houses ..." said Earlene, only she didn't finish because the phone rang again.

I was thinking the only glass house I knew of was the one at the State Fair, the one with all the mirrors, you could wander for hours not find your way out, once I saw a lady run sobbing from the exit, whoever would want to live in such a place, I was thinking, when I smelled smoke. Earlene had lit a cigarette and was walking back and forth back and forth across the room: the jitters.

    Meanwhile on TV an elevator door slowly opened.

    "Who was that?" I asked, and Earlene tripped. I pointed to her feet. She was wearing gold spike heels with rhinestone ankle straps. "Who was on the phone?" I said.

    Earlene walked over and turned the TV back up. "Nobody," she said in her jittery voice, "that was no-body."

    "Nobody, as in nobody important? Or they hung up?"

    "They hung up," she said.

    On "Twilight Zone" a mannequin moved its hand. The girl shopper screamed.

    "She don't know it yet," said Earlene, "she's a mannequin, too." She walked to the window, pulled open the gray drape, looked at the sky. Even from where I stood I could see blue.

    I said, "Did you sign up for a man or woman part? In the movie, I mean?" In her last postcard, Ma told me it was only a matter of time before I myself would be in a movie.

    "A fee-male part, darlin'," said Earlene, and pulled the drape closed again. "I was on the screen for ten seconds." She excused herself and went into the kitchen. I heard the faucet turn on and off, the microwave door snap open and shut.

    I tried holding my face in one position, smiling, for ten seconds. "Man, that's something," I said, to no one in particular.

    When the phone rang again, I answered. Automatically. I didn't think twice.

    "Dock residence." There was a pause, then a man's voice said,

    "Earl, I know it's you." Another pause, then he hung up.

    Earlene came back to the living room carrying a steaming cup with the string from a tea bag hanging over the side like a little tail. I told her about the call. I watched her turn gray as her walls and sit right down on the floor next to the TV.

    "Don't worry," I said, "it was just a wrong number."

    But Earlene wasn't buying. She downed her tea in one gulp,

then began studying the bottom of the cup like she was reading a magazine.

On TV a little motorboat circled the inside of a toilet. The little guy driving was smiling and waving up at a woman. The woman was gigantic. Gigantic or not, I was thinking, if I wandered in and found that going on in my bathroom, I'd reach for the handle. Automatically. I wouldn't think twice. I was thinking the water in that toilet was the same color as the water in Earlene's swimming pool. I looked at her, slumped there like a bag of laundry, staring into that cup.

"So what do you see?" I asked.

Earlene sighed and lowered the cup. "Oh, a passel of things," she said. "An en-tire passel."

I stole a glance: just a white cup with a mess of brown at the bottom. Though Earlene did seem more relaxed. She looked up at me and half-smiled. There was a brown speck on one of her teeth.

The first time I went with Earlene to her job at the casino, I took special pains: I moussed my spike, put new laces on my camo hightops, wore a camo T-shirt so my tattoo would show. Earlene didn't say much, just kept glancing at me out of the corner of her pointy sunglasses. We were on the way to the casino in her convertible, top down, radio blaring. She'd already decided it wasn't going to rain that day. She was driving fast, like a bat out of hell, Ma would say. My spike didn't budge.

"In my day we called that shit butch wax!" Earlene hollered, eyeing my hair. Her hair was all pulled together at the top of her head where it popped out like a pineapple. This week it was dark brown.

"At least mine's natural!" I hollered back, punching in the lighter. I'd let mine grow out from my last experiment while I decided on my next color scheme. Camo, if possible.

Earlene turned the radio down. "De-fine natural," she said.

Earlene was fond of laying these ideas on me. Concepts, she called them. She told me that if I could only learn to think beyond the surface of things, I'd get all the education I ever needed. She knew a thing or two about education, she said. She told me it was something a person could learn how to do, she could learn how to think. She said it was a sign the "Twilight Zone" Festival just happened to be on while I was staying with her.

"Y'all don't need some fool workbook askin' how many yards of cloth some lady needs," she said. "I'll lay odds y'all will never sew a stitch in your life. But *irony*," she said, "now that there's a diff'rent matter."

I touched the lighter to my cigarette. "Like I'm sure, you don't even own an iron."

Earlene laughed. "Shee-it, girl. I mean, like when the convict on the prison planet falls in love with the girl, even though he knows she's a robot? That's irony."

She was talking about "The Lonely," the episode we'd watched that afternoon. In the end, a visiting astronaut smashes the robot's face in to prove she's just a machine, which sends the poor convict into a tailspin.

"Done in by irony," I said, to prove I understood.

Suddenly Earlene floored it and we flew through an intersection just as the light turned red. I checked the rearview mirror for cops.

"On the bou-le-vard, under a tree," she said, slowing down again, "an all-black cat. I ain't waiting around for it to make up its mind about crossin', no siree," and she turned the radio back up.

It was obvious the people at the casino took Earlene for a girl. What they don't know won't hurt 'em, she said. In fact it was a rule: all the dealers were girls. And I have to say it, Earlene looked more girl than most. The others seemed harder somehow, and older. Not so much in the big rooms out front, where the lights were high and soft, but in the small bright room in the back, where they'd sit around during breaks with their shoes off, smoking and talking and playing cards.

The first thing I learned that summer at the casino, my apprent-ice-ship Earlene called it, was this: everybody was a girl. No matter what age.

"So if you're girls," I asked Mitzi Jean when I got up the nerve, "what does that make me?"

"Jailbait, hon," she said, and pinched my cheek, and the name stuck. From then on I was J.B. to the girls at the casino.

And, being girls, they all had or wanted to have or never wanted to have again so help me god, boyfriends.

"My boyfriend blew me off, that asshole," said Mitzi Jean. I pictured her with some disco dancer until Leonard walked through the door with his plaid sport coat and shiny head.

"That boy over in slots puts me in a coma ..."

"I'd take that new kid in roulette straight up ..."

"So I told the dipshit I wanted a boyfriend not a boy friend ..."

In the beginning I stood off to the side and just watched.

The door would swing open, a girl would come in, another girl leave. The new girl would kick off her red or green or black high heels, make herself a drink, toss her money on the table. The girls were partial to blackjack, a.k.a. twenty-one, they told me, the age of reason, ha ha. They played hand after hand, their rings flicking above the table like flies, their smeary mouths sipping and smoking and talking and talking: who was sick, who was shacked up, who was dead, who was out on bail.

I learned alot of things hanging around that room that summer—the smell of feet, the smoke circling the ceiling light, the changing shape of the money pile. But mostly I learned poker.

Every once and awhile this one girl, Lonna, would get the

others to play a few hands of poker because she felt Lady Luck was with her, she said. Like maybe Earlene had read her tea leaves in the bathroom or something, which wasn't possible on account of Earlene had told me mum's the word, if the girls ever got wind of her special ability they'd be brewing Lipton's and chasing her around with their cups until the cows came home.

But it wasn't until I myself sat down and played poker that I felt the calling.

From the start, I was hooked.

I'd been hanging around as usual this particular night, watching the game, circling the pushed-together tables quietly in my hightops.

"She makes me nervous, a bleedin' shark," says Lonna, gathering up the cards. "Looks like one, too, with that hair."

Everybody laughed, and Lonna patted a chair. "Come on over here, J.B., sit your ass down. Think you can handle a little five-card-draw?"

It was Lonna's turn to deal. I nodded, my spike slicing the air.

"Now we'll make this easy," she said. "Aces wild."

She glanced at me. One of her eyelashes stayed sticking straight up. Her hands moved like they had a life of their own.

"Now the main thing about poker," she says, shuffling, flapping, turning the cards, slapping them down, "it's not how you play it, it's how you *look* playin' it."

Mitzi Jean snorted. "Get off that shit, there's more to it, and you know it." She turned to me. "There's the order of hands, what beats what. You gotta learn that right off."

"And odds," said Maryanne, picking up her cards. "Like what're your chances of drawing to another queen, or maybe a straight?"

"Looks like you had the same choice, your last boyfriend," said Mitzi Jean, and laughed herself into a coughing fit.

Lonna snapped her cards into a fan. "Girls, girls, please. Don't let's confuse poor J.B. here. She needs to learn the hands, sure. *And* she needs to practice her face." She tapped a nail against her tooth. "Anyways, who is it usually wins around here? I rest my case."

I said, "My face?"

"Your poker face," said Lonna. "So you never give anything away. Or maybe you let the other guy think you have something, when you don't. It's called bluffing." She turned to the girl on her right. "Maryanne? Think you can?"

"Gimme three."

"M.J. what do you say?"

"Ditto."

They went around like that, deciding, discarding, drawing. When it came my turn, I thought for a minute. Then I said,

"Two, please."

"Polite little fucker, ain't she," said Mitzi Jean as two cards skated across the table at me.

I pulled the cards up, arranged my hand. And I couldn't help it, I thought of my face. Automatically. Lonna and another girl stayed in. I saw their bet and raised. Lonna saw the raise, the other girl folded. Lonna laid down.

"Sixes and twos, will give you the blues," she said. Another thing I was learning about poker: the dealer makes a poem whenever possible.

Lonna grinned and started reaching toward the pot. Then I laid down.

"Three sevens and the ace of spades," I croaked, and cleared my throat. "Three of a kind beats two pair."

The girls stared at me for a minute. Then they started hooting and clapping and somebody patted me on the back. Lonna raised an eyebrow.

"Well, shit," she said, "looks like we might have a shark in our waters after all."

During the next deal I lit a cigarette. Nobody seemed to mind.

◆ ◆ ◆

Out by the pool in the mornings, while I waited for Earlene to finish her beauty sleep, she called it, I'd go through the poker hands.

"Three of a kind beats two pair, straight beats three of a kind, flush beats straight ..." I'd repeat, finishing with, "... royal flush beats all." Then I'd add, "Short or tall don't it make you wanna bawl who you gonna call." Just doing my homework, I figured, and I'd march around the edge of the pool, careful not to step on any cactus flowers, doing the poker-chant.

"Like the rosary, and them lawn chairs are the stations of the cross," said Earlene, who'd been raised a catholic like my dad, though unlike him, she'd given it up, she told me, when she realized she was spending more time *in* confession than out of it, besides, it was her theory the whole business was just a way for those old whitenecks on the other side of that little screen to get their jollies.

But my homework was paying off. I'd already won forty bucks off the girls, which I'd taped to the back of the unbreakable mirror in my room. Every night I'd stand in front of that mirror and think about that money and practice my face standing in place a girl named Grace. I'd decided that, jailbait or not, I was going to become a card shark. And I'd still wear my hair in a spike.

The girls never got tired of teasing me about my hair or my hightops. And my tattoo sent them into orbit. It got to where every evening it was the same, them trying new ways to get me to change. To them it was all about how you looked. How could I ever expect to get a boyfriend or a job or a taxi, if I looked like a Martian?

I said, "Beauty is in the eye of the beholder," which was the name of the "Twilight Zone" where the ugly girl turned out to be beautiful, though nobody realized it.

"Y'all see, Sugar," Earlene drawled when I told her what I'd said, "that there is a per-fect example of irony," and she raised her head to check on the whereabouts of a small white cloud.

We'd finished spoon-diving and were stretched out beside the pool, waiting for the mailman. Other than that cloud—which had existed for nearly an hour already, a fact that hugely excited Earlene—the sky was the usual, huge and blue and empty. Once the mail arrived, we'd lay around waiting for the "Twilight Zone" Festival to start. We'd already seen sixty-three episodes. I kept track of them in a notebook Earlene had given me, writing down the title, any actor who turned famous later on, and the main concept. So far I had fifty-nine "ironies" and four "not sures."

In the mornings after the poker-chant, I'd sit on the diving board and look through the notebook, which featured a "Little House on the Prairie" cover, though I'd taped Rod Serling's face over Michael Landon's. Lately I'd started writing comments along with some of the entries, such as, *"Everybody smoked in the sixties"* or *"People look bigger when young."* Before long I'd need another notebook. I planned to show the notebooks to Ms. Alvarez-Brown, if I ever saw her again. I might be up to green and not know it.

We heard the front gate creak open, we heard a whistle. Earlene had taught the mailman to whistle so she'd know who it was. By now he also knew there wasn't a dog.

Earlene stood and stretched. Her toenails and fingernails were painted sparkly purple, her arms and legs were long and tan. My own legs were tan down to my ankles, where they turned white on account of my hightops. When I was barefoot, I seemed to be wearing socks.

Earlene's six-foot shadow wavered across the pool for a minute, then she excused herself and went into the house. I glanced at the sky. The cloud was still there, a little white dandelion in a field of blue, only it seemed to be shrinking.

Earlene returned with her first drink of the day ("Never before noon!") and a pile of mail balanced on top of a large flat box she carried like a tray. She unloaded the drink and envelopes onto a small table, held the tray toward me.

"It's add-ressed to you, dumplin'," she said, "'Miss S. Kane'."

I stared at the box, which was wider than the small table. I stared at Earlene, who was reading the upper lefthand corner.

"It's from Ok-la-homa, my stars," she said. "I am mys-tified. Go on, break the sus-pense, open it."

"Wednesday?" I said, and Earlene said,

"Well, to-day would be pre-ferable."

"No," I said, "Wednesday Wilson, from Oklahoma. She's the only one ... but what ... "

And then I knew. Wednesday had tracked me down. Sent her back to me. The Green Lady.

Ma had made me leave her behind back in Oklahoma, back in the bomb shelter, because, she said, there was no room absolutely no room for art on a Greyhound bus, any halfwit knew that. And it'd been the hardest thing, leaving her there, hanging on that wall next to the sad velvet girl. But then I thought of them hanging there together, side by side, and I'd thought, Well, at least they have each other, and Wednesday, after all, had said the Green Lady was a hoot, a real hoot, check out the star-spangled chick, she'd said.

Now here she was again. In person.

When I pulled the Green Lady out of the box and Earlene laid eyes on her for the first time, she stared as if she might be reading tea leaves in the bottom of some enormous cup. She just stared and stared, not talking, hardly breathing. Finally she let out a long breath, like she'd been storing it up for something.

"My heavenly stars," she said, "I have never seen the likes."

"It's called 'Duck and Buffalo'," I said, pointing them out. "But I just call her the Green Lady. So what d'ya think? Is she a hoot or what?"

Earlene's mouth got small. "The word is heaven-ly. This here little lady is down-right heaven-ly. I'll say it again, I have never seen the likes."

We propped the Green Lady against the little table, and while Earlene studied every swirl, every line, every color, I told her the whole story—the Double P, Nova, Judith, the buffalos. When I finished, Earlene took a few steps back, pushed her sunglasses up, studied the painting some more.

"You know," she said after awhile, her green eyes squinting, "with a little im-agination, y'all can see a rainbow up there hidin' in them sequins. I swear that could be a rainbow."

I walked over, stood next to her, slit my eyes. Sure enough, I'd have to agree, that might've been a rainbow out there in that place where the land became the sky. We stood side by side, staring, while the sun glinted off those sequins. Until our eyes hurt. Until Earlene put her sunglasses back on and walked over and slid the Green Lady back into the box. For safe-keeping, she said.

Earlene settled back in her chair, sat quiet for awhile. Finally she took a long swallow from her drink, started flipping through the rest of the mail.

"Electrical, Mastercard, Monkey Wards," she read. Then, "What's this here? Looks like somethin' else for you, Miss Kane. My, my, but you are pop-ular today."

She handed me a pink envelope, smelling like perfume, a happy face sticker on the back. I sat down and turned it over. My name was written all flowery, Ma's handwriting. I pictured Ma stopping by the perfume counter in some drug store on her way to the mailbox, spraying various interesting samples on the pink envelope, the way I'd seen her do before a big date, spraying her pink wrists.

Earlene reached over and tore open the flap with a purple nail. I pulled out a folded sheet of pink paper. A half dozen bills fell out, fives and tens, smelling like perfume.

"'Dear Sugar Kane,'" I read out loud, and faked like I was throwing up.

Once I remember asking Ma what drug she'd been on when she named me. She slapped me hard, and I couldn't help it, I started to cry. Then she started to cry, then I got mad because what right did she have to be blubbering, so I stopped. She reminded me that Kane had started out Kanezevich, but that her mother had lopped it off to be on the safe side. Probably the one act of love that broad ever managed, said Ma. The only time I remember asking my dad about my name, he said, "Your old lady's a trip, ain't she?" and narrowed his eyes and looked at me like he might be trying to memorize something.

Earlene lit a cigarette. "So what all does she say?"

So I read her the letter. Basically it said to get my ass on the nearest bus to California, it was time for me to get out of everyone's hair. It was signed with a pink heart sticker and an arrow. I turned the sheet over.

"'P.S. Tell E. Thanks!'" I read. Then, "'P.S.S. Almost forgot! Call when you get in!'" There was a phone number, but I couldn't tell if those were sevens or twos.

"'E.', that's you," I said to Earlene. Then I said, "Your name's Earlene you are a queen you know what I mean," and folded the letter back into the envelope.

"My stars," said Earlene. The ice in her glass jangled like bells. "So what's the return add-ress?"

"'Ventura, CA'."

Earlene sighed. "Well, I guess that's that," she said, and set her glass down on the little table. "The girls'll be sad to see you go, y'all have become their mascot. But you know what they say about all good things ..."

I'd heard this before. Where had I heard this before?

"No," I said, "what *do* they say?"

There was a pause ... one one-thousand, two one-thousand ... then Earlene said, "What they say is, all good things must end."

I thought about this. "Why?"

There was another pause. "Well, I'm not sure," she said, "it's just what they say ... it's just ... well ..."

"Irony," I said, "it sounds like irony to me," and Earlene said,

"That all is pre-cisely what it is, darlin'. Y'all have hit the nail on the head, right di-rectly on the head."

She sighed again, stubbed out her cigarette, glanced at the box leaning against the table. Then she glanced at her watch.

"Lands, it's festival time. Guess we can wheel the TV in where we can see it. Probably finish the di-nette today."

I'd wanted to paint a mural on the last wall, sort of a jungle theme with plenty of animals to get her thinking, but Earlene eighty-sixed that particular idea.

Now she stood up. "Y'all ready to boogie?" she said, and stepped in front of me.

And for a second she was just a shadow, the sunrays shooting out behind her. For a second I thought I saw it there, all around her, a rainbow. I closed my eyes to keep from getting dizzy. Then the shadow moved, and I felt the sun again.

"Lord have mercy," Earlene whispered.

I opened my eyes. She was staring through her pointy sunglasses at the house. I stood up, but her long fingers grabbed my arm. I turned, sideways to the sun, and looked toward the house. In the dinette, just beyond the patio door, a man stood looking back at us. The fingers on my arm tightened.

"It's him," she whispered.

"Who?"

"Him. The jig is up."

"Let's get outta here," I whispered, "call the cops, call 911..."

"Y'all don't under-stand," said Earlene. "No cops, no 911. This is it. He tracked me down. Now he's found me, it's over." She let go my arm. "I'm glad even. Re-lieved. You stay here, Sugar. It's now or never." She took a step.

"E., what're you doing?" I said. "We can sneak over the fence..."

Earlene turned her sunglasses toward me, made a tiny pointy smile. "Hon, now don't you worry none. And don't you go off half-cocked, neither, you stay put. Lookee here." She picked up the spoon lying beside her towel, tossed it high into the middle of the pool.

"One one-thou-sand, two-oo one-thou-sand..." she counted, and I watched her cross the patio and step through the sliding door into the house.

I walked to the edge of the pool. The spoon had hit bottom. I sat on the tiles, legs dangling over the side. The little cloud was nowhere in sight. Like it disappeared down to nothing again. Like maybe the sky was too much for it, it got swallowed up in all that blue. I was thinking the sky was the same color as the pool, as all the pools in all the backyards around us. And the sun sat in the middle and slanted off all that blue until, if you weren't careful, you might get dizzy. Like when you were little and spun in a circle with your eyes shut until you fell over in the clover red rover ante-eye-over.

I laid back and closed my eyes and pushed against my eyelids awhile to get those little sparkly red and blue designs. It made me think of the Green Lady, all sequiny. It made me think of something my dad won for me once a long time ago, shooting fake ducks at the State Fair, something like a telescope with a mess of little colored pieces at one end. When you looked into it, the mess became a design, like magic, everything orderly and lined up.

But mostly I was waiting. And listening. For the fight, for the hollering and swearing and maybe the sound of punches. For the sound of Earlene's voice. Not the fake girl voice she put on with her falsies and high heels, but her real voice. The one hiding behind her other voice, like a shadow. I'd never heard that voice, but I knew it was there. I was waiting for Earlene to show her stuff. I was picturing how it would be when she threw down her earrings and sunglasses and pulled off her fingernails and let fly, let this guy have it. Afterward nobody would have to know. I'd never tell, and the guy would be too embarrassed. Earlene could take a shower, re-do her make up, apply new nails.

I sat up, opened my eyes. My eyeballs hurt. I must've fallen asleep. The world looked stretched out around the edges. The sun had moved to the next door neighbor's. My arms were covered with goosebumps, my legs might've belonged to someone else, floating there in the water. I managed to haul them up out of the pool. I was wondering why Earlene hadn't called me, to come get my lil' ole ass in and help sweep up broken glass or hold her nails in place while the glue set.

I looked behind me. The box was still there. I looked at the house. Things seemed normal enough. The sliding door was pushed part way open, the way Earlene liked to do in the evening. I saw the light in the dinette. I saw the TV flickering in the archway. Then I saw Earlene. She was pushing a paint roller along the wall, now and then glancing toward the TV.

I chewed my tongue and waited for my legs to come around. When I could stand, I wobbled across the patio and stepped into the dinette. That "Twilight Zone" music, that spiral going round and round. I cleared my throat. Earlene looked over and smiled.

"You all right, E.?" I glanced around the room. Whoever

that guy was, he seemed to be gone.

"As rain, hon," she said, pouring paint in the roller pan. She moved the roller through the paint. I was thinking rain train stain cane.

I pulled a chair out from the table. My legs were still shaky. I studied Earlene. No black eyes or broken nails or pulled-out hair. She was wearing a silver cover-up, she called it, over her swimming suit, and silver sandals. She moved the roller across the wall. On TV a guy stumbled across the desert, sweating and looking worried.

"What did he want?" I asked.

"Somebody got sick. He's gone for help."

"Where?" I said.

"Just over the hill. Only he ends up in the next century, away from his wagon train. I've seen it before."

"I mean the guy who was here?" I said.

Earlene lowered her arm, kept her back to me. I counted seconds in my mind. Finally she put the roller in the pan, turned down the TV, walked over and sat down across from me.

"Y'all up for a lil' story?" she says, and lights a cigarette. I nod. She starts in. "Once upon a time, there lived a man and a lady, we'll call them ..." She stopped to think.

"Adam and Even," I said.

"Okay, Adam and Even," says Earlene. "So anyway, Adam and Even are married, everything's hunky dory. Then one day, the plot thickens. Along comes someone who steals Even away, she just falls for this new guy hook, line and sinker. So Even and the new guy, we'll call him ..."

"Noah," I said, which didn't seem right. I remember my dad telling me bible stories, but that was so long ago they probably came up with new ones by now to be more modern. Like before color, when everything was black-and-white.

Earlene waved her cigarette. "No, no, we'll call him ..."

She glanced at me. "Earl, we'll call him. So Even and ... Earl ... they run off together and get married, and poor Den ... I mean Adam ... poor Adam is left in the lurch. And not only that, he's a laughingstock, remember this is Texas."

"You didn't say that," I said.

"Well, anyway," said Earlene, "the point is, folks are sniggerin' over poor Adam behind his back. And the poor thing, he can't take it, his pride has been dealt a di-rect blow. So Adam, he vows re-venge."

She took a major drag of her cigarette. I was beginning to get the gist.

"I know what happens," I said, "what happens is, Adam goes looking for Even and Earl and ..." I thought for a minute.

"And ..." Earlene continued, "by now they're no longer together, Earl and Even, by now they're di-vorced, too ..."

"Right!" I said. "That's right! Even and Earl are divorced, only Adam, he's still pissed off. He keeps looking high and low for Earl, only Earl, he seems to have disappeared, he seems to ..." Earlene started to say something but I kept on. "But finally Adam finds Earl, he tracks him down, only ... only ... Earl is ... disguised! That's it! He's disguised, which throws Adam for a loop, he doesn't know ..."

"What to do ..." said Earlene.

"Right! He doesn't quite ..."

"Under-stand ..." said Earlene.

"Right! In fact Adam's not even sure ... he's not even sure ... this is Earl," I said. "I mean, even if it is, Adam thinks, which how could it be, but even if it is, how can he, Adam, punch this ... girl Earl ... Earl girl ... He can't punch her, he just can't do it. So it's over. The jig is up. Adam leaves."

I looked at Earlene. She was looking back carefully.

"Is that it?" I said.

"More or less," she said.

"Guess you showed him."

"I did, yes," said Earlene. "I ... showed him."

"Man, that's some story," I said.

And I was thinking, that *is* some story. Maybe there might be something to this girl business after all. I was thinking, if someone like Earl ... like Earlene ... could pull it off, could actually keep from getting walloped just by shaving her legs and getting her ears pierced, there must really be something to this. I was thinking, this was power.

I stood up, pushed my chair back. I could stand on my legs again.

"Listen, E.," I said. "Do you mind very much if I skip the painting today? I sort of want to, you know, relax. Before tonight."

Earlene looked at me in that careful way. Then she said, "That's okay, darlin'. Y'all have been such a help."

"Do you want me to make you some tea first?" I asked.

"Thank y'all, no," said Earlene. "I've had about all the in-formation I can handle for one day."

On my way out I turned the "Twilight Zone" back up. Sure enough, the guy from the wagon train had finally made it over the hill—by his own free will in search of a pill—where he'd just missed getting hit by a truck.

When I came into the living room that evening, Earlene was standing by the window with her back to the room, a cloud of cigarette smoke circling her head. I stood in the doorway and cleared my throat. She jumped, like she'd been yanked back from somewhere. When she turned toward me, I couldn't see her face, just her silhouette against the window. Like that afternoon, against the sun.

I waited. Then I couldn't help it, I giggled.

"Well?" I said.

I wobbled a little in the high heels, locked my knees to keep from falling over. I could see myself in the picture window, my hair smoothed around my head, the dress smoothed around my body. My arms looked long and stringy like ropes, a fat plastic bracelet covered my tattoo.

"Well?" I said again. "Is it okay? I found the dress in the closet. The bracelet and nylons, and a curling iron, in the bathroom."

Earlene lowered her cigarette and walked over. She looked me up and down. She turned me in a circle. She touched the shoulder of the dress.

"Gold lam-ay, my stars," she said. "I for-got about this ole thing." She touched my hair. "I can still see some turquoise."

"Well, I didn't have time to dye it back," I said. I'd experimented again, a week before. "But is it okay?" I was thinking she'd be more excited.

"Sure, darlin', it's okay, just ... diff-rent ... is all." She reached for her purse and sunglasses. "The girls'll like to die."

We drove with the top up. Neither of us smoked or turned on the radio. Earlene was quiet. Her pointy sunglasses pointed straight ahead. At a stoplight, while we waited for the light to turn green, I asked her what other "Twilight Zones" had been on that afternoon.

"The one where the people put on masks, and when they take them off, their faces are changed."

"What was the concept?" I asked, checking my earrings in the rearview mirror.

"The usual," she said. I counted to seven in my mind, slowly, Earlene-style. The light turned green.

At the casino the girls went bananas. They clapped and whistled and hovered around me like I was already a movie star, in spite of the turquoise in my hair.

"Hell, mine turned worse once," said Mitzi Jean, "a dye job in '73." She brought her face up close and studied me.

Lonna pulled her away. "You get that close to a kid in these lights, M.J., you're apt to scare 'em to death."

"Nothing scares me, and I'm not a kid," I said, and marched in my high heels over to the pushed-together tables. I sat down, crossed my smooth legs, picked up a nearby deck.

"First things first," said Mitzi Jean, and the next thing I knew I was staring at a tall pretty drink with a cherry sticking out.

"Ante up or shut up," I said, something Lonna always said.

Now she said, "Let the games begin!" and sat down across from me.

And that's how it went for the next few nights, those tall pretty drinks ("The usual," I'd say), those shiny smooth cards, and me, racking up close to twenty bucks more off the girls. Though the girls didn't seem to mind. They just oohed and aahed over my latest outfit and gave me beauty advice.

"Stick to pastels, black makes you look like a stiff."

"Smile with your lips closed, hides that space between your teeth."

"Get a Lady Sunbeam, those legs look like hamburger."

On the afternoon of the third day, I dyed my hair back to natural—dishwater, Ma called it. While it took, I sat on Earlene's gray living room carpet and watched my last "Twilight Zone." When it was over, I turned off the TV, opened my notebook, thought for a minute. Then I wrote, *"Black-and-white makes you think more."*

When I got to the casino that evening, I hurried into the Ladies, as much as a girl can hurry in four-inch heels and a dress to match. I locked the door, leaned against the wall, closed my eyes. When I felt ready I opened my eyes and looked in the mirror. I took a deep breath, flicked off the light, walked out into the room.

I laid low for a few hands, while the girls reacted to my most spectacular get-up of all, Maryanne called it, with which I was destined to break a few hearts not to mention a few laws, she said. Lonna was having herself another lucky night, more interested in the little towers she was building with her dimes and nickels than in anything else. Meanwhile, I pretended my face was a blackboard and I was erasing. The girls chattered like parakeets. Lonna's little money city grew. I kept erasing. Then it was my deal.

"Seven card stud, two down, one up, ace bids," I said. Someone checked her watch, someone yawned, someone looked at her nails. Then I said, "One-eyed jacks are wild," and shuffled and snapped the cards across the table.

After four times around, Mitzi Jean folded, after five, Maryanne. That left Lonna, after six, with four hearts showing, and me, with two threes, a nine, and the jack of hearts looking peacefully over his shoulder at the pile of money in the pot. It was now or never. I counted out eight quarters and three singles.

"That's five to stay alive," I said, and pitched it into the pot. Lonna saw, and looked at me for the first time.

"The shark's circling, girls," she said, "stay outta the water."

"Last one down and dirty," I said, and dealt the last two. I lifted the corner of mine, let it back down.

One-one-thousand, two-one-thousand, I counted in my mind. Out loud I said, "That's two to you," and tossed eight quarters onto the pile. They spilled down the sides like a little silver avalanche.

Lonna's eyebrow moved, her little finger twitched. But she saw the two, and raised three more. Her money city was looking more like a town. I took a deep breath. I stared at her glared at her bared at her.

"That's three to me ..." I said, and slid three singles over. Then I reached down the neck of my most spectacular get-up of all, pulled out a bill, and laid it lightly on the top of the pile. The smell of perfume rose up.

"And ten to do it again," I said.

Two little red spots had parked themselves in Lonna's cheeks. She glanced at her money ghost town. She waited. She blinked. Then she flipped her cards over. My throat jumped: she'd had another heart in her hand!

"Fuck a rabbit," she said.

"Now that's poetic," said Mitzi Jean.

I tried to keep from fainting. I'd pulled it off! I'd won! I started pulling in my money, when Lonna reached toward my cards. I stopped her.

"That's for me to know and you to find out," I said.

Lonna's eyes opened wide for a second. Then she sat back and lit a cigarette and looked at me like she might be trying to memorize something.

At midnight, when Earlene's shift was finally over, the girls gave me a going-away. Cake, presents, the whole shebang. Maryanne donated a pot of chrysanthemums ("From my aunt's funeral, don't tell anyone"). Lonna donated background music ("Mark my words, girls, Tom Jones is due for a comeback"). Mitzi Jean donated champagne. Between glasses of champagne and a few hands of blackjack—my big score earlier had ended all enthusiasm for poker—and a few last bits of advice ("Chew your food seventeen times, you'll never get fat"), I opened the presents. A pair of sponge dice, a six-pack of bikini underwear, two new Bicycle decks, one red, one blue.

"Bicycle don't make no camo deck, J.B.," said Mitzi Jean, and laughed herself into a coughing fit. Earlier her boyfriend had stopped by with a box of chocolate-covered cherries. While I was reaching into the box, Leonard was reaching up my nylon. Though I managed to mash a candy onto his white pants under the table.

By two in the morning the cake was history. Only a half bottle of champagne was left. The last girl had said good-bye and kissed me on the cheek, adding to my kiss collection, which must've featured a dozen colors. Earlene sighed, had a last swig of André, started gathering up the presents. I picked cigarette butts out of the chrysanthemum.

In the car I held the plant carefully while Earlene drove home through the bright streets. She drove with the top down. Block after block the lights from the casinos twirled around us. I reached behind the seat for the sponge dice, hung them on Earlene's rearview mirror.

"Just a little something, Miss Dock, to remember me by," I said, and yawned, and craned my neck toward the sky. The sky glowed dim like a curtain. I wanted to yank it open.

"Do the stars ever come out around here?" I said.

"They're out there," said Earlene, "you just can't see 'em." She lit a cigarette. She looked like she might be a girl on the midway surrounded by the lights of the rides.

I shifted the chrysanthemum to my other leg, counted three seconds. Then I said, "You don't like me this way, do you, E.? I mean, I thought you'd be glad. Would you rather I went back the other way? To my spike and hightops?"

Earlene exhaled slowly. "I like you the old way, dumplin', cuz, far as I can tell, that's the real you."

I thought for a minute. "But, look at you, what about you?"

"What about me?"

"Well, who's to say who you really are?" I said. "Take that guy, for instance, the other day. Adam."

"Dennis," she said.

"Dennis," I said. "For all Dennis knows, you're, well, you're ... well, anyway, I guess you fooled him."

"But I didn't fool him," said Earlene. "I showed him."

"Same difference," I said.

Earlene pulled over to the curb, put the car in PARK, turned toward me. "No, it's not. That's what I mean. I showed him. I really showed him."

"You smacked him?" I said. "You didn't even mess yourself

up! Man, you're good! But, I guess, why wouldn't you be, you're tall, for one." I took a chance, "And, after all, you know, you're a man ..."

Earlene looked steadily at me, even when a car roared past and laid on its horn. "No, Sugar, that's the point," she said. "What I mean is, I *was* a man. I'm not any more. Dennis didn't believe me. So I showed him."

"You showed him?" I said. She nodded.

I stared at her. "You mean ... ?"

She nodded again. I just kept staring. I didn't know what to say. I just kept watching her, even when she turned away, looked over her shoulder, pulled back into traffic. I just kept staring at the side of her face. She made a sharp right, and for a second the sponge dice were swinging there, back and forth, between us.

"But, that's what I mean," I said finally. "You don't like me this way, because it's not the real me, you say. But look at you. You ... start out one thing ... and go and turn yourself into something else. What about that?"

Earlene touched her fingers to her hair. Her mouth pointed upward. "Well, that's just not the same thing at all," she said. "Not at all. I was always myself on the inside. I just went and changed on into myself on the outside, too."

I turned my head in time to see a giant sun burst apart in a golden circle, then disappear down to nothing again. Even after it was gone, that sun still hovered in the air in front of me, in the dark there, like a wavery yellow flower. I shifted the plant on my leg and touched my fingers to my smooth smooth hair.

◆ ◆ ◆

I left the chrysanthemum on a TV tray in front of the picture window in Earlene's living room. When I pulled open the drapes next morning, the sun spilled into the room, onto the gray walls and carpet, like yellow paint.

"Now this plant needs sun," I told her, "or she'll die. Also she needs water."

"So it's a she?" said Earlene, and I said,

"Takes one to know one."

It would take me fifteen hours to get to Ventura, CA. Along with my clothes and the presents from the girls, Earlene had packed three lunches into my camo backpack. She'd also thrown in a few loose tea bags—"Don't for-get to make a tiny tear for the leaves to leak out!"—and tucked some bills and loose change into my back pocket.

"Always have a dime for a phone call," she said.

"These days it's a quarter, E."

"Just call when you get there," she said.

"But you won't answer."

She thought for a minute. "If it's your voice I hear, darlin', I will. I'll make an ex-ception."

At the depot she let me out at the curb and went to park and pick up my ticket. I could see myself in the tall front window. If I moved my hand just so, I could see my tattoo. My spike had stayed in place during the drive over. Maybe I'd dye it black when I got to California. I reached down and retied my hightop. Then I straightened up.

I pulled off my sunglasses to make sure I wasn't seeing things. But there it was, halfway between the curb and the front of the depot, sticking smack up out of the pavement: a rainbow. I glanced around. Nobody seemed to notice it. Suddenly a little girl ran right through it, laughing. I wanted to grab her, tell her, Go back, make a wish.

I inched toward it, closer and closer, and before I knew what I was about, there I was standing in a rainbow. I couldn't believe it. I closed my eyes. Could I feel something? Something like sparklers maybe? Something not inside me, but outside?

Homestudy   173

A hand touched my shoulder. I jumped.

"Sugar?" said Earlene. "Y'all okay?"

I opened my eyes. She stood there in the sun in her pointy sunglasses, a large flat box tucked up under one arm.

"You'd best get in line for a window seat," she said.

"E., look," I whispered, stepping back, pointing. "Can you believe it? Starting right here!"

Earlene looked down. "My stars, hon, that's just ... " She looked around. "See there?" She pointed toward the front of the depot. One of the glass doors was held open by a suitcase. "It's the sun comin' through that door, makin' a prism."

"Prison?"

"With an M," she said. "Just you watch."

A man grabbed the suitcase and hurried into the depot. The door closed behind him. The rainbow disappeared.

By this time the bus had pulled up, long and silver and shining, with a long silver dog streaking across the side like it might go tearing off into another dimension at any minute. I put my sunglasses back on and followed Earlene to the curb. She propped the box against her leg, handed me my ticket. She pushed something else into my backpack.

"Just a little somethin', Miss Kane, to remember me by," she said, and turned toward the bus. "Now I won-der, would it be better to put her with the suit-cases? or over-head inside?"

She bent toward the box. I looked down at my hightop.

"E.," I said, "I've been thinking," and it was true. "A bus is no place for art, any halfwit knows that."

I looked up over the top of my glasses. Earlene's were pointed toward me.

I said, "I've been thinking, she belongs in a house, you know, a *real* house. Not a bomb shelter or a motel. She could be like, you know, company."

Earlene straightened.

"Besides," I said, "that old living room rainbow is so faded, and she wouldn't be any trouble, not like a dog or cat. Or a plant."

I said, "She belongs with you, E."

Earlene's mouth opened a little, then closed.

I said, "To remember me by?"

Earlene looked at the sky ... one one-thousand, two one-thousand ... then she looked back at me. I couldn't see her eyes behind her glasses.

"Okay, sugar-pie," she said real quiet, "to remember you by."

Then her little mouth smiled. "Now give us a kiss."

"E., wait, one more thing. I was wondering, does it count, do you think?"

She looked surprised. "Of course it counts, a kiss is a kiss."

"I mean the prism. Does it count for a rainbow?"

I didn't want my wish to be wasted. Or worse, cancelled out altogether. It'd been my best shot. I wanted to save it, maybe use it later on.

"Maybe a rainbow is a rainbow," I said, "you never know."

"Y'all never do," said Earlene, "maybe it is."

Earlene's kiss was a ghost kiss, quick and light, and I felt it exactly for a long time. Even when the bus started moving. Even while I waved from my window seat far in the back, until my arm went sparkly, until Earlene became the sidewalk became the buildings became the sky. Until I turned forward, rubbing my dead arm. Some kid across the aisle was staring at me.

"What's your name?" he said, moving a toothpick around in his teeth. I stared back through my sunglasses.

"J.B." I said. I thought for a minute. I arranged my face, took off my glasses. "Wanna play some cards?"

The kid got off in Fresno minus six bucks. By then it was close to midnight. Fresno was bright as day. I was beginning to wonder if I'd ever see stars again.

While we waited for new passengers, I flicked on the light above my head, reached into my backpack for one of the lunches. My hand felt Earlene's present. I pulled it out, tore off the paper. The light shone down on the "Little House on the Prairie" notebook. My "Twilight Zone" notes, filled to the second to the last page. But there was something else.

I lifted the notebook. The light shone down on a blue pen taped to the cover of a long gray book. The corners of the book were wrapped in red, a word was written in black letters across the front: RECORD. I opened the book. It was empty. Page after page of white, with those skinny blue lines running down to the bottom like ladders.

"But what if there's no 'Twilight Zone' in California?" I said out loud. Some lady turned and looked at me.

I closed the new book, opened the old notebook to a place in the middle.

"*'Miniature'. Robert Duvall. Irony.*" I'd written. Then, "*If you wish for something hard enough, you might lose your mind.*"

That morning, before we left for the depot, Earlene had finally done what I'd been bugging her to do all summer. She read my tea leaves. What she saw was this: trees, grass, bushes, plants. My cup was one big forest. Earlene just shook her head, said she couldn't figure it out, said maybe it had to do with California, that I was headed for a new neck of the woods, something like that. Only here's what I thought: it had to do with color, the color of the forest. It had to do with green.

I leaned back, looked out at the passengers waiting in line. A baby slept on a lady's shoulder. A girl stood reading a comic. A man used one cigarette to light another. I was thinking maybe I didn't need the "Twilight Zone." Maybe I could use the new book just for comments, such as, "*Some people make better waiters than others.*" But I'd save the old notebook anyway, because when they saw it, they just might let me advance to green in California.

7
Xmas Story

Ma believed in two things: Christmas and Mary Kay. Mary Kay because a girl needed a regular routine. Christmas because she was from Up North where Christmas was a way of life. She said Up North with a capital U N. She said Christmas with an X.

"Because of the baby jesus and all that hype," she explained. "The X takes care of all that."

Ma's particular idea of Xmas relied heavily on decorations, presents and snow.

"Now, Sugar, picture this," she'd say, and start in.

And I'd hear it all again. The childhood Xmases Up North, how she and her sisters would sit before a blazing fire, stringing popcorn for the tree their smiling father had chopped in the woods, while their singing mother baked gingerbread men and mincemeat pie and the wind howled and the snow blew. Once the snow blew so hard my grandfather had to call the Fire Department to come dig them out. Which must have been before the time he ran away for good not just for the weekend.

"Enough was enough," Ma would say, "the poor man headed for the hills." And I always wondered, enough of what? girls? snow? mincemeat?

Whatever Xmas traditions she grew up with, though, Ma

had developed her own when it came to me. A week before Christmas, where ever we happened to be, she'd start crossing off the days on a calendar.

"I'm giving you the gift of anticipation," she'd say.

Once the big day arrived, I could get anything I wanted—a couple new Barbies, a half dozen My Pretty Ponies, the entire set-up for Space Invaders including a small portable TV—all of which I could keep for a week, before Ma returned everything to the store.

"What do you think, I'm a goddamn millionaire?" she'd say. "Besides, I'm giving you a gift to last a lifetime."

"And what might that be?" I'd say, and she'd say,

"Knowing what it feels like to get exactly what you want. How many people can say the same?"

According to Ma's definition of Xmas, decorations and presents were always a possibility no matter where we were. But snow was another matter altogether. For instance California, where we happened to be the year I decided I'd had it with Ma's particular tradition of gift-giving. I wanted something I could lay my hands on that would last at least until spring. Like my old run-away grandfather, enough was finally enough.

We were new to California this particular Christmas. Ma's Welfare hadn't kicked in yet, she'd already pawned everything possible. We were living in Ventura, in the rooms behind the club where Ma danced. One night during her specialty—which involved spinning around the pole on one foot while touching her head with the other—Ma's high heel slips, she falls off the stage into the Bouncer's big hairy arms. An accident, she swears. The next day we're motoring through Malibu in the Bouncer's car, a little red Toyota, which he'd lent us to haul all our worldly possessions to his place out in the Canyon.

Ma found a map in the glove compartment, I unfolded as she drove. It's another of Ma's talents, she says, knowing her way around a map. She was trying to pass this ability on to me. But faced with all those letters and lines, my eyes started to water. I was better at colors.

"Here's the ocean," I said, pointing to the large blue area off to the left. "And here's the desert." I indicated a beige area with very little writing.

"You're a goddamn genius," said Ma. "Now where the fuck is Highway One?"

I ignored her. "But I don't see Up North. Where's Up North on this map?" I was searching high and low for a big patch of white.

"Knock it off, Sugar," said Ma, and flicked her cigarette out the window. Then she flicked her pink nails above the map. "Look in this green area here for a line that goes up in that direction there, toward that brown area." I tried to concentrate, but it was no use.

I said, "Wouldn't Up North be toward the top? Where you came from? A big white place, toward the top?"

"It's not there," said Ma. "This is only one state, got that? One state. This is not the whole goddamn world."

Eventually we found a road which took us in the general direction we wanted to go. Once there, Ma drove around for awhile. Finally she slowed the Toyota and pulled back the sun roof. I poked my head through, called out to a mailman. He waved a handful of mail toward a dust-colored house with a red roof and no lawn. A porch slanted along the front of the house, black bars stretched across the windows. When Ma turned past the mailman into the driveway, he smiled and winked.

"U.S. Mail, at your service," he says, and touches his mail cap, which sat at an angle.

Men were always touching something when it came to Ma. For instance the Bouncer, who hauled himself up off the couch, touched his jeans, touched the chain hanging from his belt, then his big beard, then took us on a tour of his bungalow, he called it. Living room, dining room, bathroom, hallway. He pushed open a door at the end of the hallway.

"This here's your room," he says. I look around.

"What's with the bars on the windows?" I said, and the Bouncer said,

"The criminal factor."

In the kitchen he pointed to the Magic Slate taped on the refrigerator door.

"This here's the message center," he said. "So's we always know where each other is at." He pulled the wooden pencil from its pocket, wrote "FUCK XMAS" carefully on the gray surface of the slate. When he lifted the see-through plastic, the message disappeared.

"Dig?" he said.

"Far out," said Ma.

I said, "That's the way Ma says it, Xmas."

Ma said, "Great minds think alike, that's my motto," and tucked herself under the Bouncer's big hairy armpit.

"How's about a little pick-me-up?" said the Bouncer, and opened the refrigerator door.

Except for half a package of wieners and a few cans of Coke, the refrigerator was filled with beer from top to bottom, all of it Bud, a warehouse of red, white and blue. The Bouncer grabbed a can and shook it. Then he pointed the can at me and pulled the tab. Before I knew what was happening, I was drenched from top to bottom, beer dripping down along me onto the linoleum around my hightops. The Bouncer laughed and turned toward Ma and poured the rest of the can over her. Foam collected on her head like a little hat, or a halo.

"Yo!" said the Bouncer, "good for the hair!"

"Yo!" said Ma, "good for the complexion!"

I wiped my face and eyes and went back outside to start

unloading all our worldly possessions from the red Toyota.

At the club where Ma danced they had a rule, printed in big black letters and nailed to the wall behind the bar:

ABSOLUTELY NO DRINKING ON THE JOB
THIS MEANS YOU YES YOU

So when she first met him, Ma thought the Bouncer was a dream come true: the strong silent type, with a steady job, who, when she fell off the stage, told her she weighed about as much as a day-old kitten.

"Now that's something a girl could get used to," said Ma.

But out in the Canyon, we soon learned, the rule didn't apply.

"He runs hot and cold," Ma said after we'd been living in the Bouncer's bungalow for a few weeks.

And I agreed, picturing him as a faucet helped. He ran sometimes hot, as in whiskey, but mostly cold, as in cold beer. He spent half his time drinking beer and the other half pissing it out, usually any place handy—an empty beer can, a houseplant, the backyard.

"When ya gotta go, ya gotta go," he'd say.

The Bouncer also didn't look like he'd bounce very well. I finally informed him of this fact one sunny afternoon about a week before Christmas. By now we'd been living with him for maybe a month.

I hadn't meant to sass him that day. But me and Little Ralphie from down the block had sneaked a doobie from Little Ralphie's aunt's boyfriend's car's glove compartment, and I got inspired. The Bouncer turned a few shades of some kind of color and raised his beebee gun. He'd been sitting on his front porch making short work of a case of Bud, taking potshots at small rodents. Me and Little Ralphie were out sitting on the curb in the shade, waiting for an earthquake. I'd had to raise my voice a bit to be heard way up on the porch.

"Yo!" I hollered. "Just how high can a Bouncer bounce?"

And the Bouncer let fly. He'd filled the beebee gun with pepper. I was wearing cutoffs. Me and Little Ralphie hightailed it out of there like a couple of peppershot squirrels. We almost knocked over the mailman.

Back behind his aunt's bougainvillea, safe from the Bouncer's gun, Little Ralphie pushed his glasses back up. The glasses were held together with tape and a paper clip.

"We should've consulted Zortron again," said Little Ralphie. "Once a day is not enough. The future is forever."

Zortron was the name of the spirit who ruled Little Ralphie's Ouija board. We'd consulted Zortron earlier that morning concerning the earthquake factor, and Zortron had spelled out, "WHOSE TO SAY." Little Ralphie had said that was incorrect pronoun usage, and gave me a look. So we asked again. This time Zortron spelled, "EXPECT A MIRACLE."

Ever since getting to California, I was all, "When's it coming? What's it like?" And everyone was all, "When you least expect it, you'll know it when it happens." So I thought about earthquakes all the time. I'd wake up thinking, Could today be the day? I'd be sitting on the can wondering, What if it happens now? I'd be hanging out on the roof of the club where Ma danced, getting stoned with Little Ralphie, throwing various items at the drunks, and I'd be worrying, Is it coming? Am I too high? Should I get closer to the street?

"'EXPECT A MIRACLE'," I said. "What the fuck is that supposed to mean?"

"It's not for mere mortals to decide, Mademoiselle," said Little Ralphie.

I, however, had definitely decided something. That morning Ma had taped our official Xmas calendar beside the Magic Slate on the refrigerator door in the Bouncer's kitchen. This calendar featured a group of dogs dressed up like reindeer playing cards.

"Tonight we'll cross off our first day," said Ma, and gave me a quick hug before I could pull away. This Xmas stuff sure got her going. "You better start thinking what you want, Sugarplum."

But I already knew what I wanted for Christmas this year: my own Ouija board. I was sick and tired of Little Ralphie's board, all sticky with pop and chocolate and who knows, Clearasil, and the pointer didn't slide that well any more. And I was sick and tired of Little Ralphie never letting me ask any *real* questions, such as, Will I ever get a Christmas present I can keep? or, Does Little Ralphie's aunt give head?

Here's something else I'd learned living in the Canyon: when the strong silent type drank, they didn't stay silent for long. In fact, they became downright chatty. Sometimes when Ma was dancing and the Bouncer had the night off, he'd start following me around the bungalow with his bottle, asking over and over, would I give him some head, just give him some head? I figured this was bar talk for "let's rap." I wanted to ask Little Ralphie's aunt, who'd once been a bartender, for some pointers. She might be able to suggest a few good topics of conversation, under the circumstances. Ma was constantly warning me, Be polite to the Bouncer, don't sass, don't make waves, he's doing us a favor after all it's his house, the poor man isn't used to kids.

"But he keeps trying to start a conversation," I'd say. "I don't have a clue what to talk about."

"But that's a good sign," said Ma. "He must like you. Get him talking about himself, men love that. Ask him something about himself."

"Like what?"

Ma thought for a minute. "I don't know, like, what's his favorite movie? What's his favorite song?"

"How about Christmas?" I said. "Like what does he want

for Christmas?" But Ma said,

"Oh no, not that. He doesn't believe in any of that."

"But you do," I said, "you can change his mind."

"You can change a man's mood," said Ma, "but never his mind, that's my motto. Besides, I can't help but believe in Xmas. I've got the North in my blood, remember."

I remember the Bouncer saying he certainly agreed with that, she was a cold-blooded bitch if ever there was one. This was the time Ma refused to tell him where his car keys were until he got some sleep. He'd been roaming the house wide awake since Sunday, now it was Tuesday. Me and Ma had locked ourselves in the bathroom. The Bouncer was out in the hallway, repeating over and over how he'd run out of product, he needed to drive to the Valley for more product, have a heart you cold-blooded bitch.

Ma had locked the bathroom door to be on the safe side, though she said in this state, the Bouncer was harmless as a lamb. I was thinking, how about in some other state, North Dakota, for instance? but I kept my mouth shut. Ma was putting on her face in the mirror. I was sitting on the toilet seat watching. She kept calling through the locked door, You must sleep, go to sleep now, sleep.

I yawned. I figured this was as good a time as any to mention Xmas presents. But Ma said, No fucking way.

"Those things are evil," she said. "Haven't you seen 'The Exorcist'?"

"I don't remember any Ouija board in 'The Exorcist'," I said. "Alls that happened, the girl's head turned around."

"It's the same category," said Ma. "Bad things happen when you let evil into your life."

I said, "What's evil about knowing the future?" and Ma said,

"Who needs to know the future? The past is bad enough. Don't fuck with shit, that's my motto."

She laid her blusher on the edge of the sink. "Take that time I got drunk and went to a card reader down on East Lake. Next thing you know, I'm goddamn pregnant." I stared at her. "It just goes to show," she said, reaching for her eyeliner.

This was Ma's dancing face. Over the years I'd made quite a killing charging various audiences for the privilege of watching her build it. First she'd rat and spray her hair into a sort of tornado, then smooth the top with a brush. Next she'd pull her eyelids to the sides, draw on fat black lines like zippers. She'd draw on brown eyebrows and bright pink or purple or red lips, depending on the time of the month, she said. Then she'd add a fake mole above the lips. Finally she'd throw a handful of baby powder over the whole shebang, squirt "Charlie" or "Love's Baby Soft" into the air and walk through it. At this point I usually sneezed.

Ma set the bottle of perfume on the back of the toilet and pooched her lips in an air kiss. "One day, just you watch, you'll beg me to show you some tricks of the trade."

I thought for a minute. I made my eyes round. "How about this Christmas?" I said, and tried to look like I meant what I was saying. "I could get ... a Mary Kay Starter Kit ..." I paused, " ... and a Ouija board." But none of this fooled Ma.

"I already told you, that stuff's evil," she said, so I said,

"Yeah, but if you sell enough of it, you get a pink Cadillac."

Ma rolled her eyes. "You know what I goddamn mean," she said, and started in on her nails.

◆ ◆ ◆

Next to Christmas, Ma believed in Mary Kay. She might think the baby jesus was alot of hype, but she believed Mary Kay Yellow could save the world.

"It takes 5-7 years off your face," she'd say, "5-7 years!"

Every time we moved, she went looking for the nearest dealer.

"The word's 'distributor'," she'd remind me, "Mary Kay distributor."

Every chance she got, Ma attended Mary Kay parties, from which she'd return with tighter pores, a more positive outlook, and carloads of pink cosmetics. Often she'd be decked out in a pink headband or scarf.

"It's *the* color for blondes," she'd say, and I'd try not to look at her roots. She'd lean over, move her purple-shadowed eyes around my face. "If only you'd listen to me, Sugar, I could show you the ropes."

"Let me show *you* something," I'd say, and light a cigarette.

So when we found ourselves out in the Canyon with the Bouncer, the first thing, Ma looks in the Yellow Pages. There's a Mary Kay distributor right down the street.

"It's goddamn cosmic!" says Ma.

The distributor turns out to be Little Ralphie's aunt, who distributed a few other things as well. Little Ralphie lived with his aunt because, like me, he didn't know where his dad was—though he had it on good authority, he said, that his dad was a cowboy—and, unlike me, his mother was dead.

I learned all this the first time I met him, the first time he showed me his Ouija board. We were sitting in his aunt's boyfriend's car in the driveway, smoking and listening to Billy Idol on the tape deck. He'd been telling me about his dad the long lost cowboy, when I reached into my backpack and pulled out Diamond, who I'd been hauling around for several states now. I figured the son of a cowboy could probably relate to a little carved horse, purple or not.

I was right. Little Ralphie stared at her, his mouth hanging open, his tongue hanging out.

"An excellent facsimile," he said after awhile. I rolled my eyes and set Diamond on the dashboard.

"So what about your ma," I said, "is she a cowgirl?"

"Ma mere was an educator," said Little Ralphie, laying his cigarette in the ashtray, still staring at Diamond. "Health Sciences, Community College. But she transcended mortality."

"What the fuck is that supposed to mean?" I said, and Little Ralphie said,

"She flew off the top of a parking ramp on a Harley."

I stared at him.

"During an earthquake," he said.

I thought for a minute. I said, "How high was she?"

Little Ralphie made a sound back in his throat. He blinked his blond lashes behind his glasses. Then he said, "I'm trying to contact her."

"Contact her?"

He reached around behind the seat, brought up a smooth brown board featuring the alphabet in fancy black letters. Fancy black numbers in a half moon stretched across the top. The words "YES" and "NO" were spelled out in the corners. He balanced the board between us. On the top of the board he placed a beige plastic heart with a little round window in the middle.

He tucked his stringy brown hair behind his ears. His forehead was splattered with bright red zits. "White Wedding" came on the tape deck. I tried to picture me and Little Ralphie getting married. The thought made my teeth hurt.

"You lay your hands like this," said Little Ralphie, and placed his fingers along the edge of the plastic heart. He didn't have fingernails. He'd bitten them clean off, also the skin around where they should have been. "After awhile you can ask questions. He'll spell out answers."

"'He'?" I said, and Little Ralphie said,

"Zortron. He rules the board."

I looked at him out of the corner of my eye.

"He's a spirit or demon or something," says Little Ralphie.

"Maybe he's the son of god. The point is, this is his board."

I rested my fingers on the plastic heart and waited. The sun baked through the windshield. I glanced at Diamond. The tape clicked off. The black polish on my nails was chipped, my tattoo was fading. I wanted another cigarette. I wanted to flip the tape over. I was starting to feel pretty mental.

Then the heart began to quiver.

"Fuckenay!" I said.

Little Ralphie said, "I think he likes you. You might be a natural ..." then he said, " ... disaster," and snorted.

I ignored him. The heart moved in a small circle, around and around, then bigger and bigger, faster and faster. I closed my eyes, tried to keep my fingers in place. But I couldn't help it, I giggled.

"This is serious!" hissed Little Ralphie. "Concentrate!"

I bit my lip, squeezed my eyes tight.

"Oh Great Unknowable One ..." said Little Ralphie, and a laugh came out my nose.

"Sugar!" Little Ralphie never called me by my name, which he said was assinine. He usually called me Mademoiselle.

The heart kept spinning. After awhile Little Ralphie said, in an important voice, "If you can hear me, give me a sign."

I said, "What do you want me to do, spit?"

Little Ralphie made that throat sound again. "Pardon me," he said, "but I was talking to *her*," and I realized he meant his mother. I sighed and waited and held my breath and tried to think serious thoughts while the heart spun round.

At last Little Ralphie spoke, and I realized he was speaking to me. "Mademoiselle," he said, "what might you want to know? Is there anything about which you might like to consult Zortron?"

I thought for a minute. "I want to know ... I want to know ... what'll I get for Christmas?"

"That's assinine," said Little Ralphie. "Ask something that

matters."

I thought hard. "I want to know ... will there be an earthquake?"

Suddenly the heart stopped circling, started jerking itself around the board. I had all I could do to keep my fingers in place.

"A-B-S-O-..." spelled Little Ralphie aloud, "'ABSOLUTELY', Zortron says 'ABSOLUTELY'!"

The heart stopped moving altogether, as if it were waiting. I could almost feel it breathing. Slowly I opened my eyes. The sun shone bright on the steering wheel. A line of sweat ran down Little Ralphie's cheek like a scar. Someone was vacuuming next door.

"Anything else, Mademoiselle?" said Little Ralphie.

"Will there be an earthquake soon?" I asked, and the heart started up again. This time I watched the answer appear. "Y-O-U-L-L ..." spelled Zortron, "KNOW IT WHEN IT HAPPENS." This is what everyone was always telling me. My hair got pins and needles.

"That's it," I said, "enough is enough," and I pulled my hands away. Little Ralphie pulled his hands away. I grabbed Diamond off the dashboard and dropped her back in my pack. A crow landed in the bougainvillea and started hollering.

The night before the Bouncer shot me and Little Ralphie with the pepper gun, I finally agreed to go with Ma to a Mary Kay party. The party was down the block at Little Ralphie's aunt's house. I agreed to go on two conditions. I'd go to their blessed party, let them do whatever they wanted to me, but for payment I wanted a Ouija board.

"And secondly," I said, and I looked Ma square in the face, "I get to keep it. No return trips to the May Company."

Ma called me a goddamn little manipulator and pouted for half a day. Then she told me she wouldn't be responsible for any evil shit I brought down upon myself on account of this Ouija board, so don't come crying to her.

"Just keep the goddamn thing out of my sight," she said, zipping her pink cosmetic case. "What you can't see can't hurt you, that's my motto."

Then she wrote a note to the Bouncer on the Magic Slate: "GONE 2 GET GLAMOROUS, HOME MIDNITE," and signed it, "GUESS WHO."

"But what if he's hungry when he gets back?" I asked. The Bouncer had driven to the Valley earlier that afternoon. Me and Ma had already eaten all the food in the house, half a leftover pizza.

"Food," said Ma, "will be the furthest thing from that man's mind. Furthermore ..." She pointed a long red nail at me. "If that little dweeb is there, that Ralph person, I don't want you sneaking off. Tonight you're a girl, you're with me. Dig? You're staying for the duration."

I ignored her. I was thinking about my Ouija board, the questions I wanted to ask, what I might name the spirit who ruled it. Little Ralphie had told me to name it after his mother, for good luck. Though he didn't seem to be having much luck in that department. Besides, whoever heard of a spirit named Roxanne.

When she first saw me all Mary-Kayed up that evening, Ma screamed with happiness and started drinking. She'd been waiting for this day her whole life, she said, praying for it, she said. She always knew I had it in me, Oh lookee here girls, is she gorgeous or what? a goddamn mankiller or what? completely changed, a different person, sure I'll have another glass. Meanwhile I thought of that Ouija board and kept my mouth shut and didn't even smoke, though the dining room was so full of it I could hardly see.

Maybe that was it, after awhile Ma didn't recognize me in the haze. Between all that smoke and all that wine, maybe to her I just looked like anybody else, another party-goer. So that when I finally took a chance and pushed back my chair and stood up to leave, she didn't try to stop me. She just moved her eyes in my direction, then moved them away, that smeary smile sprawled across her face.

In the front hall I looked around for Little Ralphie. He must've been up in his room, maybe out riding his bike. After I got back to the Bouncer's, washed my face, changed clothes, I'd go look for him. I'd managed to grab a couple good-sized roaches from one of his aunt's ashtrays. And I'd thought of some more things I wanted to ask the Ouija board. Not that I expected Little Ralphie would let me. I could hear him already.

"You're a girl, you don't know serious," he'd say, then he'd ask something like, "What were your last thoughts, Roxanne, as you flew through the air toward La Cienega Boulevard?"

I walked along the half block to the Bouncer's house, past the Christmas tree lights shining into the dark from the windows of the other houses. Like the stars had fallen out of the night and scattered across the neighborhood. I was picturing Ma and her sisters, perched around some tree in their home Up North. I was picturing snow, all that snow, and in my mind, it began to fall.

The snow fell and it fell and it covered the street and the yards, it covered Little Ralphie's aunt's bougainvillea and the three pink cadillacs in her driveway. It kept falling until it reached the windows of the houses, then the roofs, then the chimneys. It piled higher and higher, until the lights from all the Christmas trees shone through, so the Fire Department would know where they were, the people who needed to be rescued, the people buried there in the snow.

When I reached the Bouncer's bungalow, I realized that when the snow came, whoever happened to be in this house would never be found. With no decorations, no starry lights to shine a message, the firemen would never know, they would pass by not knowing. This house would be passed over, just another silent white pile.

I walked around to the back, into the kitchen, grabbed a can of Coke from the refrigerator. The Magic Slate had been pulled clean. The only thing left of Ma's message was one word, "GONE."

"He's back," I thought, and listened. But I didn't hear anything. Maybe he'd left again.

I pulled the pencil from its pocket, wrote a name across the surface of the slate, "SPIRALIA." Not bad, I thought, it beat Zortron. I studied it, then pulled the slate clean. I walked down the hall to the bathroom. The lights beside the medicine cabinet flickered. When they finally blazed on, I stepped back, knocking my foot against the tub. I'd forgotten about my face.

I balanced the Coke on the sink, turned on the faucet, waited for the water to heat up. I looked in the mirror again — powdered cheeks, outlined cat eyes, little surprised eyebrows.

"Crescenta!" said the pointy red lips, and a dimple appeared, one of the eyebrows raised. Steam started to rise from the sink like a cloud. The lips tried again,

"Glowindelle!"

"Say what?" said a voice from the doorway.

"Jesus!" I said, and jerked around, grabbing the Coke before it fell.

"At yer ser-vice!" said the Bouncer, and belched.

"I-I was just . . . " I said. My face felt hot under the blusher. Then I remembered Ma's advice, about men and conversation. Carefully I set the Coke down again.

"So, anyway," I said, "what's *your* favorite name?"

The Bouncer raised the bottle in his hand, took a long swallow, held the bottle toward me.

"'Old Grand Dad'," I read. "Well, what I mean is, a name for a girl. Your favorite girl name."

The Bouncer squinted at me. "Shu-gar . . . " he said, "Shu-gar..." He leaned against the door. It slammed into the wall.

I was thinking of Little Ralphie. I said, "Don't you think that name is, sort of, assinine?"

"Shu-gar-lie ... She-gir-lie ..." said the Bouncer, and a big hand grabbed my wrist.

I tried to pull away, but the hand held tight. Then the other hand reached out, the bottle touched my cheek. Now my wrist hurt. I could smell the Bouncer's breath. I saw the white under his nose. Suddenly the bottle dropped to the floor. Now the smell of whiskey rose up and joined with the steam from the sink. I squeezed my eyes shut, my eyelashes stuck together. When I opened them again, I saw: the Bouncer had unzipped his jeans, reached in, pulled himself out. He'd pulled himself out like some old sock out of the dryer, all faded and droopy and wrinkled.

"WHAT ARE YOU D-DOING!?" I hollered, and the Bouncer shoved me.

I fell hard against the wall onto the floor. The Bouncer's eyes were closed. He was breathing hard. I tried to get around him. His boot pushed me back. I tried to stand up. His boot pushed me down. I tried not to look at that hand moving moving. There was nothing I could do. I waited just waited.

After awhile—it was like hours, like days—the hand stopped moving, and the Bouncer swore. Then he swore again, shifted position, turned his face toward the ceiling. Now all I could see was his big beard. He held onto the sink with one hand and pointed himself at me with the other and before I knew what was happening, the Bouncer let fly.

I started to scream. Then I stopped. I stopped because somehow I knew just knew: the Bouncer wouldn't remember this, and even if he did, I could hear him already, When ya gotta go, ya gotta go. Ma wouldn't believe this—I was thinking of her friend who used to visit my room—and even if she did, she'd find something to blame: Mary Kay, the Ouija board,

Little Ralphie. I could hear her already, Don't fuck with shit, that's my motto, see what happens when you fuck with shit?

So I covered my head and I waited. I sat there in whiskey on the bathroom floor while the Bouncer pissed while he pissed all over me the color of whiskey the color of the desert on the map of California the color of something ... I was thinking of something ... the color of ... straw! I was thinking of straw the straw on the floor that absorbed the piss in the place Ma danced where Grace let me smoke I could still hear that broom sweeping up straw SWICK SWICK

I could still hear the Bouncer breathing pissing so I covered my ears and I waited waited like waiting was a place a place I could be like somewhere between one thing stopping and another starting up like an earthquake like hovering in mid-air while the world readjusted a place like mid-air being suspended there like somewhere between say a parking ramp and the pavement

◆ ◆ ◆

When Ma found out the Bouncer shot me and Little Ralphie with his pepper gun (she was informed of these developments by the mailman, who'd been in the line of fire and caught some pepper himself), she slammed out the screen door onto the slanted front porch of the Bouncer's house yelling every name in the book. We could hear her down at Little Ralphie's aunt's.

"GODDAMN FAILED ABORTION!"

I wasn't quite sure who she was yelling at, this could've meant any one of us. But the Bouncer took it personally.

"SHIT-BRAINED THROWBACK!"

I could've told Ma the Bouncer was going to raise his gun at her, too, going around yelling these things. Though by the time he took aim in her direction, he was slowed down considerably from beer. Ma managed to slip through the yards to where me and Little Ralphie were crouched with the Ouija board in his aunt's bougainvillea. She took one look at that board, yanked it out of Little Ralphie's sticky fingers, threw it like a frisbee across the lawn.

"I swear you kids'll bring the wrath of god down upon us all," she said.

"L-looks more like the wrath of B-bud," I said. I could feel Ma's glarey eyes on me. She didn't say anything.

Little Ralphie started in on his thumbnail. He kept glancing toward where his Ouija board lay bumped up against the baby jesus in the neighbor's yard. It'd just missed a wiseman.

"You shouldn't have done that, you know," said Little Ralphie. "Zortron is going to be awfully upset. Why, just this morning..."

"Sh-shut up," I hissed, and pinched his arm. Ma looked at both us as if we'd just escaped from the loony bin.

"Shut the fuck up, both of you," she said, though she stared hard at me again for too long. Then she nodded in the direction of the Bouncer's house. "We'll just keep an eye on him. The poor thing won't last long, believe you me. And when he goes down, we make our move."

"And wh-what move might that b-be?" I said, and Ma grabbed my chin and yanked my head around.

"What the fuck is this?" she hissed. "I thought we were goddamn through with the goddamn stuttering! If you're going to goddamn start in again, I swear, that's it! I give up! The movies DO NOT want a girl who goddamn stutters!"

I pulled out of her grip and glared back at her.

"Anyway," she said, "as I was saying," and she adjusted one of her earrings, "we'll make our move to, I don't know, somewhere, anywhere there's..." She sighed loudly. "It's goddamn Christmas, for chrissake. I need decorations. I need presents."

"D-don't you mean Xmas?" I said.

MINIMUM MAINTENANCE

Ma glared at me. "I mean *s-snow!*" she said. "I mean *g-goddamn s-snow*! Jesus!" She turned and poofed her hair with her fingers.

Then we all turned, back toward the Bouncer, to await the inevitable, Ma called it. We watched him drink one beer, then another, then one more. After awhile Little Ralphie started in on his other thumbnail. By this time the Bouncer had started in on another case of Bud. When Little Ralphie announced he had pressing business and made a dash for his aunt's side door, Ma shook her head. Just look at him, she said, the poor thing, I rest my case, a kid needs a mother, nothing beats a mother, that's my motto.

It seemed like forever, but the Bouncer finally stood up. We watched him buckle the gun back under his belt. We watched him stagger around to his sideyard and take a piss. We watched him pass out under a yucca tree. That's when Ma pulled me out from the bushes and started running across the lawns. I was worried the Bouncer would come to, find us tearing around in plain view, start shooting again. But Ma said the state he was in, even an earthquake couldn't move his ass.

And I guess that's when I started believing Ma had been right all along about the Ouija board. Because no sooner did she say the word, when it happened. And everybody else had been right, too: I knew it when it happened. And so easy, like finally remembering something I'd always known.

It started with that sound. For a second I thought a train was coming, and looked around for it. By this time we'd reached the Bouncer's driveway, which had begun to shake. Me and Ma turned toward each other. We couldn't move. We were statues stuck in place made of cement. The ground was shaking and the trees were shaking and the leaves on the trees and that sound was everywhere. Like we were on board that train waiting at the station about to go shooting on out of there at any minute.

The whole thing lasted maybe 20 seconds. Only when it was over, it was like hours, like days. Like the next century.

Suddenly Ma snaps out of it, starts getting herself into some kind of big hurry, like maybe we really *did* have a train to catch. She's all, Get the lead out, girl, get a move on! And there we are, running in and out of the house after this thing and that, in the process of reloading all our worldly goods back into the red Toyota, and Ma's all, Shake a leg now, girl, move your ass!

Then just as sudden we're loaded up, packed in, crammed beside each other in the tiny front seat. Everything turns quiet. Ma takes a deep breath. She spreads a map out across the steering wheel. I roll down the window.

"I been thinking," she says finally, moving her fingernail along. "North is out of the question. But we'll do the next best thing. Lookee here," she says, and I look.

"Mountains!" she says. "They're sure to have snow, somewhere near the top. Take us two, three days max. What d'ya think?"

But I was thinking of something else.

"D-don't leave!" I said, and hightailed it up the driveway to the house and into the kitchen.

When I got back to the car, I held up the dog calendar.

"Almost f-forgot this," I said.

Ma looked at me. I was waiting for her to say something. Instead she picked up her purse, rooted around, pulled out an eyebrow pencil. She laid the calendar against the dashboard, drew a fat black X through the square marked "19." Then she tucked the calendar between the seats.

"I left a m-message," I said, "at the m-message center."

Ma checked the rearview mirror, adjusted her shades. "And what might that be?" she said, and slowly carefully I said,

"WHEN YA GOTTA GO, YA GOTTA GO."

Ma grinned and blew me an air kiss and reached toward the ignition. And that's when I heard it—this growl, like a faraway motor, coming from the sideyard. I grabbed the dashboard, braced myself, then I realized. Snoring. It was the Bouncer snoring. It seemed to carry, this sound, around the house, across the yard, over the driveway. I pictured it following us down the street, across the Canyon. I pictured it following us all the way to the mountains. I thought of snow, endless silent smothering snow.

That's when I did something unusual. I buckled my seatbelt. Ma glanced over.

"D-drive like hell," I said. "Head for the hills and d-don't look back, that's my m-motto."

And then we were gone. As if we'd never existed. As if during the earthquake the street had pulled up, and when it settled again, we'd disappeared. Only before we turned the last corner, I did it. I looked back. Here it was, a week before Christmas, and on that whole block only one house without decorations. Because the Bouncer didn't believe in Christmas. Ma, however, did. The Toyota, after all, was his. And we had a head start.

8

Roadsong

They were everywhere and they were looking for me. So when my aunt came to pick me up at the Seaview Trailer Court, I ducked down in the front seat of her car to keep the California Youth Authority from doing their job.

   I'd been staying at the Seaview with Maria, this homegirl from Juvenile Detention, and her family, including a couple babies and an uncle. They were nice enough to take me in. It was easier listening to the Garcias hollering in Spanish things I didn't understand, than listening to Ma hollering in plain English things having generally to do with my being a nutcase from satan who might benefit greatly from a few electrodes to the brain compliments of the State Hospital system.

   At Juvey the big topic of discussion with the counselors was Vocation, what jobs were out there, what you had to do to get one, was there training involved. The big topic of discussion with the inmates was Emancipation, who got it, what you had to do to get it, was there ass-kissing involved. In between all this discussing, I'd entertain the troops by reading aloud from the RECORD book, which is how I met Maria. The RECORD book had turned into a sort of diary featuring The Story of My Life by Yours Truly. I'd been writing in it ever since the bus ride which got me to California, and kept it in a secret zippered compartment in my backpack.

During Time Outs at the Center, Maria taught me mall hair, which she'd learned from her cousin the cosmetologist. I taught her poker. And in spite of the fact that most nights back at the Seaview we were cleaning up on her uncle and his doosh-bag buddies, Maria called them, who couldn't run a bluff to save their sorry-ass souls, she said, They know nada, she said, still I was glad to be leaving. Things at the Seaview were getting crowded.

My aunt was driving a big black Lincoln Continental she'd scored from her mother. That would be my grandmother on my dad's side—Grandma Rosa Angelina Tomassino Ganarelli—who owned a combination wig shop/bingo parlor in Toledo. That's where we were headed, Ohio, though it would take us awhile to get there. My aunt was a musician. She'd booked a few gigs on the way.

Ma, who wasn't a musician but who'd had a long meaningful relationship with a scale, she goes, Ha ha, she goes, was living in Malibu with a guy with one hand. The guy's name was Tiny. Though he was anything but, being of the six-four/two-forty variety. Just remember looks are deceiving, says Ma, he's gentle as a day-old kitten, poor thing.

He was also anything but poor, having more money than a person could spend if they stayed awake for a year. It seems one day Tiny's father—who owned a couple of factories and a forest—went for a spin in his lear jet and was never heard from again. Next thing Tiny knows he's a rich rich man, his mother having drowned a few years earlier in a swimming pool in Bel Air. So Tiny moves to a beachhouse in Malibu and becomes an animal rescuer. Say some asshole shoots a hawk or runs into a deer or porcupine, or maybe a pelican drinks gasoline. Tiny the animal rescuer would take the poor thing home and nurse it back to health. And here's the thing: he did it for nothing. I know, I asked.

Of course the animals Tiny rescued could care less if they found themselves in some joint with marble stairs and a cabana. They were just glad not to wake up roadkill. And I was glad not to wake up in a concrete room, the maid and the marble fish pond and the ocean grooving out back were just extras. But Ma. Ma thought she'd died and gone to the North Pole. She'd finally gotten all she'd ever wanted in this life, a real live man with money, one-handed or not.

After all she'd been through, she said, starting with, but never mind don't get her started, the point was, it just goes to show good things come to those who wait. I silently counted all she'd been through—starting with my dad, continuing on with Jack, Elroy, Delta Dave, the Elvises One, Two and Three, and so on—until I ran out of toes, too. Define wait, I go, so Ma goes, I said don't goddamn start with me. Then she goes, 'Tis better to have loved and lost than never to have lost at all, goddamn remember that.

I remember that my aunt and my ma didn't get along too well. Basically they hated each other's guts. My aunt blamed my ma for ruining my dad's life. My ma blamed my aunt for ruining my gene pool, she called it.

"It's the Sicilian blood makes her do these things!" Ma'd cried to the officer on duty that night, that famous night, begging him to overlook the broken liquor store window. Her lipstick was still bright pink, she hadn't said goddamn once. It was three in the morning. With Ma standing there all fluttery and helpless, that cop had wavered for a minute, I could tell. His fat cop mind was going round and round, one of his fat cop fingers was doing the same, and I couldn't help it. I spit— a good long one—across the desk, over his fat circling finger, right onto the gray linoleum beside his fat cop shoe.

Sixty days later, when I left the CYA Detention Center, I went to live with my new friend Maria Garcia with the tall tall hair. I was feeling more and more Sicilian all the time.

206 MINIMUM MAINTENANCE

I was at the Seaview for the second—maybe the third—time, when my aunt comes to get me in the big Lincoln. The car slides up, I slide in, the car slides away. That simple. An hour later we're turning off Highway One somewhere in Malibu. Coast is clear, says my aunt, and she pats my shoulder. I sit up. Then she says, Coast is Clear, that'd make a good name for a band. We drive past the familiar set of black iron gates, head down the long curvy driveway. Palm trees line up along either side like cops.

"Tiny's loaded," I said, pulling my tall tall hair off the ceiling.

"I can see that," says my aunt, dodging a coconut.

On our way out of California we're stopping in Malibu to see Ma, to say our good-byes and pick up my birth certificate (I'll be needing it, says my aunt) and, I hope, a coyote, though my aunt doesn't know yet about the coyote.

The long long driveway leading to the beachhouse in Malibu where Ma has finally settled down with a rich rich man, ends in a wide loop in front of wide steps in front of a wide front door. The door is actually two doors, each one tall and wide and wooden, carved from top to bottom with the faces of animals. Some are actual animals, others made up. But real or not, the faces have one thing in common: they all seem calm. Even friendly. The Peaceable Kingdom, Tiny calls it.

In the beginning—before that famous night, before the cop and the Center and the Seaview, before my aunt in her big black Lincoln and all the rest—I'd lived here, too, for awhile, in Malibu with Ma. For me it wasn't so much the house. I was just happy not to be in a holding pen. For me it was the grounds, Tiny called it. I loved the grounds. I loved to wander up and down the driveway, through the gardens, out by the ocean. I loved to hang out around the pens and cages where at any given time some animal might be recuperating.

But what I loved most was to stand beside that big front door and run my hands over those faces, which looked like they were just itching to push themselves right on out of that wood and take off running. They even had names. My favorite was a combination cat/unicorn called Peggy. Ma told me I had no imagination.

"How're you going to get into the movies," she said, "if 'Peggy' is all you can come up with?" She still had it in her head that I was destined to be a movie star. She'd come upon me one morning while I was standing at the door, and she'd heard me talking.

That's what I'd do in the mornings, while she was still snoring away, when the sun poked through the early ocean fog straight down the long curvy driveway onto that door. The faces looked almost alive then, in that wavery yellow sun. And I couldn't help it, I'd start talking to them. As the sun moved up, the shadowy ins and outs in the wood shifted ever so slightly, so that mouths moved and talked, eyes blinked and watched.

So when Ma made fun of Peggy that day, I couldn't tell her, I knew she wouldn't understand. Because here's the thing: I didn't make those names up. The faces told me their own names, after they'd learned to trust me. We'd been at Tiny's for ages, maybe a couple of weeks. I'd been standing in front of the Peaceable Kingdom for many mornings, when the faces decided to clue me in. I learned that, besides Peggy, there was Jeffrey, Kathleen, Mimi and Billy Boy, a combination deer/dolphin.

When me and Ma first found ourselves in Malibu, we'd stayed in the backhouse, though this particular backhouse was anything but. She just didn't want to seem too pushy, Ma said. Until, slowly but surely, the push was on. She started staying nights in the main house. She said they were only friends. She said that Timothy, she called him, didn't like being alone in that big echoey place, that she stayed in the room next to his and left the connecting door open so he could hear her moving around in her sleep.

"It comforts Timothy," she'd said between breaths, "to hear me like that." I'd come upon her, back behind the cabana, doing situps where no one could see.

As for me, I stayed by myself out in the backhouse by the ocean, practicing smoke rings and hairdos and listening to the wind and the waves and the animals moving around in their cages.

One afternoon I was following Tiny around the grounds. A salty wind tilted my hair. The ocean was big, the air so bright it hurt. We were at sea level. I looked out at the big bright water, and I asked Tiny, was he ever afraid that old ocean would just rear up, take a swipe at him and his grounds and his cages, at all his neighbors, sort of clean up the beach once and for all? Like it'd been lying low, acting mellow for centuries, when all the time it had the upper hand?

"You know," I said, "like a tidal wave?"

We'd stopped in front of a cage where a coyote limped steadily back and forth, one of its legs in a fat cast like bread dough. The coyote's eyes were the color of the waves where they stretched upward just before falling over.

Tiny tells me there's another word for tidal wave. He reaches between the bars and picks a roly poly off the rim of the coyote's water bucket, puts it in the shade of a eucalyptus outside the cage, watches it waddle away. His other arm, the one that ends in a knob, he usually keeps tucked in a front pocket. He doesn't believe in hooks. I know, I asked.

"And anyway," he says, "so what if it happens? Tidal wave? Earthquake? Typhoon? You might say life's a crap shoot."

The coyote stopped moving and stared at me. I squinted up at Tiny. "But, just in case," I said, "wouldn't you like rather live somewhere else? Somewhere higher?"

Tiny laughed so sudden the coyote jumped. "Yeah? Like where?" he said, and pulled the flask out of his back pocket.

I shielded my eyes, looked around. I pointed across the Coast Highway, to where the hills sat bunched together along the horizon like muffins. Tiny said they were mountains, but I wasn't so sure.

"How about up there?"

Tiny glanced over his shoulder. His breath smelled sticky.

"The real thing comes," he says, "a person wouldn't be safe up there either. Anyway, nobody lives up there, except a few cats, and our friend here." He nods at the coyote, raises the flask, works the cork out with his thumb and a finger.

"Not to mention snakes," he says, "big ornery things, get you in a New York minute."

He points the flask at his tall black pointy-toed boots with the curlicue designs up the sides. My hair gets pins and needles. I'm thinking this is familiar, like it happened before. Like that watchacallit, that deja view.

"Rattler wraps its teeth around these," says Tiny, lifting the toe of his boot, "it's got its work cut out."

He looks me square in the face. "Remember that," he says.

But now I'm remembering something else: Elroy, the House of Cars, getting stoned and following garter snakes around. I'm remembering Elroy's little carved horse, and the look on Little Ralphie's face the day I gave Diamond to him. The day of the earthquake back in the Canyon. I'm wondering what Elroy would say about giving Diamond away like that, or giving her away to someone like Little Ralphie, or about earthquakes or California in general.

Tiny smiles, slips the flask into his pocket, walks back across the grounds toward the house. I turn toward the coyote, who's still staring at me.

"Hey, Sue," I go. I've decided to name her Sue Nommy, after the wave.

Sue just watches me with her green eyes that never blink. After awhile one of her ears twitches. I walk to the corner of the cage, Sue limps alongside. I walk to the other corner, Sue follows me there. I fake to the left, Sue does likewise. So I sit down, pull the RECORD book out of my backpack, start filling her in on things.

Sometimes I read from the book, sometimes I just talk. But I tell her all of it. The whole shebang. My Life Story. Starting with my earliest memory, red cans rolling across a blue floor, which would've been my dad and that Beefaroni, Ma said, something that jarhead got a real kick out of, rolling various food items to his baby girl across the kitchen linoleum, she said. My dad, who could be in hell for all she cared, only the last she'd heard it was still Montana or maybe Alaska.

I just started with those cans and continued on from there. I must've gone on forever, maybe twenty minutes. Sue just watched and listened. Eventually I got to California, and that famous night: Last Chance Liquors, the Youth Authority, Maria and the Seaview.

I lowered the RECORD book. I messed with a little pile of sand outside Sue's cage. Then I started in on the next chapter, a little episode I hadn't gotten around to writing about just yet, that Ma hadn't gotten around to hearing about just yet, though I had a feeling my buddies the cops were zeroing in. That empty patrol car sitting at the curb, doors unlocked, keys in the ignition, just sitting there asking for it, I said. Like a girl would have to be in a coma, I said, to pass up an opportunity like that.

Finally I got around to my aunt, who had a gig that night up in Oxnard. Ma was taking me to hear her for the first time.

"And the best part," I said, and looked Sue square in the face, "she gets paid to do it! My aunt! Can you believe it? I'm like related to a fucking musician!"

For the first time, Sue blinked. We were at eye level.

After the big bright day, Tiny's front hall was a cave. Long and dark and cool, it might've been the quietest place on earth. I cleared my throat. The sound echoed for a couple seconds. I cleared it again. Again the echo. I took a deep breath.

"Hey!" I called, and a voice answered.

"Peace and love!" said the voice.

I spun around, ready to bolt. Then I saw: over in the corner by the marble stairway stood a tall metal cage with a green and red bird the size of a small TV perched on a swing in the middle. The bird's head made a complete turn on its body. It opened its box of a mouth.

"Sex and drugs!" it goes.

"Fuckenay!" I go, then I'm running up the cool white stairs two at a time, my heart banging.

I found Ma in the room she'd told me was hers, leaning over a dresser, staring into a mirror. Her hands rested along either side of her face, her long red fingernails pushed the skin at her temples upward. She looked Chinese. She turned her head first to the left, then the right. I tiptoed in.

"Sex and drugs!" I go, and flop onto a blue velvet couch. Ma gasps and grabs the dressertop. Her face falls back in place. Her eyes catch mine in the mirror.

"Goddamn it, Sugar! You are going to be the goddamn death of me, I swear."

I searched my pockets for a smoke and checked out my surroundings. The arms of the couch were carved tigers' heads, the back, a carved tail. The legs, which were carved paws, sat on the edge of a rug the size of a parking lot. The rug was blue like the couch and reached to the corners of the room. One wall was all windows with the drapes pulled, another closets with the doors shut. One wall was all nature paintings—trees and rocks and rivers and shit. Ma's bed sat in the middle of the blue rug, covered by a red velvet blanket with gold fringe. Matching pillows the size of Volkswagens were piled on the floor. The whole shebang could be seen again in the ceiling, which was all mirrors. I felt dizzy. I scraped a match along the zipper of my jeans.

"Like what's with the bird?" I said, and lit a cigarette.

Ma tucked her hair behind her ears and uncapped a lipstick. She leaned forward, drew on a new mouth outside the lines of the old one. She pulled a kleenex from the box, brought it up to her new lips, kissed it. She was ignoring me.

"I said, where'd the bird in the hall come from?"

Ma sighed, a little too loudly. "A commune in Topanga Canyon. Somebody gave it a hit of green pyramid and set it free. It fell off a power line into the neighbor's swimming pool. Tiny's thinking of keeping it."

I thought about this, and blew a smoke ring. "Like a butler," I said, "to greet guests? To go with the maid?" I searched for the smoke ring in the mirror above me.

"Whatever," said Ma, sucking in her stomach, looking sideways at the dresser mirror. She turned back and started the Chinese routine with her face again. I kicked off my hightops and stood up. The rug was blue quicksand.

"So what's the news from the front?" I said, which was something my dad used to say the once or twice a year he'd drop by to check up on us, and, by the way, inquire as to whether his foxy ex was back on the dole, and if so, was there a little extra laying around? By the way, he'd say, what do they call a fox's kid, a foxette? Anyway, that described the both of us to a foxy T, he'd say.

If Ma remembered any of this, she wasn't copping to it.

"Not that it's any of your goddamn beeswax," she said, "but Tiny's offered to pay for a lift and a tuck. Maybe even an augmentation."

She dropped her hands and puffed out her chest, studied

it from a couple different angles. I laid my cigarette in the ashtray and waded across the blue rug toward the door to the other room.

"It's never been my strong suit," she went on. "It's always been my legs they come for." She turned to the side again, smoothed her hand along her stomach. "But, I guess, what would be the point? Tiny says I'll never have to dance again, if I don't want to. Can you imagine? My dancing days are over, he says, gone like the buffalo ..."

But I didn't hear any more. I was through the door.

According to Ma, this was Tiny's room. This room also had a wall of closets, a wall of windows, and the bed, like Ma's, sat in the middle facing the open doorway. But as for the rest, plain as dirt. No velvet couch or rug, no pillows or pictures or mirrors on the ceiling. Just that small bed with a plain white blanket and a small wooden table alongside. I was thinking, Now *this* is a room, if ever I wanted a room, *this* would be it. In here, if you looked at a thing, you knew it was the thing itself, not some reflection. This room was simple. Easy. Nothing to trip over, nowhere to get lost. Just walk on in, kick off your shoes, flick off the light, catch some Zs.

I walked on over to the table beside the bed and switched on a small lamp. The tabletop was glass, smudged and dusty. I could see my face there, only blurry, like looking through smoke. Hazy, like in a dream. I pulled at a small drawer. It jerked open. A syringe rattled out. I stared at it.

"Nam," Ma said suddenly from the doorway. My arm jerked around, knocking over the lamp. The bulb shattered against the floor.

"Fuckenay!" I said and stepped back, my foot crunching glass. Ma was staring at the closed drapes across the room like they might be a movie screen.

"He could've gotten out of it, I'm sure," she said, "all this money. Only he wanted to go. He enlisted, he told me. His father was still alive." She yawned, started toward the window. "He did it to spite the old man, is what I think."

I was thinking something didn't feel quite right. My foot felt hot. I lifted my foot and looked over my shoulder. A chunk of glass poked from the bottom of my stocking, in the middle of a red circle growing redder. I grabbed the edge of the bed.

"Ma..."

She reached out and pulled open the drapes. Light blasted the room.

"I guess things happened over there," she said, stepping back. "Things ... happen. Whatever."

I pulled off my stocking. Dark red drops fell onto the shiny white tile. I squeezed the skin together, the drops fell faster.

"Ma ..." I said again.

She turned toward me. "What *is* it?"

I looked up, saw her face, looked away. "It's just ... it's ... what's green pyramid?"

"Oh for godssake," she said, and glanced down.

Then she said, "The maid'll get that, she's doing this floor today. Tile wipes up easy."

She started back toward her room, talking over her shoulder. "A goddamn maid! Can you imagine? Whoever said money isn't everything? I goddamn beg to differ."

And I was thinking, A maid. What about maiding? I'd have to remember to ask Ma more about it. After all, I'd been cleaning up after Ma all these years. To hold up my end of the bargain, she'd say, and when I asked what bargain that might be, she'd say the one she made with god to go through with it and have me in the first place.

I was thinking, As a maid, I might be a real shoe-in.

◆ ◆ ◆

My aunt's stage name was Road Warrior. She did a combination acid polka/sit down comic routine, she called it. The first time I met her, she was on the western leg of a three-month tour.

"I like to mix it up, keep 'em guessing," she told me, when I finally caught her act, at an all-night bowling alley in Oxnard.

Me and Ma had driven up in Tiny's special-made Vette, which we parked in the blue handicap slot. My aunt had tried to time her jokes with the crash of balls hitting pins. When that didn't work, she ran the accordion through a phase shifter, turned the reverb up to ten.

"This here's the acid part!" she shouted, and we never heard another strike.

My ears were still ringing a few days later when Ma got the phone call. They'd finally tracked her down at Tiny's. I was there, too, and accidentally picked up the hall extension. It was the Youth Authority, concerning my latest adventure. The one featuring that empty patrol car. I replaced the receiver and stood in the long still hallway, grinding my teeth, listening to Ma in the other room.

"Mm-hmm, mm-hmm," she repeated, in her Barbie-doll voice, I called it. Finally she hung up, dialed again, asked for my aunt.

"Francesca Ganarelli, room three-o-six," I heard her say, a little too loudly. That's when I hightailed it.

I could hear Ma screaming into the phone all the way out by Sue, whose leg seemed much better. In between paces, Sue stood like a statue in the middle of her cage and stared at me. Her eyes were see-through. She might've been trying to tell me something. We were just visiting.

On the way back to Maria's that afternoon, Ma went on and on. Her pupils were wide and black, her fingers shook on the little leather steering wheel.

"Three weeks out of lockup," she hollered, "you're back at it! Just another goddamn JD nutcase, stealing whatever isn't

216 MINIMUM MAINTENANCE

nailed down, trashing a police car for godssake! How goddamn stupid can you get?" She took a big breath.

"And you think you have a case for Emancipation?" She glanced over. "Yeah, that's right, don't think I don't know what you're up to with all your little dirtball friends, making all your little ridiculous plans. The rate you're going, they'll laugh you right out of court, if they don't goddamn haul your ass to jail!"

Suddenly the Vette veered toward the left lane, a station wagon laid on its horn.

"JESUS FUCKING CHRIST!" I hollered, and punched her.

Her head jerked toward me, tears squirted out of her eyes. "WHAT THE ... WHO DO YOU THINK YOU ARE?"

"YOUR FUCKING KID THAT'S WHO!" I hollered, and punched her again.

Her arm flew up away from me, her head jerked back toward the freeway. I raised my fist to hit her again, then I couldn't help it. I started to cry. Really bawl. In fact I started to scream.

Ma managed to pull over onto the shoulder. She waited, calmly, and smoked a cigarette. She sat with the window rolled down, smoking while I screamed, her bangs moving lightly back and forth, the Vette rocking like a cradle in the wind from the freeway traffic.

After awhile, between screams, I started to notice something. Something in the background. Each car made this sound. Not the steady whooshing sound of traffic, but a long single note like music. I could hear the note approaching from way off. Then as the car passed, the note changed to a lower note, until that car-note faded away, and I started listening for the next one.

I stopped screaming in order to hear better. That's when Ma laid down the law.

"That's it, it's settled," she said, in a voice I'd never heard before. "You're going with Francesca, back to Ohio. Let them deal with you. I can't do it any more."

This new voice was quiet and steady and careful. Like she might be announcing for Bowl-A-Rama, or trying not to stutter. She hadn't said goddamn once. I looked over. Her arm was turning color where I'd hit her. I opened my mouth, but my words disappeared in the note of a passing semi.

Ma kicked me out the first time for setting one of her costumes on fire.

We'd been living in Venice, a block from the beach, waiting for our ship to come in. We'd been waiting for this particular ship across half the country, and so far, nothing. Nada. But Ma goes, Look out that window, what do you see? a goddamn ocean, that's what, and what sails the ocean? I rest my case, keep your eyes peeled.

Our apartment had a small balcony where I'd sit for hours, smoking Thai, keeping my eyes peeled. Not for ships, for rollerskaters. One of Ma's acquaintances, Barry from Bozeman, had provided the Thai. He'd also provided me my own pair of skates.

"Oberhamers," he'd told me proudly, "City Roller wheels."

Barry claimed to have known a guy who knew a guy who knew my dad in Montana. Ma believed him, but I wasn't so sure. Barry also claimed to leave his body while he slept and travel the planet. He called it projection. I wondered if he projected to Bozeman then, or somewhere else. I never asked.

The Oberhamers were barely broken in when I knew I'd never be a skater. I had scars on my knees and elbows I figured would be there when I croaked, a tingling in my shoulder which wouldn't quit. In the end what I liked best was the look. So I hung out on the balcony in cut-off T-shirts, leather wrist guards and neon short-shorts, listening to Eddy Grant and INXS on a big yellow headphone radio, getting stoned and watching the *real* skaters down below through my Foster Grants.

There were skaters alone, skaters in pairs, skaters in long curvy lines like snakes. Skaters who'd spin for minutes in a blurry circle, then stop on a dime and skate away, as if they'd suddenly had a conniption and now it was over. There were skaters who'd skate by backward in the morning, then backward again in the afternoon, and in between, when I went down to the beach to profile, there they'd be skating backward.

Sometimes I hung the Oberhamers over my shoulder and took them with me down to the beach. I rubbed beach tar on the big red wheels, scraped the toe stops against a curb, bit off one of the laces. I'd hang out on a bench along the paved bike path trying to sweat and look exhausted. After awhile I pawned them, forty bucks. Nobody asked what happened to the skates. Meanwhile, I continued my balcony routine.

Ma, meanwhile, continued hers: dance, sleep, watch for that ship, pick up the Welfare check. Her latest thing was tanning topless on the balcony behind a Mexican blanket. So I'm all one shade when I dance, she goes. Most of the time I skipped school, she didn't seem to notice. I worried that sooner or later she'd put her foot down about the pot, until one day she asked for a hit and told me I rolled a good doobie. When she showed up in the afternoons with her blanket and her cardboard sun reflector, I'd grab my yellow radio and well-rolled doobies and head for the beach.

And I had my chores. While Ma slaved on stage, I did my bit to earn my keep, namely, keep the apartment from being taken over by cigarette butts and Jack-in-the-Box wrappers and empty boxes of wine, not to mention all the little shifting dunes of beach sand.

I was gathering the laundry one day when I came upon one of Ma's costumes—uniforms, she called them—lodged in the foot of her bed. At first I thought it was a tarantula and started to have a conniption. Then I saw what it really was, and I couldn't help it. I took the thing out on the balcony, threw it in the Webber, squirted it with lighter fluid and lit a match. Then I lit a joint and sat back to watch. The flame died down, so I tore up the sheets one by one and added them. When the Mexican blanket caught fire, I burned that, too. For safety's sake.

Next morning I was yanked out of bed by my hair.

"You're outta here!" Ma screamed. "You're a goddamn nutcase! I don't want to see your face for a goddamn long time!" She stomped out to the balcony, clothed, and smoked a cigarette, while I threw some things in my backpack.

That first time lasted three weeks.

Mostly I hung out at the beach, begging change, getting stoned, trading a joint with some rollerskater for a place to crash. A couple skaters let me stay in their cars. One skater, Ramone—who could come out of a toe spin skating backward—let me stay in his apartment. A few other kids were staying there, too, and it was at Ramone's I learned to cook.

Ramone had shaved his afro, wore five earrings in one ear, was a Virgo and a vegetarian, and ate mostly Italian. So in exchange for our beds, the prima veras, he called us, did the cooking. We learned three-cheese ravioli, spaghetti marinara, fettucini al fredo, and how to mince garlic and tear lettuce and open a wine bottle without eighty-sixing the cork.

"I'm getting in touch with my roots!" I told Ramone, and he flashed me his gold tooth.

"They're getting the fuck outta here!" Ramone's boyfriend told him, when he got out of jail, and the prima veras were back on the street.

By then Ma had calmed down and bought new linen.

Ma kicked me out the second time for the cigarette contest.

I was having this little party, just a couple of the prima veras. We'd stayed in touch. We'd been drinking tequila and chianti in the kitchen of the Venice apartment, I was entertaining the troops with the RECORD book. Then we started doing hits of hash. I can't remember who started the contest, but I won: I held a cigarette on my wrist, right in the middle of my spider tattoo, longer than anyone. When I lifted it off there was this funny smell in the air, and Ma was flipping out in the doorway.

 I didn't go back to the apartment for a couple months that time. When I did, Ma had moved. The lady next door with all the cats told me where. To a beachhouse in Malibu, some guy named Timothy.

◆ ◆ ◆

Road Warrior pulled the big Lincoln to a stop in front of the wide front steps of the beachhouse.

 "How'd she book this gig?" she asked, craning her neck to see the top of the house.

 "A dealer at the casino where she used to work," I said.

 "And . . . ?" said Road Warrior.

 "Earlene had this friend Tiny in California, she said. So Ma says she's leaving for greener pastures, so Earlene says, here, take this, this is like as green as it gets, and she gives Ma Tiny's phone number."

 Road Warrior twisted around to check out the marble fountain.

 "Earlene thought Ma and Tiny might get along," I said. "It might be in the cards, she thought."

 "And why, pray tell, would she think that?"

 "She like read Ma's tea leaves. There it was, this big 'T'."

 "So that's it?" said R.W.

 I thought for a minute. "Earlene used to be a man."

 My aunt looked at me.

 I said, "Earlene and Tiny met at the State Hospital."

My aunt blinked.

"Ma thinks I might benefit from the same thing," I said.

"A sex change?" said my aunt, and I said,

"No, shock treatments."

"I see," she said, nodding. "You know, that'd be a good name for a band."

"Sex Change?" I said, and my aunt said, Actually I was thinking Shock Treatment, but that'd be groovy, too.

"So anyway," I said, "Ma gets to California, she calls the number, he's not available. She calls again a few days later, same thing." I thought for a minute. "I wonder if that was the maid she talked to? Anyway, Ma just keeps calling, you know, like a routine, like smoking or stopping by Welfare. Until like what do you know, one day he's there."

Then I said, "The rest is history," which is what Ma said the time I asked her how I happened to get started in the first place, let alone born. First she'd said, The way your dad held a cue stick.

"Anyway," I said, "Tiny, he's like always been rich—and a man, too—but the main thing about Tiny . . ."

"Yo, Princess," says R.W., raising her palm, "too much info, no more about the Tiny thing," and she turns off the ignition.

Road Warrior combed her eyebrows in the rearview mirror, checked the back seat to make sure the blanket hadn't fallen off her sound equipment. Then she popped the trunk release and got out and walked back to check on her accordion. It lay in its big black case like a coffin, surrounded by piles of loose clothes and bedding and a few empty whiskey bottles.

It was hot. The sun had baked the fog away. The heat sat on top my hair like a cap. I could hear the ocean, like traffic, back behind the house.

R.W. slammed the trunk and took a few steps, then stopped dead in her tracks. She was staring up at the Peaceable Kingdom, mouth open, hands stuffed in the pockets of her black leather jeans. I remember my dad telling me one of his sisters had been Queen of Toledo. I tried picturing Road Warrior with a crown, then dropped it. Though she did have eyelashes. Not to mention hair.

"What have we here?" she said, moving up the steps toward the huge door, her spurs flashing in the sun.

I listed them. "Peggy, Jeffrey, Billy Boy, Mimi..."

"My, my," said my aunt.

"It's called the Peaceable Kingdom," I said, And yes, I said, that'd be a groovy name for a band. I pulled the bell chain, the Peaceable Kingdom swung open.

"Nice threads," said R.W., and the maid blushed and looked down at her apron. I was picturing myself in just such a get-up, wondering if you got a color choice, or if black-and-white was the name of the game.

We followed the maid's big bow across the entrance hall. I glanced toward the cage in the corner.

"Peace and love!" I said.

"Sex and drugs!" said the green and red bird.

"Holy shit!" said my aunt.

The maid led us into the morning room, she called it, and pulled the hall door closed behind us. Ma and Tiny were waiting for us, perched on bamboo chairs around a bamboo table, sipping drinks with little bamboo umbrellas sticking out. Plants dripped from the ceiling, waved from the corners, sprouted from the floor.

"Yo, Tarzan," says Road Warrior, looking at Tiny.

"Sugarpie," says Ma, looking at me.

I looked at the three of them.

"Check ya later," I said, and headed through a set of glass doors out onto the grounds to look for Sue.

In my backpack in the car I had a red leather collar and matching leash I'd pocketed from the Pet Peeve near Maria's, and a red rubber bone Maria had given me that morning as a going-away. We'd been standing out in front of the trailer at the Seaview, waiting for Road Warrior, when she gave it to me—wet, from one of the babies chewing on it.

"So are coyotes allowed in motels or what?" she goes.

"If they're on a leash," I go.

Then I go, "Your cousin, the cosmetologist. I was wondering, is that like only in California, or do they have them in Ohio do you think?"

"I'd say they're like pretty much everywhere," she goes. "So maybe I'll like visit you, or whatever, in Toledo. So how far away is that?"

I was thinking of something Road Warrior had said.

"Like it's not the end of the earth," I go, "but you can see it from there."

I hurried in out of the sun, back through the glass doors into the morning room, just as Tiny handed R.W. a wad of cash. R.W. folded the money away. They glanced up.

"Where is she?" I said to Tiny.

"Pardon me?" he said.

"Sue ... the coyote ... did you like move her somewhere?"

They all three stared at me, their faces blank as boards. I was thinking about the Peaceable Kingdom. I tried to look calm. Even friendly.

I tried again. "She's not in her cage ..."

It was like these people couldn't understand English, like I'd come upon them in a dream. Only there'd been some sort of mix-up, this was somebody else's dream.

Finally Ma cleared her throat. "Sugarplum, look what I ... what we ... have for you." She smiled at Tiny. "You first."

Tiny reached under the table, held up a pair of pointy-toed boots with curlicue designs up the sides. The boots were tall and black, the curlicues yellow. He held the boots toward me.

"Now you can lose those," he said, smiling, nodding at my

camo hightops. My foot moved all on its own.

"Now me," says Ma.

She set her drink down on the table beside an envelope. She tapped the envelope with her long pointy fingernails. I could smell the polish.

"Your birth certificate," she says. "I found it, buried with some old stuff. I thought it was lost."

She kept her hand on the table. There was a big bright ring on her third finger. It might've been a diamond. She tapped the envelope again. The diamond flashed. I ignored her.

"Tiny," I said slowly, "what happened to the coyote?"

Tiny lowered the boots, looked from me to Ma, back again.

"Timothy?" I said, and he shrugged.

"She's gone," he said. "She recovered, I let her go." My knees started to shake. He looked me square in the face. "They get better, they leave. That's the way it works."

Then he said, "You know that, Darnelle."

Road Warrior's chair leg scraped the tile. Ma's new ring scraped her glass.

"What did you call me?" I asked Tiny, and maybe he said it again.

Only I couldn't hear. Tiny's mouth moved, my aunt's mouth moved, but I couldn't hear. My ears had started to ring. The ringing got louder and louder until everything else was drowned out. Like I'd fallen into a giant bell and all the air was one long sound.

I grabbed the envelope with my birth certificate and ran—back through the entrance hall, out past the Peaceable Kingdom, down the steps, up the driveway toward the Coast Highway. I was in a contest. I had to keep running. Running and running. I had to see how long I could stay in that bell of sound before it faded away.

When the ringing finally stopped, I was in a small valley between two hills. It might've been the quietest place on earth. I stood and listened and heard nothing. I turned and looked back and saw nothing. No ocean, no houses, no highway. Only the low muffin hills covered with flowers and rocks and brush and shit. I looked up. The sky was a wide blue bowl. I was under it. I was thinking, Now this is grounds, if ever I wanted grounds, this would be it.

"Fuckenay!" I said out loud, and waited. For what, I don't know. Nothing happened. Nada.

I sat on a rock. I pulled the envelope from my pocket, opened it, read the paper inside, folded it up again. I looked around. Then I stood and cleared my throat.

"Darnelle." I said the name.

I said it again, louder.

"Darnelle!" This time I heard a faint echo.

I took a great deep breath, and opened my box of a mouth. "DARNELLE!"

And suddenly there it was, filling the air, coming back at me just like I'd said it,

"DAR-NELLE! -NELLE! -NELLE!"

I hollered my name again, and again my name came back. I started to laugh, and the voice laughed, too, so I laughed harder. It was like I wasn't alone. Like the voice belonged to someone, someone who'd been waiting there, maybe for a long time. Someone who'd been following me, one step behind, just waiting for me to turn around. All I'd had to do was turn around and call.

I threw back my head to call her again, when I heard a scream. High above in the blue sky bowl, a hawk was circling, slowly. As if it had all the time in the world. As if maybe it was following its own shadow on the hillside below. I tried to imagine how I might look to that hawk, a small beige blur in all that green and brown, hollering my beige head off.

And that was it. The big quiet sky, the quiet circling hawk, and me, standing there hollering. Suddenly I felt embarrassed. I closed my mouth and looked down, away from the sky toward the ground, toward the place the hawk seemed to be circling. Then I saw: a coyote stood in the brush at the foot of the hill, silent and still, watching me.

◆ ◆ ◆

Tiny never believed me about the coyote.

By the time he came huffing and puffing over the hill, waving those black boots around with that big lonely hand, and found me running back and forth and twirling in circles, the coyote was gone. We'd been chasing around, me and the coyote, just dancing and goofing and generally acting mental, when all of a sudden it stopped dead in its tracks and looked me square in the face. That coyote just stared. Its eyes were the color of the waves. Then it turned, and in a New York minute, it was gone. Like it vanished into thin air. Like it projected to Bozeman. That's when Tiny came over the hill.

I never mentioned the coyote to Ma, who was too busy crying and carrying on and generally acting sappy, while she followed Road Warrior's car up Tiny's long curvy driveway and pleaded with me to get off my goddamn vegetarian kick.

"You are what you eat," she sobbed, "and in your case, that makes you a goddamn noodle." I was watching her in the sideview mirror, thinking noodle was a step up from nutcase.

"And another thing," she sniffed, wiping her eyes, "it wouldn't hurt you to send a goddamn postcard now and then. They're small, you can write big."

By now she was really blubbering, and she must've forgot about it for a second, she almost gouged her eye with the diamond.

My aunt sort of believed me, but she didn't think it was Sue

I'd seen.

"Life isn't that groovy," she said. "Shit like that only happens in the movies."

"I'll never be in the movies now," I said, and blew a smoke ring.

This was a few weeks later, after my adventure in the muffin mountains. Me and Road Warrior were sitting on a bed far from California, leaning against the padded headrest, in a motel room on the outskirts of Des Moines. R.W. liked the idea of outskirts.

"More privacy," she said, "cheaper booze." Also it would make a good name for a band, she said.

We were watching the TV test pattern, listening to the rain, passing a pint. She said after all I'd been through, I deserved a good belt, only don't make it a habit. We'd spent the afternoon playing poker. I was twelve dollars and thirty-five cents richer. Now the cards lay jumbled around us like leaves on the flowery bedspread. Tomorrow we'd be back on the road, headed for her next gig on the outskirts of Milwaukee.

I'd stayed mad at her through four states, so it must've been the whiskey made me finally blurt it out, there on the bed: I knew Tiny had paid her to take me off their hands.

"I saw him give you money," I said, "in the morning room in Malibu. You like tried to hide it, but I saw."

R.W. stared at me for a minute. Then her eyebrows lifted like two jets taking off.

"That was for weed, for chrissake. You stayed pissy halfway across the country for a lousy half ounce?" She shook her head and passed me the Jack Daniels. "Here, Puss, snap on this. It was all for nothin', nothin' at all."

I thought about this, and blew a smoke ring toward the black boots, which I was wearing. I lifted my leg. The ring caught perfectly around the pointy black toe. Also I was wearing the red leather dog collar, which fit perfectly around my white neck.

"You know, that'd look groovy on a drum set," said R.W., pointing at the test pattern.

"How 'bout a T-shirt?" I go.

"How 'bout a bumper sticker?"

"How 'bout a tattoo?"

Road Warrior grinned. "Yo, Peaches, let's check it out," she said, and pulled at the neckline of my T-shirt.

The night before, while Francesca Ganarelli was cranking up her accordion at the American Inn out on the highway, I'd borrowed the Lincoln and drove around until I found an open tattoo parlor, run by a guy named Frank, who tried talking me into something a little more elaborate. I know what I want, I go, take it or leave it. So Frank hands me a lude, pops the Stones in the tape player, smokes a bowl, and tattoos my name, "Darnelle," real pretty, just above where my heart would be. I was back at the motel before Road Warrior would've had time to dust off her phase shifter.

"So like, my whole life, how come no one ever told me my *real* name?" I said, peeling back the bandage. "Just tell me that much."

R.W. leaned in for a closer look. The bed crabbed loudly.

"Because no one *knew* your real name, for chrissake," she said. "Except your old lady. We all just figured she'd named you Sugar."

"But, my whole life," I said, "what the fuck kind of a name is that?" I tried looking at my chest, only this made my neck hurt.

"It's your fucking name, is what," said R.W. "This new one'll take some getting used to." She had a swallow of whiskey. "And while we're at it," she said, "could you do something for me? Enough with the Road Warrior bit. Could you like call me Fran?"

I said the new name to myself a few times, then out loud. "Fran. Yeah, sure. Fran." I looked at her. "It'll take some getting used to."

Fran slapped me a high five, reached over and touched the flowery letters on my chest. She had no fingernails to speak of. She bit them on purpose, she said, on account of they interferred with more important things, for instance, beer can-opening and/or accordion-playing. She herself had four tattoos, none of them visible at the moment. She'd only showed me three. The fourth, she said, was at heaven's gate, to be seen by those who'd died and gone there. I'd pretty much decided it wasn't Aunt Fran who'd been that queen.

Now she said, "I know! You could wait tables in some cocktail joint! You wouldn't have to wear a name tag!" She laughed and had another hit of J.D.

Then she said, "That broad we called, when we went through Nevada? She seemed pretty groovy, bet she could get you a waitress job."

I looked at her, then back at the test pattern. I was thinking, You're right about that, nobody's groovier than Earlene, who actually answered the phone after one ring, then actually started bawling when she heard my voice. But waitress?

I was thinking, If you're a queen or former queen, you'd probably never be a waitress. You probably basically had it made. Like being a movie star. And I'd lay odds you won't find many queens in Juvey Hall. Say Aunt Fran had been a queen. Would she still have turned into Road Warrior? Or Ma, would she still have danced? Would I even be here?

I was thinking, Well, I'm fucking here. I'm no queen or queen's daughter. I've got to come up with fucking something. Waitress, maybe. Though the counselors at the Center probably wouldn't think much of that one. I could hear them now, The word's Vocation, ladies, not Vacation, ha ha, set your goals high, ladies, reach for the stars.

So maybe maid, then. Or cosmetologist. Bartender. Dealer. Card shark. Artist. Stock car racer.

Only none of these felt right, none of them fit. And not on account of what the counselors would say. The more I thought about it, the more I wasn't sure. All I knew was, if possible, I'd rather work *outside* than *inside*. If possible, I'd rather drive truck than like dance.

Then, all of a sudden, it came to me. Out of the blue. Like I might be having a vision or hallucination. Only this was different, this was real: musician! I could be a musician! It was fucking perfect! I could drive around *outside* through the land and scenery, from *inside* job to inside job. After all, my aunt was a musician, it was probably in my blood.

I glanced around for my backpack. I wanted to write this down in the RECORD book. In fact, I might start a whole new chapter: The Future. But then I realized, blood or no blood, to be a musician you needed to know how to play. You needed to have had lessons. And I'd never had a lesson in my life. So it was back to the queen thing. It's either in the cards—or the tea leaves—or it's not.

"I've never had a lesson in my life," I said. "Fuckenay," I said.

"How's that?" said Fran.

"I mean like even if I wanted to, you know, do what you do, I can't play. I don't know shit about it."

Fran looked at me. "Play? You talking about music?"

I nodded, my cheeks felt suddenly hot.

"Shit, girl," said Fran, "you wanna learn about music? I can teach you about chords and shit, give you a few pointers. It doesn't take much to get the general gist. You know, close enough for rock 'n roll."

She sat up straighter. "So what brought this up?"

I flicked the seven of diamonds off the bed with my thumb and finger. "I was thinking of, you know, jobs and shit. I was thinking like maybe I could, I don't know, play accordion ... or something."

Fran was quiet. Then she says, "Well, I could teach you what you need to know on that old box. But I've sort of, let's say, got the corner on the accordion market. Now you, you'd be better off with something ... well, smaller, let's say."

I studied the big black case propped against the wall by the door. I sat up straighter.

"How about harmonica!" says Fran, digging in her pockets. "Or even better, drums! All you need are a couple of sticks, you can practice anywhere."

"Like a drum set is small?" I go, and Fran goes, You got a point. Only I was thinking of something else.

Fran yawned and rolled over and popped another quarter in the Vibra-Bed. I watched the ten of clubs vibrate its way across the flowers to the edge of the bed.

"D-did you know what Ma said when I asked her about my b-birthday?" I said in my vibra-voice.

"Your b-birthday?" said Fran.

"I saw it, on my b-birth certificate. I was l-like born in the s-summer. M-Ma always said I was b-born in the fall. When I asked her, sh-she said what d-difference does it make, a g-girl has a right to h-hedge about her age."

"Oh b-brother," said Fran, and yawned again and reached for the pint.

When the ten of clubs finally fell, I got up and walked into the bathroom. I flicked on the light, pulled down the neck of my T-shirt, studied my new tattoo in the mirror. The light was too bright and it hurt my eyes, but I studied that mirror for a long long time. Like I was looking for something. For what, I don't know.

Then suddenly, I saw. Plain as day in those nice flowery letters, I saw it: "ellenraD."

I blinked and read it again: ELLENRAD

My ears started to ring.

I hurried back to the other room and crawled up next to

Fran. The bed had hit 4.5 on the Richter, a few more cards had fallen. She held out the J.D., but I shook my head. I'd started to notice something. Something in the background, like behind me somewhere. My ears were ringing, and in the ringing I was hearing this voice, like maybe it was a story, or maybe a song:

> *Toledo didn't work out so she went back to California. She applied for Emancipation and was never in a movie. She learned to be a waitress, got her own backhouse, cut her own hair. Made her own pasta, grew her own weed, had many pets, bought a guitar. She called her band the Prima Veras. One day she went into the mountains to look for a coyote. If this coyote was still there, the girl would find her. But the beauty part: no one would ever find the girl. She'd have become somebody else, a different person. Like the old one had just vanished and the new one's mother, Mrs. Rad (who thought movie stars were silly), had had the goddamn good sense to name her daughter Ellen.*

Beside me on the big motorized bed Road Warrior snored evenly. Her eyelashes lay still, her hair sprawled across the pillow like a map. I reached over and turned off the lamp. I turned the dog collar around so the buckle wouldn't pinch. Then I laid down, my head resting on the hair. It smelled like Prell and traffic, like cigarettes and trees. My hand moved through the hair until it found a shoulder.

I was thinking they were everywhere—cars, restrooms, police stations, store windows. I was thinking that from now on, all I had to do to remember who I was, was just find a mirror, just look in a mirror. It was that fucking simple. I could read, couldn't I?

I was thinking I could write. I was thinking maybe tomorrow I'd send Ma a postcard. From the rack in the motel lobby, the one with the old white horse walking along a trail through a field toward a barn. You can tell the horse is old by its back. You can tell it's evening by the sunset. Across the top, in the middle of the sunset, are the words, "ONE FOR THE ROAD." On the other side I'll write, "*We're halfway there*," and sign it, "*Peace & Love*." Or maybe "*Sex & Drugs*," depending. I might send one to my dad, too, care of General Delivery, Alaska. Like sending a letter to Santa, I was thinking. I'd have to remember to tell that one to Fran. But I'd decide about my dad tomorrow.

Across the room the test pattern glowed like a nightlight. I was listening to the cars out on the rainy highway, watching the headlights surf the walls. After awhile my ears stopped ringing. Then the bed stopped quaking, and I couldn't help it, I fell asleep. Or maybe I projected. Either way, with my boots on.

Epilogue

(August 1970)

Afterward Donna always said her baby was worth a can of beans. That's what she could afford. Others brought boxes of Tuna Helper, cartons of Pop Tarts, bags of granola and trail mix, six packs of Shasta. One guy brought an entire packing crate of Wheaties, Breakfast of Champions, wallpapered with "HHH" stickers. Grace from the Kum On Inn, where Donna had waited tables until a few weeks earlier, was bringing the restaurant-size can of green olives and the quart jar of maraschino cherries she'd copped from the supply closet.

Donna had arranged to meet Grace at the concert, only Donna was late. She'd had trouble getting out of bed that morning. When she was finally standing, she'd been too exhausted to shower or dress, so she'd wrapped the India print bedspread around her belly and squeezed into a tube top.

The nurse at the Free Clinic had told her she was a week past her due date. Donna figured it was just her karma not to have had this kid a few days before, when the temperature dipped below eighty for the first time in weeks. The sooner she got this kid out the sooner she could lose some weight in preparation for Vic's tour of duty to end. He'd sent her a photo a few months back, a real hard-on in his marine get-up against all that jungle green, think of the tan that boy would have. And won't he be surprised, though, Donna was thinking, her hand resting on her belly, Real goddamn surprised.

But the cold snap hadn't lasted, and by Saturday, the day of the concert, it was back to ninety degrees, ninety percent humidity, like a jungle, Donna was thinking. Mid-morning, not a cloud in the sky, traffic at a standstill outside the stadium, heat shimmering above the cartops like a mirage. Donna sat in the Beetle with the windows rolled down, dragging on a roach—she'd found it in the ashtray, probably months old, what the hell it might get things moving down there—listening to the radios in the cars around her, all tuned to the same station.

"Where it's happenin'! Where it's at! The Concert for Sharing!" belted the deejay. "Head on over with food for the foodshelf! Bread for your brethren! That's your admission to groove all day! And speakin' of groovin', here's the Moody Blues ..."

The Beetle's radio didn't work, or its left turn signal. And when a Home Juice truck smashed in the left front fender awhile back, Donna had promised the driver not to press charges, then pocketed the fifty he'd slipped her and written "OUCH!" across the dent in red primer paint. The heater didn't work, either, like this mattered in the dead of summer. Besides, Donna had her intuition, she'd been getting signs: this was it, her life was changing, she wouldn't be putting up with thirty-below-zero Januaries any goddamn longer.

The Doors came on. The people in the VW bus next to her held up a box of Creamettes and flipped her the peace sign. Donna smiled back and held up the Van Camps in Heavy Syrup.

By the time she'd circled the parking lot twice, almost sideswiped a television van, and finally managed to wedge the Beetle into a space between a couple of Harleys, Donna could hear that one of the bands had already started. She turned off the ignition and listened for the song: Steppenwolf, one of her favorites, another sign. She checked her watch. Probably the second act, maybe the third.

The drums pumped through the August heat, knocked against her forehead, her temples, the bridge of her nose. She was sweating. She closed her eyes, only this made her dizzy. She grabbed the car keys and the Van Camps, and squeezed out the door. The drums stuck in her throat. She tried to swallow as she maneuvered across the asphalt.

At the gate she waited while the people in front of her handed over their bags of groceries. The drums had reached her chest. When she held out the Van Camps, the ticket guy held up his hand in protest, then saw her belly. He shrugged and stamped the back of her hand with what appeared to be a giant woodtick.

" . . . And Pillsbury says it best . . . " he whispered as Donna pushed past him. The drums had reached her ribs.

Donna made it as far as the bleachers. She caught a brief glimpse of the wide stadium field, overflowing with people, criss-crossed with blankets like an enormous quilt, dotted with lawnchairs, umbrellas, dogs, a horse! And at the far end the band, high on the stage, a skyline of amps piled around them.

Then the drums reached her belly, and what Donna saw last, before all the rest—before the legs and the hands and the tent erased the sky; before the screaming pain; before her own screams and the screams of the ambulance in the distance and that man kneeling beside her asking what she'd be naming her new daughter and Donna opening her mouth to tell him just where to go and at the last second seeing the camera, the mike, seeing the man's smiling familiar TV face, at the last second saying "SUGAR!" and not "SHIT!", my god she'd almost said "SHIT!" on TV (*TV!*), a girl couldn't swear on TV, a girl had to be cool on TV, jesus what did her hair look like?

Before all that, before everything changed, what Donna remembered along with that can of beans was this: someone had been flying a kite, a bright yellow kite, and in an instant she'd felt it, a love so big it took her breath away. She'd grabbed her belly and whispered the words and for one long moment had watched that kite prance and kick, a runaway bottle-rocket, high above the crowd against the impossible blue.

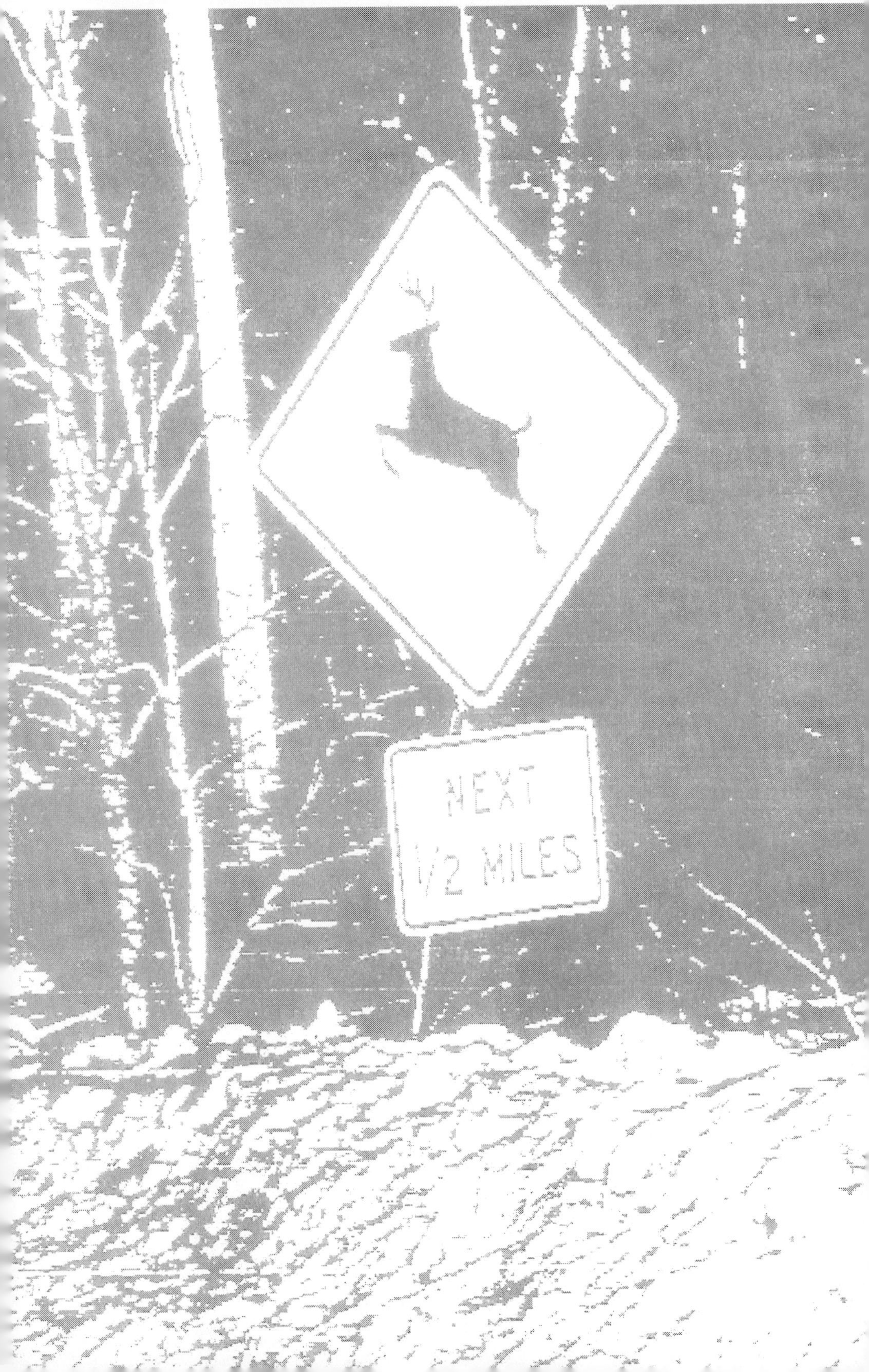
NEXT
1/2 MILES

About the Author

Carolyn Colburn received a B.S. degree from the University of Minnesota and an M.F.A. degree from Goddard College. She has worked as a musician, typesetter, teacher and contract writer. She has been awarded a Minnesota State Arts Board Grant and a Loft McKnight Fellowship. Ms. Colburn divides her time between her home in Duluth, Minnesota, and a cabin on Lake Superior near the Canadian border. Her blog can be found at sixspruce.blogspot.com.